The Blue Ho

Born in Lima, Peru, in 1954, Alon
childhood in Paris and Washingt
at the age of seven. He studie
Universidad Católica del Perú and later at the University
of Texas at Austin. He is married with two children
and lives in Lima.

The Blue Hour

ALONSO CUETO

Translated from the Spanish by
FRANK WYNNE

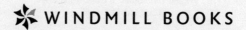 WINDMILL BOOKS

Published by Windmill Books 2013

2 4 6 8 10 9 7 5 3 1

Copyright © Alonso Cueto 2005
Translation copyright © Frank Wynne 2012

Alonso Cueto has asserted his right under the Copyright,
Designs and Patents Act, 1988, to be identified as the
author of this work.

First published as *La hora azul*, by Editorial Anagrama, Barcelona

First published in Great Britain in 2012 by William Heinemann

Windmill Books
The Random House Group Limited
20 Vauxhall Bridge Road, London SW1V 2SA

Addresses for companies within The Random House Group
Limited can be found at: www.randomhouse.co.uk/offices

The Random House Group Limited Reg. No. 954009

www.randomhouse.co.uk

A CIP catalogue record for this book
is available from the British Library

ISBN 9780099533092

The Random House Group Limited supports the Forest Stewardship
Council® (FSC®), the leading international forest-certification organisation.
Our books carrying the FSC label are printed on FSC®-certified paper.
FSC is the only forest-certification scheme supported by the leading
environmental organisations, including Greenpeace.
Our paper procurement policy can be found at:
www.randomhouse.co.uk/environment

Typeset by Palimpsest Book Production Limited
Falkirk, Stirlingshire
Printed and bound in Great Britain by
Clays Ltd, St Ives Plc

For Quinta Chipana and his friends in Vilcashuamán

A young prisoner, an underage girl, was persuaded to spend the night in the bedroom of one of the senior officials of Los Cabitos. [. . .] On the morning of 3 March, the prisoner escaped.

Ricardo Uceda, *Muerte en el Pentagonito*

'Yeah,' I said, and, almost without realising it, added, 'maybe a person isn't only responsible for what they do, but also for what they see or read or hear.'

Javier Cercas, *The Speed of Light*

I

NOT LONG BEFORE THIS STORY BEGINS, A PHOTOGRAPH of me appeared in the 'Society Pages' of *Cosas* magazine.

It was a full-page photo. I was smiling, facing the camera, head held high, wearing a designer suit, my right hand resting gently on the shoulder of my beautiful wife Claudia. I looked the part – that effortless elegance some people can pull off when we know the paparazzi are around. My tie was neatly knotted, my hair elegantly tousled, the ring that bore witness to fifteen years of happy marriage visible on the fourth finger of my left hand. Standing next to me, Claudia, my business partner Eduardo and his wife Milagros . . . all four of us turned towards the camera, holding glasses of whisky, an affectionate smugness in our smiles, as though we'd just been awarded a prize for being the happiest couples that night.

One day, over breakfast, Claudia handed me the magazine open at the photo. Later that day my sister-in-law called me at the office. 'You look like the perfect couple,' she said. I was flattered but not surprised that the photo was the biggest on the page.

Back then, I was often in the papers and I think I always looked good. Statistics, so to speak, were in my favour: I was forty-two, earned $9,000 a month and weighed twelve and a half stone – the perfect weight given that I was six foot one. I spent an hour every day at the gym. In addition, I was a partner in a prestigious law firm with a list of over a hundred major clients. I had a lot of work, but I had a lot of help at the office. I remember back then a friend enviously telling me that every time he saw me I looked happier.

I'd always wanted to be a lawyer. At school, I'd once written an essay entitled 'The Law in Everyday Life'. My basic thesis was that all social relationships – including love and friendship – are based on an implicit contract. Fathers, children, husbands, wives, lovers, friends, siblings come to an unspoken agreement about how they behave, and habit establishes the boundaries of the contract. Should one of the parties deviate from that behaviour, they are breaking their promise and hence violating that tacit contract. The law was based on human relationships. Or that was what I believed back then.

As a boy, I wasn't only interested in the law. I also had fantasies about being a writer. I even wrote a swashbuckling adventure novel once.

I've been brooding over my frustrated vocation as a writer for a couple of weeks now.

I've been thinking about it because I wanted to write this story down. I'm not sure why. I certainly don't ever want to come face to face with someone who's read it (I've hired a ghost writer to put his name and imprimatur to it).

In the book, I call myself Adrián Ormache. But I'm sure

some people will work out who I am. They'll recognise me, or my wife Claudia. My wife Claudia. It feels strange calling her that. As though she were a stranger. The arc of her name reminds me of a rainbow – at least that's what I told her the night we met at a party twenty years ago; it was a ridiculous chat-up line, but she thought it was funny.

At the point when this story begins, Claudia was the perfect wife. She dressed well, accompanied me to cocktail parties and was friends with the wives of other lawyers.

You couldn't find a better wife, my mother-in-law used to tell me. And she was right. Claudia's impeccable taste in clothes and her faultless manners invariably impressed friends and acquaintances. She would organise sumptuous informal dinners, the tables groaning with platters of meats and salads and desserts. Eminent lawyers – the del Prados, the Muñizes, the Rodrigos – would linger into the early hours and were always effusively kind when they said goodnight. The guests included prominent members of congress like Carlos Ferrero and Lourdes Flores; President Belaúnde himself came once. They were good friends.

I liked it when my daughters saw these people coming to our house. We have two daughters who are completely adorable – corny, but that's the only word that springs to mind.

These days, the elder, Alicia, is studying law at the Universidad Católica. She is happy in her vocation. She'll be a lawyer like me. She is a beautiful, smart woman – and I'm not just saying that because I'm her father. She's at the age when she thinks she knows everything, but she's still sweet, even indulgent with her elders. She is – and I don't think this

3

is an exaggeration – exceptionally intelligent. Our younger daughter, Lucía is a sensitive, rather dreamy girl, still scared of spiders, still afraid of the dark. She has a vivid imagination and a desperate need for approval and is constantly telling jokes and stories. With her green eyes, her silken hair and her long legs, she is one of the most beautiful young women I've ever seen. Her chattiness these days belies the efforts she had to make, as the younger child, to be noticed in a house with three grown-ups.

Lucía is a huge fan of grunge; she and her friends shut themselves away in her room and listen to Kurt Cobain. Back when she turned thirteen, I bought her a bass guitar. Thankfully, it's not too loud. It hardly matters, though; our house in San Isidro is 5,000 square feet so there's room enough for everyone – including the maid, the cook and Claudia's driver – to get away from her playing.

Before her obsession with playing bass, Lucía was great company. She used to tell me stories, confide in me about her problems and those of her little friends; she'd hug me and ask for a kiss. These days, those hugs are among my most precious memories. I miss those moments and I feel that, after everything that's happened, they now belong to the past. Back then my daughter was hugging a different man, a man who has gone for ever.

My wife Claudia had inherited her mother's skill for changing nappies, answering questions, soothing the girls' fears. She read child psychology books about typical behaviour from the ages of seven to ten and eleven to thirteen. My mother-in-law had given her daughters a loving, well-balanced education and sent them out into the world armed with a mixture of strength, moral rectitude and a reasonable love of their fellow man, and Claudia was instilling these same values in Alicia and Lucía. It should be said, however, that her parenting skills were underpinned by our financial security. My practice was going pretty well thanks to a good working relationship with my clients (if I do say so myself). In addition, my in-laws had managed to amass a considerable fortune in the many years they had worked at their factory. My father-in-law was outlandishly generous when it came to inviting us on holidays. He would stump up for the best five-star hotels, open a tab for me at the bar, buy presents for the girls. The Caribbean was among his favourite places, and as a result, Claudia and I sported a healthy tan even in the winter.

I was not immune to vanity. I enjoyed having a nice house, a wife who was beautiful, loving and a perfect hostess, two dutiful daughters who worked hard at school. I'm not ashamed to say that I liked to dress well. And yet these things I loved, sometimes (and that part of my life seems so long ago now) . . . what I'm trying to say is that sometimes I felt gripped by a sort of pain, a hand squeezing my throat making it difficult to move, to do even the most ordinary things. From the simple matter of getting up in the morning, brushing my hair and getting dressed to everything else: facing the world, dealing with the noise and clamour of the day, meeting my responsibilities, the gruelling effort required to dress, to shave, refashion myself and emerge transformed into a gentleman.

Maybe it was this heaviness I felt, this general ache, that

triggered my dreams. They were not depressing dreams but rather vivid scenes in which I felt free to act on my desire to indulge in wanton violence.

A good example: I'm naked. I dimly realise I'm in my father-in-law's house at an elegant dinner party, a buffet. My father-in-law looks at me and smiles. There are lots of people in black tie helping themselves from the buffet. Suddenly I have something in my hand. What is it? It's a bottle of ketchup. I unscrew the top and spray tomato sauce all over the table. The white tablecloth is spattered red. My father-in-law is not smiling now, but the other guests congratulate me. Suddenly I realise that it's not a bottle of ketchup. It's a gun. A gun. And it seems the most natural thing in the world to use it. I start shooting at everyone and they die laughing. Finally, I fire a bullet into my temple. I wake up. Dream over.

Though somewhat grotesque, they were always entertaining.

Another recurring dream. I punch my father-in law on the jaw in his own house while his whole family clap and cheer. He gets to his feet and I hit him again. And so on and so on.

These violent visions were like powder flashes. I was astonished, I laughed to see myself do such things. But I succumbed to these images with a certain pleasure.

Maybe I'm making too much of it. It wasn't really like that. I felt basically content with my family, my job, my friends and acquaintances. I got on well with my father-in-law, who constantly invited me to go on trips with him (I often declined). I liked to sit at home on the terrace gazing out over the swimming pool. I felt proud and happy to be able to invite friends round. I didn't need to do anything to maintain the solid wall surrounding me. Success was like a sleeping pill. I wanted things to carry on like this for ever. The dazzle of my designer suits was my gift to myself. My voice, a precise, leisurely drawl, gave a glossy patina to conversation – to quote an admiring comment Claudia once made.

And then, one morning some years ago, everything changed. On the day my mother died. The death of my mother has probably been the most important event in my life.

It had been a long illness and when her time came, I was expecting it. Even so, when I heard that she was dead, it plunged me into a grief that I will never get over (does anyone ever really get over anything?).

The morning her nurse, Norma, rang and gave me the news, the words were like blows all over my body. 'The *señora* has passed away. I was in the kitchen and I heard a noise. I rushed to her bathroom and found her just lying there on the floor, I didn't know what to do. She'd been washing her hands – she's been washing her hands all the time recently.'

I've often pictured her, standing gazing at herself in the mirror – her blue dressing gown, her slender frame, shoulders held high – just before she collapsed. It's as though I can hear everything, the dull thud of her body, the rustle of arms and fabric falling, and the silence until she is found.

I drove over to her house and I was alone when I finally saw her as she was: an ethereal body sprawled on the bathroom tiles, swathed in her dressing gown, legs crossed, mouth open in amazement.

7

The hairbrush had fallen from her grasp and was lying in a corner. In a last flirtation with the world, my mother had just brushed her hair. She made a handsome corpse, ready to receive guests at her wake. I cradled her, tried to talk to her, but though I have had little experience of death, I realised that what I was holding was not a body but a piece of meat. And yet her face looked somehow magical. Calling an ambulance was merely respecting the formalities, a reflexive gesture of hope. I can still feel the fabric of her dressing gown, the last trace of warmth on her skin, still see the funereal paleness of her cheeks. Though some years have passed, that pain has never left me, the admiration I felt – that I still feel for her – the admiration, the love, the gratitude I feel for her . . . all these things I carry with me.

My mother had died with strategic suddenness – no rituals, no goodbyes, no pronouncements, no family reunions. She had made her will well in advance. From time to time, in a soft voice, with no drama, she had been making small bequests.

'Keep whatever you want from the clothes and the shoes, the rest you should give to the Carmelite parish church in Sicuani. I'm leaving you the big mahogany clock, you can take it when it's all over.'

These were not dramatic statements, just simple instructions she would give as she was getting into the car, or on the phone just before she said goodbye. Don't talk like that, I would say, before she changed the subject. She had told me now. She was perfectly serene.

Claudia was by my side at the hospital and at the funeral home. With her help, I let our relations know. The most important and the most distant, obviously, being my brother Rubén who was living in New Jersey.

And so, after many years, I got to see him again.

My brother Rubén. That afternoon, in the airport, waiting for him, I was distracted by grief. The traffic jam on the motorway, the harassed taxi drivers, the two filthy urchins in the parking lot who begged me to let them wash my car.

When Rubén came through customs, I rushed over and hugged him.

The premature paunch, the beginnings of a double chin, the coarse teeth. The paunch was the result of too much high living funded by his successful career in New Jersey. As we drove from the airport to the church, Rubén reminisced about Mamá. His voice faltering, high-pitched, ragged with sobs.

'I keep thinking about Mamá, I can't get her out of my mind; I can still hear her voice, still see her. I have all these memories playing over and over in my head. That time she made me a cake with icing-sugar strawberries spelling "Rubén", that time I broke my leg and she stayed with me holding my hand, the times she'd pick me up from school and we'd have lunch together. What mother does that?'

Sitting there in the car next to me, Rubén sometimes threw up his hands and let out a howl.

We arrived at the Iglesia de Fátima for the vigil. Seeing the coffin, he threw his arms around it, pressed his face to the lid and wept. At first loudly, and then in great wails. Some of our relatives came over to hug him or pat him on the back.

He and I sat together through the night, getting to our feet every now and then to accept condolences. The following day, he walked with me at the head of the funeral cortège. From time to time he wiped away his tears. He had been the last to leave the vigil and the first to arrive for the funeral. For my part, I had spent the night repeating the same litany to friends and relatives: thank you; thank you for coming; thanks; yes, it was very sudden; she'd had cancer and she'd beaten it; it was a heart attack that killed her.

Claudia never left my side except to comfort Lucía when she was crying. Alicia was holding up better. I watched everyone from a distance: friends, colleagues, relatives in groups, chatting, smiling, asking questions. I saw them through the grief, the politeness and the hugs as through a thick pane of glass. In the end, my whole body ached from greeting all these people.

It all went so fast: the slow, measured procession to the cemetery, the last words of the priest, the coffin lowered between the flowers and wreaths. Then the slow procession home. That day I talked to people I hadn't seen in years . . . To uncles and cousins, to all the friends who came to express their condolences. Everyone was there. It was like a party; Mamá was the guest of honour, but it was my brother and I who greeted everyone.

Rubén had inherited our father's rasping voice, calloused fingers and tubercular nose. He was, in a certain sense, his reincarnation. With age he grew more and more like him; a gnome slowly turning into the ogre that begot him. My father's face – an image I pieced together from fragmented memories of the few occasions I had seen him – had been a craggy wilderness. It was difficult to imagine Mamá's delicate fingers caressing it. It was as though the images came to me from opposite extremes. On one side, the whispered echoes of lullabies my mother sang to me, her slender figure waiting for me at the breakfast table. On the other, my father's hoarse stony laugh, his red-raw knuckles.

Papá. I had done everything in my power to put the few memories I had of him out of my mind.

His death had caused me only the vaguest twinge of sorrow, a dutiful, obligatory grief. The day before, I had gone to visit him at the Military Hospital. I found him leaning back against the bedrails. He had a ragged beard, his pyjamas were stained and he was talking incessantly to a priest.

That day, when he saw me come in, he sat up and opened his arms wide.

'*Hijo*, you came, I can't fucking believe you finally came.'

Papá's hoarse voice which came out in short barks, his grubby striped pyjamas, the eyes tight shut, the hands thrown up; I didn't know what to say to him, he babbled on at me, his hands raised, about the things I'd done wrong, about how we hadn't seen each other since and how now . . .

'I've got so much to tell you. How are the girls? Good?'

'They're fine.'

'That's good, but there's something I need to tell you, *hijo*, listen, if you ever . . . Have you seen Rubén recently?'

'No, no, I haven't seen him.'

'OK, but listen, there's something I want to ask you. There's a girl, a woman I knew a long time ago . . . I don't know, maybe you can find her – I want you to find her if you can – I knew her during the war. Up in Huanta, when I was stationed in Ayacucho. She was from round there. I'm begging you, please. Before I die.'

He was saying something like this when the nurse came in with his injection.

'Get out. Get out, can't you see I'm talking to my son? As I was saying, *hijo*, this woman, she was from Huanta . . .'

'Hey, Papá, take it easy, let the nurse give you the injection.'

They told me later that he argued with the nurses that night, with the duty doctor.

'Get my son Adrián here,' he screamed, trying to rip the IV out of his arm, 'I want him here right now.'

Eventually he calmed down. The next day he woke up, asked for his breakfast, then curled into a ball and stayed that way. He was dead.

At the vigil, my mother and I came to leave a spray of flowers, talked to a few of his friends and left. All told, we weren't there more than an hour. The rest of the time was spent organising the formalities for the burial and accepting vague expressions of sympathy.

My mother, from whom I inherited my idealism, my melancholy nature, my militant optimism and my passion for music and literature, had committed the sin that is derived from such virtues. Her innocence had spoiled her; in a sense it had perverted her. Her first, her only contact with the outside world had been meeting my father.

Mamá had been a gentle, slim, refined, dreamy girl who, after a conscientious education at the Colegio Belén, had found herself at a party talking to a Marine cadet who wore a dark uniform glittering with insignia. According to my aunts, my father's gallant posturing – the uniform, the heroism decked out with courtesy, the insolent cheerfulness – created a fantasy figure in my mother's mind. It deceived her.

My father in full dress uniform had shown up unannounced at my mother's house and she had blithely gone with him, climbed into his Chevrolet and listened to his tales of naval school.

'Hello, Beatriz . . .' he had said, offering his hand to lead her down the front steps.

'You look so pretty, my little queen. We were taken out to sea at six this morning and forced to swim for two hours. It's amazing, seeing the world from down there, the wonderful underwater world – some day I'll take you with me to explore the depths of the ocean.'

My grandfather's tantrums and my grandmother's sad resignation – may they both rest in peace – were all for nothing. My mother had decided to marry this officer who promised to give her a life of adventure that, according to her, he had never had.

My father's one talent had been his ability to keep up the facade during their courtship to hide what he truly was . . . he had kept it up until they were married and my mother finally slept with him (I don't think she had counted on this, seeing him sleeping next to her, seeing him wake up). After that, she had to put up with the late-night drinking binges, the early mornings waiting up for him, the screaming matches . . .

In keeping with the good manners instilled in her as a child, my mother had been a model divorcee. She never spoke ill of her ex-husband because she never spoke of him at all. Nor did she ever go out with another man – although several passionate suitors beat a path to her door. Perhaps her silence was an admission of her foolish naivety. She had a variety of stock phrases she used when Papá's name came up in conversation – 'I wonder what he's doing these days?', 'Let's hope he's doing well for himself.' Once she sent him a document by courier.

My mother gave herself over to the exquisite rituals of her solitude – classical music in the drawing room, blue-and-white trouser suits, conversations with friends. And yet, she once confessed to Aunt Flora that an ex-husband is a millstone a wife is never free of.

'People will say you used to be married to him. There's nothing you can do about that.'

I would never be free of him either. I saw him quite regularly while I was in secondary school, much less when I was at university, and only five or six times after he got back from Ayacucho where he'd done a number of tours of duty – *caimans* he once told me soldiers called their stints in a war zone.

Over time, I came to agree with my mother's subtle, unspoken contempt. Her discretion was a mark of her sophistication but it had a practical purpose too, since, as an aunt later told me, my mother thought it important that we be proud of our surname. Since we were stuck with it, it was better to give it some prestige through our own exemplary behaviour conveniently underscored by a deliberate artlessness.

Only once, and at my insistence, did my mother ever speak to me about her relationship with my father.

'To tell you the truth, I think that I only realised who I really was after we split up,' she told me. 'Before . . . I don't know, I was so naive, I genuinely believed my life would be this wonderful adventure, I don't know what I was thinking. And now I'm on my own, and I accept that. But I know my marriage had its compensations, at least I have you and Rubén, I have my darling granddaughters, I have my friends. I barely have a minute to myself: I have the book club, the knitting club where we make clothes for poor children, my music group, my card games. I lead a full life, Adrián, what with you and the girls – if your brother would just write a bit more often, everything would be perfect . . . but, well, I suppose he's busy . . .'

Otherwise, from time to time, I had my own ideas about my father. Sometimes I liked to give in to my fantasies, to pretend to myself that he had been a great soldier, a hero in the war against the Shining Path – Sendero Luminoso, a guy brave enough to go to Ayacucho and tackle a group of organised murderers. Who would do something like that?

More than once I had talked to Alicia and Lucía with a certain respect, even a vague admiration about their soldier grandfather. A child with a stable family environment invariably has more things in life she can be sure of – that was how Claudia and I reasoned. My mother agreed, obviously.

'What's important is that the girls know they come from good stock, that the weapons they have as they go out into the world are the result of family tradition, of effort and discipline,' Claudia said to me. 'Like every soldier, your *papá* was a man of discipline and that's obviously got to mean something.'

And so, for many years, I lived with the certainty that my father had been in Ayacucho in the early eighties waging war against the communist terrorists of Sendero Luminoso, that he had done something to defend our country and that, for this, we owed him our respect.

Besides, as kids, Rubén and I had always been excited and thrilled to see him. Whenever he came to visit, he would take us to the cinema and afterwards we'd eat *pollo con papas* liberally seasoned with fatherly advice (you've got to work hard in this life, it's no good being a shiftless layabout), and his cheesy jokes (what did one egg say to the other egg?).

The insolent, cheerful shadow of my father sometimes flitted through my mother's fortress. I looked out onto the world from its high windows. Even as a little boy, I felt comfortable and happy in those lonely rooms. My mother had never set foot outside. The delicate courage she had taken such pride in during her first months as a divorcee had set like concrete; her fortress was now impervious.

Marriage had been a difficult cross for her to bear, my aunt Flora told me.

'She put up with your father for two and a half years. She made his breakfast, she made his dinner, she went with him to his reunions with his army buddies, twice, with heartbreaking tenderness, she bore him children and she patiently put up with her role as a meek, submissive wife. That all changed the third time he stayed out all night. The very same afternoon she stood in front of him in the living room, told him in no uncertain terms that she was disgusted with his gambling and his womanising, and gave him his marching orders from the house and the family. He listened to her in disbelief. The very same evening I watched him move out for good. She gave him precise instructions about the suitcase she'd packed. Not long after that, she took a job in my uncle Lucho's studio.'

All this I was told by my aunt Flora, who – herself a militant spinster – followed my mother's misfortunes like a soap opera in which she was simultaneously the privileged viewer, the narrator and one of the supporting cast.

My aunt Flora told me that my mother's first inkling of what he was like came within days of their wedding.

'I think even at that stage she realised something was wrong. Well, after the shock of that first realisation, she became determined to get shot of him. Your father only made it worse with his boorishness and his coarse manners at the table and in conversation. I can't think how she hadn't noticed it before. Well, anyway, when they'd been married three years, she finally decided to divorce him,' Flora told me.

'You and Rubén were only babies at the time. So, anyway, your mother phoned your father. He'd been living in an apartment since they separated. And she said, "I need to send over divorce papers. Can you make sure you're at home at seven o'clock?" And your father said, "Listen, you little bitch, I won't have you divorcing me. I'll take you to court." So your mother said, "Take me to court – you'll only end up paying more alimony." And then in a soft voice she said simply, "I'll send a courier with the papers at seven. It's in your best interests to sign, Alberto. You have to do this one thing for me. Don't be a pig-ignorant fool." Those were her very words.'

After the divorce, my mother had a little more colour in her cheeks. She threw herself into raising Rubén and me with a passion, having come through the catastrophe with some shreds of dignity intact. She had proved to the world that she could rise above her misfortunes. Her courage was the result of the tragedy of her lost illusions. She refused to see my father, speak to him, or ask about him; she made sure she was always impeccably dressed, kept her head high, a smile on her face, organised afternoons of tea and music with friends – these were the hallmarks of her grace in the face of tragedy. It was a grace she had constantly tried to pass on to us. She advised us to always keep our cool.

'When you have a problem,' she used to say to us, 'you need to put the problem in perspective and consider every possible solution before making a decision.'

She was also obsessed with clothes.

'What you wear is a reflection of who you are on the inside,' she told us many times.

One of my mother's abiding obsessions during our childhood was that we be well dressed. She liked to buy us jackets, shirts and ties from Harry's in Miraflores. I always wore mine but Rubén was never really comfortable wearing his, nor was he ever really comfortable in the big white-carpeted living rooms of our house. As soon as he could, he went off to live in the US. He had been back for short visits several times since. And although she had rarely said so, my mother never stopped missing him.

Thankfully, this was something I didn't talk to him about during the few days he spent in Lima for her funeral. My mother's sadness was a subject which, I felt, he didn't deserve.

II

WHILE RUBÉN WAS HERE, I SAW HIM ALMOST
every day. Together, we read her will which left
everything to us in equal parts. We talked to the
lawyer, had a meeting with the solicitor. We gave away some
of the things in the house. Meanwhile, I went through the
process of mourning alone – the patient self-control during
calls offering condolences, the toll taken by insomnia, the
release of tears, reading the notices in the newspapers, the
gradual acceptance of her absence, the lucidity of empty spaces,
the cards and letters that still came for her.

One night, at a dinner at Aunt Flora's house, I sat next to
Rubén. Seeing him close up, I was struck again by how different
we were: my close-cropped hair and grey suit, his thick greasy
mane and leather jacket; my cheerful, circumspect pronouncements and his harsh, curt sentences dotted with swear words.

He had put on quite a bit of weight, and obesity simply
highlighted his other shortcomings. He swaggered through a
world that revolved around him. The love handles and the
sagging jowls called attention to the fatty deposits in his veins,
the coarseness about his face with its bushy eyebrows and

beady eyes; the man did not simply walk, he insulted the world with his body. The hoarse voice was a product of the obesity. He looked faintly ridiculous and slightly repulsive, yet somehow I still felt close to him. The duty of memory in my mother's tearful eyes whenever she talked about Rubén. This was no time to reproach him for his meagre letters to her, or his failure to contribute to her medical bills. It was better this way, it gave me the moral high ground, something I had often said to her.

A week after the funeral, the day before he was due to fly back to New Jersey, Rubén and I had lunch. We'd agreed to meet up at his hotel, since it was convenient for both of us (Claudia didn't think much of Rubén and I didn't want to put her through another meal with him at our house; to tell the truth, I wasn't too keen on our daughters spending time with him either).

At 2 p.m., the appointed time, I was just arriving at the Hotel César. I parked in the car park and walked a couple of blocks along the Calle Diez Canseco.

I don't know why I paid particular attention to the state of the pavement that day, it was something I didn't usually notice; the cement was cracked and pitted with holes, boards covering certain sections. A dank smell seemed to rise from the dusty crevices and potholes.

I bumped into Rubén as he was getting out of a taxi. He was laden with shopping bags.

'I've got this *gringa* girlfriend who wants me to bring her back some alpaca. It's fantastic stuff, she'll love it.'

I told him to take it up to his room, that I'd meet him in the dining room.

I had a coffee and read the papers while I waited. He showed up a little while later, his hair wet and his bovine eyes glittering. He sat down opposite me and waved to a waiter.

'A pisco sour, make it a double.'

'Coming right up, *señor*.'

I ordered the same. I was hoping the drink would help me deal with this conversation.

The hotel dining room was full of fair-haired tourists. It made the place feel strange, like a parallel universe inhabited entirely by blond beautiful people, in which Rubén and I looked like ethnic dolls in a display case. The tourists stared at us with faint smiles as though wondering if they could have us gift-wrapped to take home.

After the pisco sour, I ordered duck with rice which the waiter, thumb and index finger forming a circle, enthusiastically recommended.

'It's very good, *señor*.'

Rubén ordered the same with a portion of *frijoles* and a fried egg on the side. When he asked after the family I said, 'Fine, everyone's fine,' and quickly shut up as though I had just confessed a secret. He said he would have liked to see my daughters.

'Some other time,' I said. 'They've got a lot on at school at the moment, exams coming up . . .'

'Let's get another pisco sour. Two more pisco sours, *señor* . . . You not having another one?'

'Better not, I've already had one and I have work this afternoon.'

'So, anyway, when are we going to see each other again, dickhead?'

'I don't know.'

'Hey, I wrote to you and you never answered.'

'It's just I've had a lot of things going on, what with work and Mamá dying, you know.'

'You should have written, you should have told me, in the end I was the one who had to phone you, remember?'

'Yeah, I know.'

'OK, let's forget it, I'm going to order dessert. Another pisco sour and a *mazamorra*, *señor*.

'You want the truth, the truth is the US is a great country,' he said, 'but *gringos* can't make pastries like you get here. In the States, they're all flour, there's nothing like a *mazamorra*, I'll tell you.'

I lit a cigarette.

I felt unexpectedly comfortable, sprawled in a chair here next to Rubén, with waiters dancing attendance on us. The food was good. It was a perfect day.

Rubén wolfed down his *mazamorra*, and told three dirty jokes in a row, leaning over now and again to punch me in the arm. He talked about his ex-wife, about his visits to high-class brothels, about how much money he was capable of spending in a single night. Then he explained what he called his philosophy of life:

'Fuck today, my friend, for tomorrow you might be fucked. Just look at Mamá.'

'I don't think she ever had fun in her whole life,' he went on. 'She should have travelled, should have come to see me in New Jersey.'

'She had fun in her own way,' I said.

'What do you mean in her own way?'

'For some people, having fun means *not* going out – they like staying at home, reading a book, listening to music, watching a film.'

'Jesus, bro, you're full of shit.'

We went on talking about Mamá; he asked me about her last months, I told him she had prayed a lot, listened to music, had tea with her friends, that sometimes she had asked after him. Eventually, I told him what I had always believed.

'I think splitting up with Papá was the best thing that could have happened to Mamá.'

Rubén's face tightened. He raised a finger and shook it sternly.

'What are you saying that for?' he said. 'Papá was a great guy. I mean, Mamá was great too but she wasn't the right woman for him.'

'Of course she wasn't.'

'Anyway, she always looked down her nose at him. I mean, what was a man like that to do with a stuck-up society lady like her? Don't get me wrong, I have every respect for my mother. My *mamá* is always here,' he thumped at his chest, 'and I'd beat the shit out of anyone who ran her down. But Papá was great too, I mean, he was a regular guy, he may have had his faults, but he was decent. That's how people are, that's what men are like, you see what I'm saying? I don't agree with you at all.'

'I don't know, I think they were completely different people. To me Papá always seemed so macho.'

Rubén went on eating, took a sip of his pisco sour and stared at me. Something suddenly flared in his eyes.

'I never thought of him as macho.' Rubén paused, glanced out the window, then thumped the table. 'You want to know something? I saw him cry his eyes out one night. He hugged me and said he didn't have any money. "A poor old solider like me," that's how he put it, "I don't even have enough to put clothes on my back, by the time I pay the electricity and the water I barely have enough to buy food." He puffed out his chest and thumped it. "Me," he said, "who fought for my country against terrorists," then he raised a finger, "but at least I have my sons. At least I have my two sons." He said it over and over, thumping his chest.'

The image of my father thumping his chest seemed slightly grotesque though I didn't say anything. But I was determined to defend my mother.

'If Mamá married Papá it was probably out of a romanticism fed by too much music and too many love stories. Marrying him was a silly mistake. Personally, I think she fell in love with Papá's uniform, with some image she had of him, but not with him. Later, when she got to know him, that's when disappointment set in.'

Rubén wiped his mouth with a napkin, then quickly raised his finger and wagged it from side to side.

'I don't believe it,' he said.

'No?'

He finished his pisco and immediately ordered another one.

'You know I used to bring him to New York every year for New Year. Well, the last time he came with some friends of his. Two friends it was.'

It irked me to think Papá had spent more time in the US with Rubén than he had with me in Lima. But in a sense it was understandable. It didn't take a genius to work out that my father would have felt more comfortable spending time with my brother than with me.

'So what did you do?'

'I took him to Ranch X, him and his mates,' he said. 'A brothel like you wouldn't fucking believe. You walk in and there's this huge fountain,' he flung his arms wide, 'and this pretty little thing comes right up to us. "Hi guys, nice to fuck you." I swear, that's what she says and offers you a drink. The place is fucking awesome, we had a ball. Obviously I picked up the tab, because the Peruvians were all flat broke. But I swear, the old man was amazed. I tell you, when it comes to whores, the *gringos* have us beat. In the States they're tall and attentive, they know how to look after a guy. *Gringo* women can be ladies when they want to be.'

The waiter brought the glass of pisco which he knocked back. He then ordered a beer and a coffee and started chewing on a toothpick.

'So, how did Papá seem when he visited?' I asked.

I felt strange. Only now, with my mother dead, could I allow myself to show any concern for my father.

'Fine. He was fine. I mean, OK, he was in a bit of a bad way because he was scared. He was convinced someone was going to go poking their nose into all that shit about Ayacucho and the war. He was a bit worried about journalists too, at least that's what he told me.'

'What?'

'Well, he'd been a bit of a bastard, the old man, there was some stuff he didn't want getting out.'

The waiter brought the beer and the coffee.

I took a sip of water.

'A bit of a bastard? How do you mean?'

He lifted his glass, seemed to be muttering into the beer, then he went on.

'You know what Papá did, right?' he said, poking at his teeth with the toothpick. 'You know what sort of shit he was up to when he was posted up in Huanta, the kind of things he did when he was working at the barracks?'

'Sure, he was fighting terrorists. Like lots of people back then. Had to be fucking difficult.'

'No, not that . . . Like I said, he could be a bit of a *cabrón*, the old man.'

He took a sip of his coffee and sat staring at the swirling liquid. It was a thick cappuccino. There was a fleck of white foam on his upper lip. The waiter stood next to us, hands clasped.

'Anything else I can get for you, *señores*?'

Rubén ordered a brandy and insisted I drink something. Every time I suggested something he shook his head.

'So, a glass of mineral water, *señor*?'

'Please.'

Rubén sat staring at me harshly.

'For Christ's sake, have a drink.'

'I told you, I have work this afternoon.'

'*Puta madre*, just have a fucking drink. I mean, face it, when are we next going to see each other?'

'OK, but I'm still here. I haven't gone anywhere. So, tell me about Papá?'

He gave a heavy sigh, splayed his hands.

'Shit, I don't know, you probably know all this stuff already, but the old man sometimes had to kill terrorists. But he didn't just kill them right off. The men, well, he'd have them worked over . . . to make them talk. And the women, well, you know, sometimes he'd fuck the women and sometimes he'd let the rest of the troop fuck them before he put a bullet in their heads.'

The waiter brought the brandy and the mineral water. Rubén took a long sip.

I sat speechless, as though paralysed. Even the bubbles rising to the surface of the water seemed astonishing.

'He'd fuck them and hand them over to the troops?' I echoed his words as though to confirm what I had just heard. 'How do you know?'

'One of his men told me.'

'Who?'

'An officer, Capitan Martínez. I met him when he came on that trip with Papá, I met him in New Jersey. "El Guayo" Martínez they called him. I saw him last night over at a friend's, "Chacho" Osorio. Remember Chacho? We had a couple of drinks at his place. He was telling me what the old man used to get up to. How sometimes he'd screw a female terrorist and pass her on so the rest of the troop could gang-bang her, then he'd just put a bullet in her head. He'd tell the girls he was going to let them go after, so they'd agree to whatever he wanted. He told me that's how they dealt with the fear.'

I looked away. The tourists were gone and a nervous-looking boy was clearing the table. I felt an emptiness. Sometimes he'd screw a female terrorist, pass her on so the rest of the troop could gang-bang her, then put a bullet in her head. That's how they dealt with the fear. Was it that simple?

A faint glow came through the windows, barely enough to light up the line of tables. On the far side, cars passed. A black tricycle passed, towing a cart of empty bottles. An old man pedalling slowly.

'And you believe that?'

'Sure, that's what they said.'

'I don't know, a lot of these stories are made up, or they get exaggerated,' I argued.

A fly had found its way into the restaurant and was buzzing around Rubén's head. He tried to shoo it away.

'But you know something?' he added with a smile, arms out in front of him. 'One of them got away. One of the girls escaped.'

'One of them got away?'

'That's what they told me, something like that. Well, you know what they say, even the best hunter misses sometimes. Even the old man wasn't infallible. And – get this – the girl managed to escape because he fell in love with her.'

'Did he ever say anything about this?'

'No, he never said anything. What would he say? Guayo told me. But you have to see the old man's side of it . . . the war must have driven Papá half crazy. They say that's how it is when you're at war – things get so bad that that's just how it is.'

'I don't know. I can't believe it.'

'What can't you believe?'

'Any of it.'

'Why not?'

'I don't know.'

'War is always fucked up, little brother, all wars.'

'I suppose.'

Rubén finished his brandy.

'That was good. Hey, have a brandy with me, kid.'

'No. I think I'd rather have a pisco.'

The waiter said he would bring me another pisco sour.

'We'll drink a toast to the old man. To Mamá too.'

We were silent for a while. Eventually, the waiter brought my drink. It was thick as syrup and the barman had gone a bit heavy on the lemon juice. I polished it off. We talked for a bit longer.

I checked my watch, told Rubén I had to go. He shrugged.

When I stood up, he followed suit. I gave him a hug and we exchanged email addresses. He had several email accounts and spent some minutes jabbing at them with his fat finger, explaining which ones he checked every day.

By then, I had decided not to see him again for a long time.

I got into my car, turned on the radio. One of them got away, one of them managed to escaped once because – get this – he fell in love with her. Obviously the war drove the old man a bit nuts.

The traffic lights at the junction of Óvalo and El Pacifico were red.

* * *

Back at the office, as I was checking through Señor Cano's contract, I suddenly saw my father – the sagging jowls, the puffy eyes, the big teeth – talking to me in his voice like sandpaper: 'It's not like that, son, it's not like Rubén says it was.'

He was standing at my desk facing me, peering over my paperwork with a vague smile as though aware he was guilty of something but wanted me to hear his side of the story. I saw him hold out his hand to shake mine, his fingers huge, his knuckles tensed. Here was my father standing, looking at me as I sat at my desk, intensely aware of everything I'd just learned. With all that was going on in his face, the thick skin, the stony lips, the damp eyes, I felt I was seeing his uniform for the first time. The black-and-green camouflage pattern, the cap, the thick belt . . .

My father had once ordered me to go and study law in the United States. 'Listen to me, it's what's best for you, don't be a bloody fool, *hijo*.'

It was one of the orders he liked to give. There were others. When I was in secondary school he'd asked me to phone the children of his army buddies and hang out with them.

'Jesus Christ, why don't you call General Salvatierra's boy, I gave you the number, just fucking call him. Tito and Chacho Salvatierra are posh kids, they can get you into that club of theirs and you can all play football.'

The image vanished.

The gruff voice that ordered me to carry on my studies abroad or hang out with the kids of his army friends was the same voice that had ordered the deaths of women he had just fucked. As he said it, he might even have hit them with those thick, hairy knuckles I remembered so well.

I suddenly felt hot. I walked over to the window. Down in the park, everything suddenly seemed lonely and sad. The flowers in small rectangular beds on the lawns. The stone statue. The posts. The patches of yellowing grass. A guard in a blue uniform pacing the dirt path.

Suddenly, I heard Jenny's voice.

The telephone had just rung.

'Adrián, Señor Cano has arrived.'

'OK. Send him in.'

When I got home, Claudia asked how my day had been, how things had gone with Rubén. I told her it was nothing out of the ordinary.

'I don't think I'll see him again,' I commented.

But that night, when Claudia was asleep, I called the hotel. The answering machine in his room picked up. I left a message.

I went to bed and slept fitfully.

The following morning, I went out for a walk.

The street stretched away: a couple of houses, a few trees, the black road.

When I got to the office, I called Rubén's hotel again.

He answered, his voice hoarse.

'You want me to drive you to the airport?' I said.

'Don't worry about it, I've ordered a taxi.' His voice trailed off in a yawn.

'But I'd be happy to drive you, *compadre*,' I said. 'Then we can talk on the way.'

'OK, whatever,' he said. 'I'm supposed to be at the airport at noon, but if I get there at one o'clock that's fine. Swing by half an hour before.'

I pulled up to the door of the hotel at 12.30 and there he was. He shot me an alligator smile, held out a ten-dollar note to the porter who had carried his bags and told him to buy himself a drink. The minute he got into the car, he confessed with a self-satisfied sigh that he was desperate to get away from some girl who'd been hounding him since the previous night.

'Soon as she found out I'd got my green card, she was all over me. She's supposed to be coming to pick me up at one o'clock, so put your foot down.'

As we drove, he launched into a series of predictions about the future of American society.

'They're completely materialistic,' he told me. 'All they think about is money, and after a while you get bored talking about it, but that's how it is there, it's all about money. That's why one of these days I'm going to take my wad of cash, come back here and buy a little farm down in the Lurín valley somewhere, keep chickens and sheep, just a little place with a couple of animals, and I'll sip my beer and watch TV. Fuck all those *gringo* women, what I need is to find myself a *chola*, a nice little honey to look after me, cook for me, and I'm here.'

'So when are you thinking of coming back?' I said.

'Fuck, that's a couple of years away at least.'

The grey midday sky above the trees. Rubén's harsh voice. The grimy snail's pace of the traffic.

We finally made it past the traffic lights and set off down the Avenida Elmer Faucett, towards the flags at the airport that were fluttering with eerie desperation.

I was driving as fast as I could by this point, it was almost half past one.

At the checkpoint, I gave the security guard an ironic salute, showed him my papers and helped my brother unload his luggage. Then I managed to convince the guard to let me join the queue with him.

Once in the queue, pushing the suitcases along, I made the most of the first pause in the long rambling spiel about some *gringa* with 'awesome legs' Rubén was giving me to ask the question that had been plaguing me for hours now.

'Hey, what you were saying last night, that stuff about Papá, were you serious?'

'What?'

'That stuff about Ayacucho and the terrorists.'

'The terrorists?'

'You know, about raping them and then having them killed, was it true?'

He looked at me. The queue shuffled forward and he pushed his suitcase another few inches. We were coming up to the security check.

'Oh, yeah, that . . . That's what they told me. Why?'

'What exactly did they tell you?'

'What I told you, that he used to screw the female prisoners – I don't know if they were terrorists or not, I really

34

don't – that sometimes Papá would screw them and pass them on to the troops. But only sometimes.'

He slung the strap of his case over his shoulder. Some guy came up alongside us.

'Hi, Rubén,' he said. 'You guys don't remember me. I used to be friends with you in the old neighbourhood, we used to play football in the park, remember? I'm Hugo.'

'Ah, Hugo,' Rubén said. 'Of course I remember you.'

Eventually the guy left.

'So, one of them got away from the old man?'

'That, oh yeah, one of the women escaped. That's what they told me.'

'What exactly did they tell you about her?'

'Jesus, I'm fucking telling you what they told me. There was this *chola* the old man took a fancy to, he didn't pass her on to the rest of the troop, he kept her for himself. The old man always was a sentimental fucker.'

He started laughing, then stepped forward to the security guard and answered his questions.

'Kept her?' I said.

'What?'

'The girl. He kept her?'

'He made her stay with him until she did a runner. That's how I heard it.'

'Who told you?'

'Who? I already told you, El Guayo Martínez.'

We were coming up to the check-in counter.

'Where did you see him?'

'I have to go.'

'Just tell me where you saw Guayo Martínez.'

'I already told you, I met him over a couple of drinks.'

'But where?'

'I met up with him and Chacho Osorio, I told you. Fuck's sake, what's with all the questions?'

'Nothing . . . it's nothing, I just want to know. So where can I find this Chacho Osorio?'

'How do I know? This is the first time I've seen the guy in years.'

'So where did you meet him?'

'Jesus Christ, what is it with you?'

'Nothing, it doesn't matter. Just tell me, how do I get in touch with this Chacho guy?'

'Look, I don't exactly have his number on me right now. Why do you want to know anyway? I don't want you jerking my friends around. You planning to call him or what?'

'I don't know. It's just in case there's any trouble. I mean, I could be asked about this shit.'

'Best thing you could do is forget it, never mention it again.'

'OK. Don't worry . . . I'll see you, Rubén. You're next at the check-in.'

I clapped him on the back. 'Let's keep in touch,' I said. 'Have a safe trip.' I tried to dismiss him with another pat on the back and took off as fast as I could. And yet before I reached the glass doors, when I turned and he raised his hand to wave again, I felt a little sad.

III

A S I WAS DRIVING ALONG THE AVENIDA DE LA Marina, my phone started vibrating in my pocket. It felt like a small, angry animal.

It was Claudia, calling to remind me about the parent–teachers' evening.

'They asked us to come early because there are a lot of teachers to see, Adrián. At these things punctuality is taken as a sign that our children matter to us, being late shows a lack of respect,' she said. 'And it's not just mothers who go to these things, fathers are expected go to them these days.'

'Let's meet up there,' I said. 'I'll come straight from the office.'

'OK. How did things go with your brother?'

'Good, they were good, but it's not going to change anything. He's never going to change.'

That afternoon, I went to meet with a group of businessmen hoping to launch a new brand of beer.

I gave the speech I give all new clients: production permits, shareholding opportunities, filing patents, costs of testing.

They asked for a discount. I wasn't listening. I was staring at one of them, a plump, pinkish man with a square head mottled with bald patches as though he'd been rubbing them for years.

I arrived at the school before Claudia. Some of the parents were hanging around the door, laughing and chatting about politics. Claudia turned up, impeccably dressed in a lime-green suit. The whispered conversations carried on until the headmaster came into the room.

The headmaster was a man of about fifty and wore a bright, well-fitted suit. His voice was strange and cold like the voices you get on public-address systems at airports. He gave a reasonably appropriate introduction in which he talked about order and creativity, the twin virtues which the school strove to foster. Afterwards, each of the teachers talked about the aims and objectives of their classes.

The meeting ended early. I dashed down the stairs. A feeling of emptiness made me stumble as I walked across the immense courtyard. Suddenly my mother, my mother's face, appeared, staring up at me from the blurry concrete.

It was unacceptable that she had passed away. It was impossible. I would never be prepared to face the facts. The world was so vast and I felt crushed from all sides . . . A yawning silence like the explosion of absence.

Claudia caught up with me and we walked to the gate. I chatted to some of the other parents, then we walked quickly to the car. Claudia took my hand.

When we got home, I found a letter of condolence:

I waited a few days before writing to you, but you have
been in my prayers. Beatriz will be sorely missed, but she
is with God now.

The letter was from Señora Laura, an old school friend of
Mamá's. There were a number of other cards. One of my
mother's great talents had been her ability to sustain her childhood friendships.

'*Tonight, we went to the cinema with Laura and afterwards
to a cake shop where they serve coffee and wonderful pastries, we
had a lovely time.*

'*Today I went to mass with Rebecca who told me her fifth
grandchild had just been born – imagine that. She showed me
the photo, a beautiful baby boy.*'

My mother's voice floated over these cards from her friends.

'I'll save the addresses,' I said. 'I want to send thank-you
letters.'

'Of course,' said Claudia. 'You should do that tomorrow.
Your mother had wonderful friends.'

'She had a lot of friends, she loved people.'

'Are you sad?'

'I'm fine, don't worry.'

She stroked my head.

'You coming up?' she said, one foot on the stairs.

'No. I'm going to go over some papers. And I need to sort
out Mamá's trunk.'

'You want me to help?'

'No, you go. I'll be up in a little while.'

I watched her go.

I went into the study.

I had feared and deferred the moment I would have to face my mother's trunk. It was black leather with a metal strap and a buckle with a padlock.

I took the key out of the drawer.

There, tied up with blue ribbons, were the papers she had kept her whole life. Documents, receipts, probably letters and photos.

My first thought, half-fearful but half-expectant, was that I might stumble on letters from a lover, letters that out of passion or pride my mother had not been able to throw away.

I didn't know whether my mother had had a secret lover during or after her marriage to my father. If she were still alive, I might not have forgiven her, but now I was almost hoping that she had. I was fascinated by the prospect of discovering the secret side to an all-too-well-ordered life. But I also thought that her integrity, her elegance and her fear would probably have proved insuperable obstacles to getting involved in an affair. No. She had not had a secret lover. She had not put on make-up, got dressed up for some special man. Even moderation has its excesses.

In any case, if she had had a lover, she could easily have got rid of his letters and cards. Cancer had been patient, it had given her more than enough time to cover the traces of any secret life. She had had time to shape the memory she would leave behind. But it was also possible that she wouldn't want to throw away such letters; that she might secretly want the world to discover her affair, an affair she would not have had the courage to admit to while she was alive but which she might have dared to confess to me after her death, perhaps even with a sort of bitter pride. Even so, even now, would she rebel against the image of herself as a woman of elegance and restraint? The need to pass on a shocking secret; it is tempting, a form of revenge from beyond the grave. A love letter, a photo, some scandal out of the silence . . .

In fact, what I most feared was stumbling on some private diary and finding out what she really thought about us. Disappointments about me, gripes about Claudia and the girls, wistful memories of Rubén, the private pain of her loneliness. Perhaps somewhere in here was a piece of jewellery or a dress she had worn as a little girl, an old rag doll, symbols of her desire for fantasy, for beauty she had felt she had to pack away in this trunk full of dreams.

But there were none of these things.

That night, I spent two or three hours untying the ribbons and going over the documents one by one. Some of the envelopes gave off little clouds of dust as I opened them, every puff the herald of some new revelation. She had kept copies of letters to cousins and friends.

I'm so happy to see my grandchildren growing up, sometimes I still go and pick them up from school, it's a pleasure I can't deny myself.

I saw Angélica and Rebecca last night, we had a lovely evening at La Tiendecita Blanca. Rebecca has ten grandchildren now – even she finds it hard to believe.

The letters were consistent with my memories of her. Her face, her bearing, her white dresses were all written here in these ribbons, these envelopes. I felt the gentle terror of knowing that she was looking over my shoulder, reproaching me for having hoped to find something more than this.

I went on looking. I noticed that over the years, her hand-writing had become increasingly drawn out and distorted.

I came upon a bundle of large envelopes. Inside were photos of Mamá as a little girl – in a swimsuit, in her nightdress, at children's parties – and at the birthday parties of her children and her grandchildren, vestiges of a lost happiness cherished for its modesty.

In another envelope I found a sheaf of papers: income tax returns, property tax, receipts and records and more receipts. In another were old school reports, photos of her looking young and serene, almost smiling with her beret and her good grades.

I felt I was playing out a scene she had known I would play. Bent over this trunk, the harsh light of the lamp on my face, going through her papers one by one . . .

There was a bundle of papers related to the house, receipts for payments (she clearly held on to everything, there were receipts here from forty years ago), more photos of her with my grandparents, with my aunts, photos of me and my brother when we were little, always with her, always without my father. I found family letters, from my aunt when she was living in Canada, from my grandmother when she was travelling in Europe, birthday cards Rubén and I had made for her when we were children, party invitations, school reports.

Before I knew it, it was midnight and I was sitting, wiping

my cheeks, overwhelmed by the heat from the lamp. Suddenly, I noticed an envelope different from the others, a creased envelope written in a slow deliberate hand, the words joined together like a line of ants.

There was no return address, only a name: Vilma Agurto.

Carefully, I took out the sheet of paper and words sprung up on the lined paper, a sheet torn from a school exercise book. I held the letter up to the light and began to read.

Señora Beatriz Ormache,

Your husband, Officer Ormache, is a wicked man who has brought great shame to our family. My niece was tortured and injured in Huanta. My niece was a good girl, she was never involved in anything to do with terrorism, but soldiers came and took her away and your husband, Señora, your husband hurt her, he raped her. For this reason, Señora, you and your children have been cursed. Cursed for ever. A curse that will linger for years over your children and your children's children. And that's how it will be.

Vilma Agurto

I folded the letter and slipped it back into the envelope.

I wondered if maybe my mother had not been able to find it to get rid of it in her last months when she had probably gone through this trunk clearing away all traces. Maybe she had dropped it – after all, I'd found it on its own, not tied up with ribbons like the rest of the letters and papers. Had she discussed this letter with anyone in the family or outside the family?

43

I put the papers back in order, tied them up just as I'd found them. Yet again I was acting as though I was afraid she might come in and catch me.

I locked the trunk and put the key back in the drawer.

There was nothing that urgently needed to be dealt with. Her income tax and property taxes were all up to date. We had set up joint bank accounts so that I could access the family money.

And yet that night, my insomnia returned even worse than usual. It was like a sharp pain, a burning sensation, the bed felt too small.

I lay awake, staring at the ceiling.

At about 2 a.m., I got up and turned on the TV.

They were showing old comedy reruns. After a while, I turned it off.

Suddenly I realised what was happening. I got to my feet and went back into the study. Vilma Agurto's niece was clearly the same woman my brother Rubén had talked about, the one who ran away, the woman he said my father had been in love with.

I went down to the bathroom and got a glass of water. My every step seemed to echo like a drum. I opened the trunk and reread the letter. *Your husband has brought a terrible shame on my family. My niece was tortured and violated in Huanta. Soldiers came and took her. Your husband, Señor Ormache, hurt her, he raped her.* But one of them got away, Rubén had said. Even the best hunter misses his mark sometimes. The old man was pretty crazy what with the war and everything, wars do that to you.

IV

I WOKE AT 7 A.M. AS USUAL. IT WAS WEDNESDAY AND I was having a breakfast meeting with my partner Eduardo at La Tiendecita Blanca.

Eduardo's much more of a lawyer than I am; he has shorter sideburns, a bigger paunch, a shinier briefcase and his blue ties. His manners are both gentler and firmer than mine. His car is just a little bigger. He knows more about the law than I do. He's always talking to me about new phones, new gadgets he's buying.

I wouldn't want it to seem as though I was just making fun of these things. I'm grateful for the way Eduardo manages the office, his contacts with people in key companies and obviously for his warmth, his friendship. But there's something about him that bugs me. I don't know what it is. When I see him all happy and serene, I want to hurt him in some way; I'd like to reach inside him, find the right cable, unplug it and watch Eduardo crumple to the floor.

At eight o'clock, La Tiendecita Blanca was full of guys like us. Guys in suits, chatting, smoking, some buried in their newspapers.

That day, Eduardo and I were meeting up there to work out the sackings at the office. We chatted about a couple of staff we had problems with, the secretary who was always late and whose spelling was atrocious, the courier who disappeared for two hours every time he had a job, the young lawyer who was always asking to leave early.

When I arrived, Eduardo was sitting waiting for me at a table at the back. I ordered a coffee and said, 'Do you realise, Eduardo, there's all these people sitting in here, checking each other out, chatting, going about their business and they all seem happy being who they are, calmly doing what they're doing when life's going on just outside. Don't you find it funny?'

Eduardo said he didn't know what I was talking about and asked if I was feeling OK.

'You've had a lot to deal with since your mother died.'

While he was giving me the speech, his hand jerked as though he felt a sudden pain in his side; he took out his mobile phone and brought it to his ear. He jotted a number down on a napkin.

'It's amazing how valuable numbers are,' I thought out loud. 'Seven has great expectations, it can hold its head up, stare into the abyss, while nine and eleven are sinister and two is an innocent you feel you have to protect. Yeah, I know, I'm thinking crazy shit, I don't know what's got into me, I don't know why I'm thinking this, maybe I should see a shrink . . . know any good ones?'

'What's the matter with you?' Eduardo stared at me. 'You're all over the place. Cut the crap and let's deal with our business.'

I looked down, took a sip of coffee and burned my lips. 'Let's deal with our business.'

We agreed on our assessment of all the employees we intended to fire. We drew up a list and swapped numbers of friends and acquaintances who might be able to suggest replacements. I didn't feel any the worse for not having slept but I had three coffees and two glasses of orange juice just in case. I could easily have drunk a vodka too.

I talked to Eduardo about my brother's visit though obviously I didn't go into the details.

We said goodbye. I got back in my car.

I moved in fits and starts along the slow river of traffic down Avenida Pardo. I was thinking about Vilma Agurto's letter.

Sitting in the car, gripping the steering wheel, I could hear my father's words slipping through the chill morning air. His sentences like tiny monsters scurrying all around me on the avenue. He'd warned me. Told me straight out. Someone behind me honked their horn and I heard the clatter of my father's words at the Military Hospital the day he died.

'There's a woman, in Huanta, up in Ayacucho, you have to get in touch with her, you have to find her. I need to ask you this before I die.'

I was watching him as he spoke. His voice was gruff and hoarse.

The trees along Avenida Pardo led me directly to the ocean. I kept driving and came to the seafront.

I hadn't given what he said a second thought in years; I'd dismissed them as the ravings of a dying man.

I turned right. I was two blocks past the Avenida Espinar. I would have to take the long way round. I headed slowly for the office.

When I got there, I sat in the car for a while. What worried me most was that this whole episode would taint my hard-won reputation. If it came out, this story about my father would obviously affect my professional standing. A lawyer can't afford to have even the slightest stain on his designer suit or his immortal soul. Papá raping and killing girls in Huanta. And one of the girls escaped . . . If news got out it would be a catastrophe. I'd have to deny everything.

I needed to protect my reputation. Being an upstanding man from a good family with a good name . . . that's the sort of thing that reassures clients. Seedy stories aren't good for business. This was why I was glad Rubén lived abroad – if he were living here in Lima, his disgraceful behaviour would be difficult for me to cover up. News of Rubén's whoring and his drinking binges would turn the family name into fodder for the gossips and scandalmongers who flourish in this business.

The fact that my father talked to me about this woman shortly before he died incriminated him to some extent.

I went up to my office, past the receptionist who handed me a couple of letters. I threw my briefcase onto a chair. I suddenly felt uncomfortably hot. I took off my tie and turned on the computer. Jenny came in and asked if I needed anything. I told her I didn't. Since my mother had died, she'd been more considerate to me.

I was still grieving for my mother, obviously. I had to go

through the stages. I knew I was still on the lower slopes of grief. I had to skirt the cliffs, carry on until I reached the summit; only then could I begin my calm descent, return to the tranquillity of sea level – that was how I saw it, that was the geographical metaphor I used to get me through. I had to keep climbing until I could finally begin to come down again.

But that morning, sitting next to the window as the light streamed in, suddenly, I don't know why, I wasn't thinking about my mother, I was thinking about the woman in Huanta.

The woman appeared against a background of hills, like a body without a face. She appeared alone, covered only by a black veil. She was lying next to my father. She was a dark shadow by a wall of smoke. In the unexpected silence that invaded the office, the image of my father next to her appeared again and again. I saw them together, him in his uniform and her, naked now. And I think that image marks the beginning of everything that would happen later.

V

I SAW THE TELEPHONE DIRECTORY ON A SHELF. OSCAR
Osorio. Chacho Osorio. He was a friend of Rubén. There
he was in the five pages dedicated to people called Osorio.
I dialled the number. The call was answered by a young
woman, possibly a girl.

'Señor Chacho is not here. He left this morning to go
travelling. I don't know when he'll be back, *señor*. Can I tell
him who called?'

I hung up. I opened the phone directory again, intending
to look up Vilma Agurto's number. I checked through all the
Agurtos, but couldn't find her; what I did find however was
a V. Agurto. It could be Victor or Victoria or Vanessa. It
would have been ridiculous to call: 'Hi, good afternoon, is
there someone there by the name of Vilma Agurto who wrote
a letter a couple of years ago to a Señora Ormache about the
rape and torture of her niece? Well, you made a mistake. My
mother was Miss Miller, or rather she was Señora Beatriz
Miller who, as a result of some romantic accident, an episode
that's never been clearly explained, married Señor Ormache,
the man who abused your niece, *señora*.'

I realised I'd been thinking out loud when the phone rang. It was Claudia. She'd just had a call from her father. I listened.

'Adrián, listen, I've got good news. Papi called me and asked what we were doing for the girls' school holidays. He said why didn't we all go on holiday with him and Mami, what do you think?'

'Where?'

'The Caribbean, Isla Margarita in Venezuela, what do you think?'

'I don't know. I've got a lot of work on. We'll see.'

'OK, let's talk later.'

'Did anyone phone for me?'

'Yes, actually, some woman with a strange voice called for you . . . Hang on, I've got her name here, someone called Vilma Agurto.'

'Vilma Agurto?'

'Yes, that's right. She had a strange voice. She said she saw the notice about your mother's death in the paper. She wants to talk to you. Who is this woman, Adrián?'

A silence, a lump in my throat. 'I'll tell you later,' I said. 'But what did she say?'

'She asked for you, like I said – she sounded funny. She said she'd call back, then she hung up. That's it. To tell you the truth, I was a bit worried. Have you any idea who she is?'

'I think so, but it's a long story, I'll tell you later.'

'What should I tell Papá about the holidays?'

'Let's talk later, we can talk about the holiday then too.'

I rubbed my face.

Vilma Agurto had my home phone number; she had called

me and she would call again soon. I knew she would phone again, it was just a matter of waiting. In the meantime, it was best to do nothing.

Sitting at my office, I forced myself to work on the Guerra family business. They wanted to expand their chain of poultry shops into the provinces.

At midday, I called on my uncle Federico, my mother's cousin. Federico was a doctor with a list of well-heeled patients on the Calle Lord Cochrane, a quiet street in the upmarket Miraflores district. His success was due in no small part to the wealth of his wife, my aunt Pepa.

The distinctive thing about my uncle Federico was his voice. He spoke in a sort of extraordinary baritone that burnished even trivial comments – 'I had an interesting patient today', 'I'm going into the office for afternoon surgery', 'I think perhaps it's time to watch the news' – to a fine lustre. The house was impeccably neat, the only element of chaos being a cocker spaniel which he addressed with great formality; he would eject it from the room by opening the door and saying, 'If you would be so good . . .' Uncle Federico treated us much as he did his dog, invariably pleasant but never quite affectionate. The greatest gift he wished to bestow upon his nephews was his voice, which he himself considered the hallmark of elegance. Family legend had it that when Uncle Federico watched the Peruvian team score he didn't shout 'GOOOOOAL!', but '*Anotación, anotación!*' and that before making love to my aunt Pepa he would say, 'If you could wait a moment, I need to hang up my clothes.'

I called on him at his consulting room – luckily he wasn't

with a patient. I found him sitting in his armchair, head high. The knot of his tie seemed to be the only thing holding him up. Sometimes I thought that knot was a button that turned him on and off.

I asked how he was. He told me he was well, tolerably well.

'Listen,' I said, 'I've had a call from a woman called Vilma Agurto who says she knew Mamá. Do you know who she is?'

'No, I can't say I do, I've never heard mention of the name Vilma Agurto. A friend of your mother?'

'I don't know.'

'Is everything going well in your life, *sobrino*?'

'Everything's fine, everything's good.'

That night when I got home, I found Claudia and her sisters eating chocolates and drinking wine one of my sisters-in-law had brought back from Argentina. Claudia heated up some food, brought it to me in the dining room and asked me how things had gone at work.

'We need to lay some people off, but otherwise, things are fine.'

'Everything's fine?'

'Yeah, no problem.'

After I'd eaten, I went into the study, turned on my PC and started playing chess against the computer.

Computer chess has only two emotions in its arsenal: green light and red light. The numbers and letters that flash up indicating the virtual brain's moves are implacable and usually chillingly astute. There's a particular pleasure in beating a computer. It's like beating a god. You don't have to feel any sympathy for a computer. Humiliating it, bringing it to its knees, watching the hapless machine flash up its red light . . . I've become addicted to this stuff.

That night, maybe because of the chatter of my sisters-in-law, I couldn't quite concentrate. The computer beat me in twenty-three moves, which was faintly embarrassing given my recent track record. I was prepared to take my revenge. Then, unexpectedly, I turned off the monitor and wrote down the name Vilma Agurto.

The following day, I said Hi to my secretary, Jenny, as I passed, then holed myself up in my office.

Jenny has long, silky hair, silver earrings and radiant olive skin. Everything about her seems to project itself outwards. Her eyes radiate light. Her hair, like shimmering gossamer, seems to float in the air. She speaks with passion, her vowels perfectly articulated, and she gestures as she talks. Her conversational gambits range from the weather to the menopause to former clients.

Jenny has a fierce intelligence which she uses to hide her tender heart. An amateur psychologist, she's constantly trying to work out the motives of clients and colleagues: 'Poor guy, obviously wasn't breastfed as a baby,' or 'Just because he's not the boss at home he tries to play the boss here,' are typical things she might say. When you ask her to get a document from the Public Registry Office, she has a series of stock phrases like, 'If they don't get back to me, I'll go over there and smash in their faces.' Yet she's capable of bringing a sweetness to her voice as she picks up the phone and says, 'Good afternoon, Señor Cano, such a pleasure to hear from you.'

I'd hired Jenny on the recommendation of Claudia's family. From the day she arrived, she took to her role like a duck to water. She typed contracts, arranged meetings, checked the civil code, managed calendars and, most importantly, got along with everyone. Her questions and remarks were always pertinent, she was cordial with clients (equally gracious with those who were presumptuous, long-winded or brusque) and she was a willing and candid chatterbox when it came to me.

She had two minor flaws: a voice that was harsh, almost grating, and a taste for garish dresses that I requested she tone down. She was not particularly pretty, but I liked looking at her because she had all the right curves in all the right places.

I liked, admired, perhaps even fancied Jenny. She'd lived life in a hurry: married by the time she was twenty, divorced at twenty-four, married again at twenty-eight only to end up a childless widow the following year. She had been sad and angry when she broke up with her first husband – a nice enough guy, but a liar and a womaniser. Her second husband had died in an accident driving round one night to patch things up after an argument (she sometimes cried when she talked about him). She was a feisty 'mother' to her two nieces and a gifted executive secretary to her three bosses. Sometimes I imagined that I was a sort of surrogate husband. Her unswerving loyalty to me consisted of a spirited defensiveness when anyone criticised my work and an arsenal of excuses and a persuasive tone when it came to telling callers I wasn't in.

That day, Jenny was waiting with a list of appointments

that included the people to be fired. Eduardo and I had agreed to handle the dismissals in person, each taking two from the list of four people we needed to sack. This was not the first time I had been called on to fire someone. I would do it calmly, with just a hint of pleasure if I particularly disliked the person.

With a secret smile I fired the courier, an insolent, surly youth, but I felt sorry at having to dismiss the secretary whose letters were constantly littered with misspellings. She was a skinny, quiet, chaste-eyed girl who, when I told her I had to let her go, asked if I could help her find another job. I said it would be my pleasure. They both headed down to human resources to collect their last pacheque. The whole business was over and done with by noon. I might feel a little bad over lunch, but there was time enough to compose myself before dinner that night.

Around midday, just before I headed out to lunch with Eduardo, Jenny came into my office.

'I have a Señor Chacho Osorio on the line. He said he's returning your call.'

Hearing his voice on the telephone, I immediately remembered his face. Chubby cheeks, nose pitted with acne, square head. I'd seen him a couple of times, always with my brother; going out while I stayed at home.

'Adrián, how are things? What's up . . . ?

'Hey, Chacho. Long time . . .'

'Yep. Hey, it's good to hear from you. Rubén came by my place a couple of days ago. A little reunion.'

'Yeah, he told me.'

'Hey, I'm really sorry about your *mamá*, Adrián. She was a good woman, she really was.'

'Thanks, Chacho.'

'Well, I'm not going to ask how you're getting on because I know you're doing well for yourself. Seen you in the paper and everything.'

'You know how it is, journalists will write about pretty much anyone.'

As we talked, Chacho's face slowly came together in my mind.

'What are you talking about, anyone? They write about you, you're a big guy these days, Adrián. So what miracle has you calling me?'

'I'd just like to meet up. When could we see each other?'

'I don't know, you tell me . . . whenever suits you. I'm easy.'

I paused.

'What do you say we have lunch today?' I said. 'You free? I'll pick up the tab.'

'What, now?'

'Yeah.'

He hesitated.

'Yeah, sure, great.'

'OK. I'll pick you up at one thirty. Give me your address.'

I hung up, and got to my feet. I paced around the office a couple of times.

It occurred to me that my office was too small. Maybe one of these days I should think about getting a bigger one.

* * *

Jenny came in with a bundle of cheques for me to sign. I stared at her. As she sometimes did, she was wearing mascara that made her eyelashes stiff. Her eyebrows were carefully and precisely pencilled.

'You OK?' she asked.

'Sure. Why?'

'I don't know, you don't look too good. Is something wrong?'

'No, everything's fine.'

I'd agreed to pick up Chacho at half past one, but I set off early.

The day was steel grey, the light casting shadows on the concrete walls. Traffic along the expressway known as 'The Ditch' was moving slowly, there seemed to be a hold-up of some sort. When I came to Javier Prado, I took the ramp and drove into the maze of narrow motley streets in San Borja. Almost immediately I saw the name of Chacho's street. Liszt. I was right by his place, but I was still fifteen minutes early. I decided to ring the bell. A black metal grille, a dilapidated door with glass panels surrounded by a feeble, faintly disgusting, climbing plant.

The door was opened by a woman of about twenty, maybe twenty-two, wearing an orange sweatshirt with a University of Miami logo across the chest. She let me in. In the middle of the room was a big plate-glass table. I sat on a blue sofa facing an egg-shaped mirror. A Sacred Heart of Jesus stared down at me from where it hung in a spotlight. I heard muffled voices from upstairs.

Then, finally, I saw him.

Chacho Osorio. A face that had materialised from my childhood. Square, solid, thick lipped, a sharp pointed nose. His eyes were too small for the size of his head, while his mouth on the other hand seemed too big. His hair was like a carnival. He was grinning at me like a dirty skull. He shook my hand.

'Jesus, Adrián, how long has it been? I just saw Rubén the other day. I was really sorry to hear about your mother.'

'Thanks.'

'You fancy a glass of rum here before we head out?'

'Sure, why not, a quick rum and we'll go.'

I knocked back the drink as quickly as I could to make it clear I wanted to get going.

He moved like a pent-up athlete. Every movement – picking up a glass, pouring from the bottle, adding the ice – seemed faster than necessary.

In the car, I suggested we go to Café Café in Larcomar. He nodded. Obviously I didn't want to go anywhere that might be particularly crowded. Café Café was a nice enough place, it had a good view, served delicious salads and at this time of day it would be almost empty.

That day, as I stepped out of Chacho's house, the street seemed to shimmer in the sunlight. A shaft streamed briefly through a gap in the clouds. In that moment, Chacho seemed a radiant being. Sitting next to me, he started talking.

'When you were a kid, I was round your house all the time. I can still see you now. I'd call round to see Rubén and you'd say, "He's not here, *señor*." That's how you used to talk, all polite, you were a serious kid. I'd call round to take Rubén to your *papá's* place, that's why I used to come to yours, remember?'

I parked in the underground car park, climbed out and was immediately harassed by some guy in blue overalls begging to let him wash my car for four *soles*. How long will it take? I walked one step ahead of Chacho across the upper terrace. As we went down the steps along the seafront, I saw a long queue of fat tourists in shorts lined up at the railings.

We got to Café Café: wicker chairs, brownish yellow tables, Jaunes playing on the stereo. On the far side of the glass wall, the ocean stretched away. Chacho stopped in front of the windows.

'This place is fucking awesome, isn't it, *compadre*? The waves breaking out there in the distance. I think I'll bring my niece here, she's just started at university, I'll bring her here and buy her an ice cream, sort of a reward for all her hard work.'

As I listened, my attention wandered and I stared out at the low clouds.

I ordered steak and salad, a glass of red wine and a coffee. Chacho asked for *lomo saltado*, a beer and dessert. I'd told him lunch was on me.

Chacho spent a while bitching about money. 'These days, ten *soles* doesn't buy you anything. That's just how it is. Since I got out of the army, I've been working odd jobs here and there. A mate of mine got me a job at Petroperú but then when Fujimori got into power, I had to leave. Right now, I'm doing odd jobs for someone, but only until the end of the month. After that, who knows? Suppose I just have to keep on looking, that's how it is.'

Watching him eat, I steeled myself to say what I needed to say.

'Chacho, there's something I wanted to ask you.'

'Shoot.'

'You were stationed with Papá up at the barracks, weren't you. The barracks in Huanta?'

'Yeah. Fuck, that was some fucking situation. I don't know how we survived.'

'I can imagine. I mean, the weather up there's bloody awful.'

'Fucking weather was shit, the food was shit. And if that wasn't bad enough, we had to fight a fucking war against those fucking terrorists.'

'Yeah. But there was something I wanted to ask, Chacho.' I looked him in the eye, almost smiling. 'Is it true that some girl got away from Papá?'

Chacho put down his fork and picked up a napkin. He went on talking with his mouth full. There was a smudge of tomato next to his mouth.

'Who the fuck told you about that?'

'Rubén told me.'

He looked down, spearing strips of steak and fries and rice onto his fork.

I asked the waiter to bring him another beer.

'Your *papá* was a great man, a fine soldier.' He waved his arm up and down, fingers splayed. 'Fuck that, he was a great Peruvian, that's what he was.'

'I know, Chacho, I know. You know what, Chacho? The truth is, I want you to tell me about him, to tell me everything you know about him. That's why I wanted to talk to you, I didn't want to talk about anything else, I wanted to talk about him, I want to know what he did. I know things were tough up there. Here in Lima, we couldn't imagine what was going on. I know that. I'm not trying to wind you up.'

He looked at me as he speared a potato.

'OK, man.' He was calmer now. 'Maybe we should change the subject.'

We made brief stabs at conversation. I asked after his family. He told me he had two sons, one was studying accountancy and the other one was studying law. He was just about to graduate. One of them was thinking of getting married at the end of the year.

In a stupid attempt to get him in a good mood, I commented that he'd be a grandfather soon.

He gave a faint smile. 'What about you? You've got two daughters, don't you?' he said. 'Rubén told me you've got two daughters.'

'Yes, I've got two daughters. One of them is just finishing secondary school.

'You know, Papá talked to me about that woman,' I whispered abruptly.

He finished his glass of beer and set it down. His eyes were puffy.

'He told you?'

'When I went to see him in the hospital, that last day, he was talking a bit strangely that day, he seemed confused.'

'What did he tell you about her?'

'I don't know. He said there's a woman, a woman in Huanta up in Ayacucho, you have to find her. Something like that.

At the time, I didn't think anything of it. You think he might have been talking about her?'

'Could be, could be.'

He started drumming his fingers on the table.

'You're still angry. I'm sorry. I know how hard it is to talk about what happened back then.'

He glanced at me, then turned away and stared out into the distance.

'What do you know about any of this?' he muttered eventually, and went back to eating.

'You're right. I don't know anything. That's why I'm asking.'

They brought him a coffee and he took a few quick sips.

'I'm fucking roasting here,' he grumbled.

'You're right. They've got the heating up too high. I'll ask them to turn it down. You want a glass of water?'

The waiter brought us iced water. Chacho finished his coffee. We talked for a bit. He wiped his face slowly with a napkin as though postponing the moment when he would be free to talk again. Then he folded the napkin and set it down.

'You want a drink?' I asked.

'No.'

There was a pause. Suddenly, he picked up his glass.

'Since you're picking up the tab here, I'll buy you a drink somewhere else,' he murmured.

I glanced at my watch. Somewhere else?

'Sure. Let's go,' I said.

We got in the car.

'We're going to visit a friend,' Chacho told me.

'Who?'

'Just a friend. You'll see. He'll be happy to see you.'

As we drove, Chacho talked to me about his problems with his wife. He was planning to split up with her.

'She's a selfish bitch, doesn't think about anyone except herself. We're always fighting. There's times I have to hit her, give her a good slap to get through to her, the woman's a fucking animal.'

Now and again, he laughed. Short terse laughs through gritted teeth.

As we drove down Avenida Salaverry, Chacho gave directions. Turn here, straight on. He brought his finger up to the window.

'Where are we going?' I asked.

'You'll see.'

We were coming into the Breña district – a tangle of shabby, run-down narrow streets, potholed, cracked and caked in mud. By Avenida Arica, everything seemed to be covered in a layer of filth. I parked in front of a big door.

It was opened by a brawny man who hugged Chacho and clapped him on the back.

'This is Guayo,' he said.

He had the beady eyes of a rat. His unbuttoned shirt revealed a forest of white hair. He had a big belly, fat stubby fingers, a face mottled with blotches and freckles, and arms covered in moles. His voice, like a girl's, was completely at odds with his huge rat-like face. Next to Guayo, Chacho looked like a puppet. We sat at a table covered with a blue-and-white striped plastic tablecloth. The floor was covered with patches of concrete and traces of sawdust.

'So come on, Guayo, you not going to offer us a drink?'

At the back, a midget waitress was washing dishes. Guayo called her over. 'Carmencita, Carmencita,' his shout cut the air.

The midget had a snub nose and eyes like ground glass. She dried her hands, wiped them on her apron and came over with a couple of large bottles of beer, carrying them disdainfully as though they were animals whose throats had just been cut.

'So what brings you here, mate?' Guayo said to me. 'I've seen you before somewhere, what the fuck's with the clothes? You look like those lazy fuckers you see in the papers, always wearing a suit, or maybe you just wear it so everyone knows you're a big man, huh?'

'Fuck's sake, don't be rude to my friend, Guayo,' Chacho said.

'I'm not being rude, *compadre*. Just telling it how it is.'

'You don't know who this is?' Chacho said, putting a hand on my shoulder. 'This is the *comandante*'s son.'

'The *comandante*'s son? Comandante Ormache's son?'

'Guayo, this is Adrián Ormache. Rubén's brother.'

'What? Fuck, I don't believe it. Comandante Ormache's son?'

He got to his feet and hugged me.

'A pleasure, it's a pleasure,' he said.

We sat down. Guayo picked up his glass and raised it towards me.

'I can't believe it . . . You're Adrián?'

Before long we'd finished the bottles of beer.

The afternoon wore on. Guayo and Chacho reminisced about old friends: 'I wonder what happened to that guy, I never heard from him.' 'Someone told me he's got a little farm up in Arequipa.' A network of beads of sweat began to trickle across Guayo's skin. Chacho on the other hand was dry and talking faster.

'So how are things going with the restaurant?' he said.

'Good, really good, but we don't let just anyone in here. We have to close up at nights because the streets round here are getting to be pretty dodgy.'

Guayo explained that he'd worked as a policeman, then later as bodyguard for some businessman. This, he had decided, was his vocation: looking after important people, keeping them safe, until eventually he could be St Peter's bodyguard.

'It's my destiny, *compadre*, you understand. But we're still friends, we still meet up here, Chacho and me,' he said, putting a hand on his friend's shoulder.

From time to time, they'd interrupted their conversation to offer another encomium to my father. I thanked them as effusively as I could.

At about half past four, I called Jenny and told her to cancel the rest of my appointments for the day. I said I was in a meeting.

'So this is where Chacho and I always meet up,' Guayo said again. 'We still meet up because it's a miracle we got out of that hellhole alive, a fucking miracle. Because a lot of guys died up there.'

'Who, for example . . . ?'

'Well,' Guayo threw his arms wide, 'you remember Rosas, the engineer?' He turned to Chacho who nodded.

'What happened?'

'I'll tell you. I'll never forget it. There was this one time, we'd been tracking a gang of terrorists and we saw them going into this house, hiding. So we surrounded the house and shouted for them to come out, but they wouldn't. It was just a wooden shack – we chucked grenades and torched the place and they scurried out of it like fucking rats. Bang, bang, we shot the fuckers, just like that. They'd just killed the mayor in a little town called San Francisco and come here and holed up, but we surrounded them, shouted for them to come out and when they didn't we torched the place and as they came running out we fired, bang, bang, and killed every last one of them. Even the last guy who came out shouting and waving a red flag, we shot him too. We didn't show our faces until they were all lying dead on the ground. But it was a sad day, a sad day for us. That's where my friend Rosas died.

'We'd all been trained to fire a *coup de grâce*, make sure the fuckers were dead, but there was one guy we must have missed, I don't know how, but one of the terrorists wasn't dead. He'd been shot, he was wounded, but he wasn't dead and with his last ounce of strength the fucker aimed his FAL semi-automatic and fired at Rosas, setting off the grenade hanging from his belt. But Rosas didn't die right away. He hung on for two hours. There was my mate, lying dying for two hours. We called out a 'copter but it didn't come and it didn't come and Rosas was praying and I was holding his head, talking to him,

67

trying to keep his spirits up, telling him to hang on, and he was giving me messages for his son: "Tell him I love him very much, and take care of him for me, do whatever you can to help him, and my wife, and my mother, but promise me you'll tell them, Guayo, tell them I was thinking of them, tell them I died happy and that I'm in heaven, that I'm up there looking down on them, that I'll watch over them, tell them I died defending Peru, that's the most important thing, tell my little boy, tell him to look up into the sky, tell him I'm there with the stars, tell him to talk to me, don't forget, promise me." And I tried to keep him calm: "Don't say things like that, you'll see your little boy again. How old is he? You'll see, you'll be around to see your grandchildren, the helicopter will be here in a minute, don't talk like that." "Just promise me you'll tell them." "OK, if you want, I promise, but you'll be fine, I swear, the 'copter is on its way, it's coming."

'I watched my mate bleeding out and I tried to reassure him, but then he just lay there, like he took one last breath and lay there, my friend, lying there in front of me, I swear, he just closed his eyes and his body stopped, his whole body stopped working, stopped moving, like he was paralysed, like he was already dead. Fuck. Still the chopper didn't come and when it did it was too late, there was nothing we could do, we just had to let him die. But I can still see his lips moving, his lips were dry and they had that white crust they get when you die. But I hope he died thinking he was going to live, that he was going to pull through. That's what we all wanted.'

While Guayo was talking, I felt as though I was sailing on a sea of beer, listening to his words through a pleasant haze of seasickness. Chacho and Guayo went on talking, sometimes to each other, sometimes to me. Talking loudly as though they were preaching to each other. From time to time they'd stop and pour me another beer or tell me about some woman they'd been with, but mostly they just told stories about the war. After a while, they started reminiscing about the ways they used to torture people.

'Sometimes, we'd push their heads into a bucket of water to make them confess. If we weren't doing it to them, they'd have been doing it to us, that's just how it was. Sometimes we'd attach wires to their balls or their tits. But only sometimes.'

In the four or five hours I spent with them, it was as though I was seeing them through a screen: two excitable monkeys performing for each other, juggling vivid balls of memory.

Then suddenly, everything shifted. I can still clearly remember the moment when Chacho, pointing at me, laughingly said to Guayo, 'Hey, this guy's been asking about what happened that time with Miriam.'

It was the first time I'd heard her name. Miriam. As I picked up my full glass of beer, I realised something was happening. I had spent the past five hours drinking with my father's favourite torturers and now they were about to tell me her story.

VI

'MIRIAM. WHAT HAPPENED WITH THE GIRL, Miriam?' I asked.

Chacho looked away, Guayo poured himself another glass of beer and started talking.

'Thing is . . . what happened is . . . this one time we brought your father a young native girl we'd found in one of the villages, and he screwed her, then gave her to us to screw and then we killed her. Well, after that, we did the same with other women. We told the girls we'd let them go if they let us fuck them. That's what we told them. Or at least screw the officers. Two or three times we did it. At least we shot them in the head. The female terrorists had it a lot worse, we killed them by smashing their heads in with a big rock.

'One day, we found this girl in a village right nearby. She was really pretty, really young. She was slim with long hair and big dark eyes – like I said, pretty. We picked her up in a village near Huanta. The minute we saw her, her *mamá* grabbed hold of her and wouldn't let her go, she wouldn't let her go. "You're not taking my daughter," she said, so we pistol-whipped her and the old woman fell on the ground howling and we dragged the girl off kicking and screaming to the truck and took her to your *papá*.

'Your *papá* slept with her that night, and next day there we were waiting for him to pass her on, to give her to us, but the door to your *papá*'s room never opened. I swear, it didn't open. Your *papá* didn't want us to have her. I don't know what got into him. The whole platoon was there waiting but he just kept this girl for himself. When he finally came out, he left her in the room. Round about noon we saw her again, she was at the window. She only opened it for a minute, she was scared shitless. She stood there with tears in her eyes and her hair all nicely combed and then she closed the window. And that was that. Your old man was in love with that girl and he didn't want the troops getting their hands on her. He didn't want her executed, and all the soldiers were bad-mouthing him but we shut them up. And just like that, I don't know how, but your *papá* went soft. He was happy, he'd ask us to bring avocados so he could have breakfast, with her. Your *papá* was mad about that girl.'

Guayo raised his glass. Chacho had been nodding at every-thing he was saying. I'd listened in silence, and I don't know if I showed any reaction.

'And this was the girl who escaped?' I asked.

Guayo held up his hand and shook his head as he poured himself more beer.

'She didn't escape,' he said. 'You got that wrong. She didn't escape. We let her escape.'

'She fucking escaped,' interrupted Chacho. 'She smacked us both and she got away from us, dickhead.'

'You mean she got away from you, because you had to get involved, you couldn't leave it alone.'

'If you'd left it to me, no way she would have fucking escaped.'

'You had a thing for her, Chacho, that was the problem, had a thing for her.'

I looked at Guayo.

'What was she like, this girl?'

Guayo started to say something.

'A hot little *chola*,' Chacho interrupted. 'We picked her up in Luricocha, just outside Huanta. That's where we found her. But she got away. She escaped and we never found out what happened to her. When your *papá* came back and found out what had happened he was furious, he put us in the slammer. It was like he was crazy, he started searching for her all over. He put us in the cells for two days, your old man. Eventually, he came with the key and let us out himself and he hugged us and we all got hammered and he was taking the piss, saying we didn't know anything about her. And the other soldiers were laughing at us too until we gave them a good beating and wiped the smiles off their faces.'

'But how could she have escaped from the barracks?' I asked.

'Because your *papá* went off to Huamanga one night,' said Chacho. 'He went to meet with some general from Lima. He went off and left her with us. That was his mistake. And, well, our mistake was to start talking to her, we started talking about everything, and we broke out some beer and had a drink with her but she only pretended to drink, she hardly drank anything, but we didn't realise that, she'd lift her glass but she'd just take

72

little sips. We were in your *papá*'s office, he'd gone off to this meeting with the high command, he'd be staying in Huamanga overnight so we could spend the night with her, so we turned on the radio, put on some salsa, knocked back a couple of beers and then we asked her to dance and she started dancing, first with me, then with him and then this guy tried to kiss her and she pulled away and I bawled him out, said what was he doing trying to sleep with the *comandante*'s girl and we started fighting and then suddenly I felt something hit me on the head, the little *chola* had grabbed a beer bottle and smashed it over my head and then she did the same to him. Smashed them right over our heads. We were pretty bombed, hadn't a fucking clue; we wound up sprawled on the floor and that's where we woke up the next morning. Guayo woke up before me because he was cold.'

'But how could she get out of the barracks?'

'Because she put on Guayo's uniform, that's how, that's what I've been telling you . . . The girl put on Guayo's uniform and walked straight out of the barracks, told the sentry she was leaving and he thought it was Guayo.'

Chacho lifted his glass.

He pointed a finger at Guayo as though he was going to shoot him. Guayo listened to him, stroked his chin, shrugged his shoulders and looked at me.

'The *chola* put on the beret and everything,' Chacho went on. 'Lit one of Guayo's cigarettes and walked out of the *comandante*'s office, didn't give the guard a second look, and in Guayo's voice – she impersonated Guayo's voice – she said, "I'm just going out for a walk," that's what the guard told us next day, "I'm just going out for a walk," and the guard said she sounded exactly, I mean exactly, like Guayo, said she looked like him, with the cigarette dangling from her mouth, because Guayo was always smoking . . . Anyway, so the guard opened the gate and let her out. He let her leave, he had no idea we were right inside, drunk and unconscious because of her.'

'And she was never found?'

'We never found her,' said Chacho. 'Your *papá* searched all over for her, but he couldn't find her. In the end, he forgave us and after that we never heard a word about her, about Miriam.'

'Miriam what?' I asked.

'How would I know? Just Miriam, that's all I knew.'

'But he fancied her,' said Guayo, pointing at Chacho.

Guayo was patting him on the back.

'He had a thing for Miriam, he fancied her – you fancied her, didn't you?'

Chacho glared at him angrily.

'He says he didn't,' Guayo went on, 'but he fancied her too. You'd see her and you'd be like a little fucking lapdog.'

'Get the fuck out,' said Chacho.

'You fancied her. You loved Miriam. That's why you wanted to have a drink with her, to dance with her, remember? Besides, you knew she had nothing to do with Sendero Luminoso. You knew she was just some girl we took off the streets because we wanted to bring someone, to bring a woman back for the *comandante*. Maybe you thought if you brought him a girl like that, he'd be happy and he'd be grateful

74

to you, but then you fell for her. That's why you brought her, remember? You went to her house, dragged her away from her mother and took her. You wanted her for yourself, didn't you?'

Guayo's words and his little-girl laugh drowned out the voice of Chacho who was staring at him. Guayo's white hair glistened with sweat. Chacho shoved him hard, then seemed to retreat into himself. His ears were flushed red.

'Hey, what's up, Chacho?' Guayo laughed. 'What's the matter?' He pushed his friend's shoulder gently.

Guayo tried to pat his face and Chacho gave him a slap that rang like a whip-crack.

They struggled to their feet and started scuffling. They were pummelling, pushing, faces pressed together, the squeak of shoes sliding on the concrete.

I stood up too, though I made no real attempt to try and separate them.

It was the waitress who pulled them apart. The dwarf waitress strode over brandishing a bottle, stood in front of them, stared at Chacho and screamed, 'That's enough, Señor Chacho.'

Chacho looked at her, stepped back and thumped the table, making it jump. One of the beer bottles fell and smashed on the floor. He was breathing heavily, staring at the bottle, his eyes wide. He said, 'You always were a fucking shit,' and disappeared out the door.

I suddenly heard the roar of traffic from the *avenida*. Outside, the street was dark now.

* * *

'Fuck, stupid shit didn't have to get heavy,' Guayo said, nodding towards the door and very slowly taking his seat again. 'Come on, let's have another beer. What d'you say?'

'Sure.'

'Carmencita, couple of beers,' he roared, sweating like a pig.

'But were you serious, was Chacho really into the girl?'

Guayo took great gulps of air.

'Sure, that's why he tried to take her off me,' he said eventually. 'There we were with her, I was about to kiss her and he got between us and next thing I knew she smashed beer bottles over our heads. I think she knew he had a thing for her. Then she stole my uniform – she knew she had a better chance of imitating my voice, 'cause I've got this high-pitched voice – and talked her way out of the barracks. Crafty little *chola*, she was. "Just going for a walk," she said to the guard, with a cigarette in her mouth. And she fooled him. Sometimes I'd go for a wander round Huanta just because it was dangerous, but at night I just strolled round the barracks if I felt like a walk. She knew that, that's why she said, "I'm just going out for a walk," and the guard obviously thought it sounded like me – or maybe he opened the door because she was about my size and she was smoking a cigarette. Walking around Huanta in uniform alone, Jesus fuck, a guy could get himself killed. I think she was a bit loco, you know?' Guayo tapped his head. 'She wasn't all there. Though I guess she'd say better to die on your feet than live on your knees. I don't know, maybe the little *chola* had a point.'

He wiped his forehead with his hand. He looked away.

There was a long silence. I heard a dog barking. The barking rose to become a persistent howl. I figured someone was probably beating the animal.

Guayo stroked his chin, ran his fingers through his hair, took a long slug of beer.

'But you know what I think? I really think he had a thing for that girl. Straight up.'

'Looks that way.'

'Yeah. Hey, let's have a couple more beers – one for the road, yeah? Carmencita, two more beers. A toast, to Comandante Alberto Ormache. A toast to Adriáncito. Adrián, that's your name, isn't it?'

Guayo went on talking. I was barely listening.

'Your *papá* was a very organised man. He always got up early, he'd have us drilling and marching. He was strict, your *papá*, but off duty, he liked to fuck around too. He changed while he was with that girl, with Miriam. He was nicer.'

I drank some more beer. The thick bitter taste, the bubbles rising to the surface, my father's name fluttering round the table, I barely remember what was said after that.

'So this girl, you found her in a village near Huanta?' I said. 'What was the name of the village again?'

'Luricocha, it was called Luricocha. It's just outside Huanta. That's where we picked her up. Well, I didn't pick her up, that was Chacho. Dragged her away from her *mamá*, he did, told her we were taking her in for questioning and left her mother standing there sobbing. I think he fell in love with her the minute he set eyes on her. But obviously he had to take her to your *papá*.'

The midget brought over a tray of *chicharrón de pescado* the colour of olives. Guayo speared a couple of the deep-fried strips of fish and wolfed them down. He opened his mouth wide as though he was yawning.

'Your old man never told you?'

'No, he didn't. I mean, why would he have said anything to me? Anyway, I didn't see much of Papá back then.'

I was about to get up and say my goodbyes when Guayo reached over and stopped me.

'Hey, hang on, let me tell you something,' he said, chewing as he talked. 'Don't know if I should, but I'm gonna tell you anyway, out of respect for your father's memory, OK.'

'Tell me what?'

'Keep your voice down, shit, what's wrong with you? You pissed off with me or something?'

His eyes were huge and damp, his face puffy like a child's.

'No, I'm not angry, honest. Actually, it's been really nice meeting you, talking about Papá. So, tell me, what happened?'

Guayo glanced around, mopped his forehead.

'OK. You sure you're not pissed off?'

'No, honestly.' I paused a moment. 'How could I be angry with one of Papá's friends, Guayo?'

'Ah, OK. All right then, I'll tell you.' His lips broadened into a smile. 'I'll tell you. I ran into Miriam again later.'

He had pushed his hand across the table and was staring at me, his eyes shining. I felt a shudder run through me.

'You saw her? The girl who escaped? I thought you said the two of you never saw her again?'

Guayo raised a finger.

'Chacho never saw her again, but I did, yeah? I saw her.'

'When?'

'Shit, I don't know, one night when I was working for Dasso, the engineer. I used to be his bodyguard, used to go with him to the bank over in San Isidro when he had to talk to the manager. Anyway, I asked Dasso if I could go and get a bottle of Incakola while he was in the bank and he said OK, so I go into this little corner shop nearby and the girl behind the counter, she stares at me hard, I remember it like it was yesterday, she was wearing a gold chain round her neck and a polo shirt and her eyes were huge – it was her, I couldn't fucking believe it. I'm telling you, she stared at me and then I gave her the money and took the bottle of cola and I realise she's still fucking staring at me. She gave me my change and stared at me, then looked away. And I recognised her, I knew it was her. It was Miriam. Here she was, working in this shop. This was later, a couple of years at least, but it was definitely her. And when I recognised her, I put the bottle down on the counter – I'd hardly touched it, hardly had a sip, but I put it down – and I got the fuck out of there and went back to the bank, shit, and I looked round and she'd come outside and she was standing at the door of the shop. Standing there staring at me, in her blue jeans and her white polo shirt with her long hair and the gold chain round her neck, and for a second I thought she was going to come after me but luckily she stayed there and I went back to the bank. I went into the bank and I sat down and I waited for Dasso to finish. Every now and then I'd look out at the street to see if Miriam was coming. Shit, I tell you, I was fucking scared.'

He threw his arms up.

'I don't know why I'm telling you all this, I wouldn't want this getting out. You can't tell Chacho about this.'

'Don't worry, I'm not going to tell anyone.'

'I'm only telling you because I'm drunk. It's just, if your old man had still been alive, I'd have gone straight round and told him. I'm sure I would. That's why I'm telling you, because I can't tell him. Miriam was there in that little shop in San Isidro staring at me.'

He gave a long pause. Down the back, the midget was making a racket, washing dishes in the sink.

'Tell me, where exactly was it? The shop where you saw her?'

He shook his head.

'Dasso always went to the Banco Weisse on that big street with all the trees – Avenida Dos de Mayo, it's called – just off Javier Prado in San Isidro. It must have been right round there somewhere. I've never been back there. And that was a while ago now. And I never told Chacho. Luckily your *papá* never knew. Another beer? This really is the last one. You know, you look a bit like your old man. It's been really good meeting you.'

I can remember everything that was said that afternoon in Guayo's restaurant in Breña; his pockmarked face, his reedy voice, that shirt he was wearing.

Sometimes, we'd hold their head in a bucket of water to make them confess . . . Chacho here loved to attach electric wires to the women's tits, he really got off on that . . . This one time, we brought this girl we'd picked up in one of the villages to your papá . . . *If we weren't doing it to them,* compadre, *they'd have been doing it to us . . . Her* mamá *grabbed hold of her and wouldn't let her go, she wouldn't let her go, "You're not taking my daughter," she said, so we gave her a slap but the old woman wouldn't let go.'*

While Guayo had been talking, an image of this girl appeared before me, of her and my father against a black background.

Finally, I said my goodbyes to Guayo. I don't remember what I said as I was leaving. I might even have hugged him. I felt protected by the windows of the car. That afternoon, a dirty drizzle was falling over the traffic as I drove back along Avenida Salaverry; the treetops were swaying slowly. *'But how could she get out of the barracks? Because the bitch put on Guayo's uniform, I told you already. Your* papá *was furious, he started looking for her all over the place.'*

When I got to the Avenida del Ejército, I stopped the car and got out. The sea air whipped my face.

I stopped off at Helena de Pezet, a café that sold expensive chocolates. I went into the Gents, washed my face and combed my hair. I bought some chocolates. When I got home I straightened my tie. It was nearly eight o'clock. Obviously I didn't want my daughters to see the state I was in.

As for Claudia, well, she would have understood that you don't meet up with your father's friends and not come home a little drunk.

I opened the front door, went into the bedroom and explained briefly to Claudia what had happened. 'Why don't

81

you just go to bed,' she said as she left the room. Alicia was in her room studying and Lucía was listening to music. I went in and gave them a chocolate each. I tiptoed to the shower. I saw my reflection in the mirror, my features flattened by eyes puffy from the drink. I could barely remember driving home. The men I had met that day . . . each justified himself, blamed everyone else.

I put on my pyjamas and felt a wave of relief as my head touched the pillow.

If one of my clients, if Eduardo or anyone at the practice had seen me at the moment, they wouldn't have believed it. A drunk, lying curled up in bed at his wife's suggestion, eyes wide as headlamps, thinking about his father, about his officers, about the native girl in Ayacucho who had got away.

VII

TWO IN THE MORNING. I GO TO THE BATHROOM, I have a splitting headache. I take a couple of aspirin. I can't bring myself to look in the mirror, I must look terrible.

When I come out of the bathroom, Lucía is waiting for me. Skinny legs, puffy eyes, one hand in her mouth.

'I heard noises, Papi, is everything OK?'

'Everything's fine, *hija*. Don't worry.'

Lucía feels scared in the dark. Is someone going to jump out at her, she asked me, some old woman going to come out of the wardrobe and hit her?

I brought her back to her room, opened the drawers and the wardrobe with her.

'There's nothing here, see?'

'Can I sleep in your bed anyway, Papi?'

'Of course, *hija*.'

She lies next to me, hugs me to her. Claudia doesn't move. I fall asleep and wake up with Lucía's hand on my face. I sit up. For a while, I give myself over to that most comforting of pleasures, watching my daughter sleep. The suspension of her skin, the distant density of her eyelids, the abandon of her legs. Only children sleep with such complete surrender. Watching them is restful. Lucía is ten years old and I fear the future her sensitive heart holds in store for her. Her eyes well up with tears when she sees a bride stepping into a church and she gets gooseflesh if she reads a horror story. Watching her sleep, I indulge in a fantasy of the future, wondering who her friends will be, what her life will be like when she finishes school, what countries she'll visit one day, whether she'll be strong enough, strong enough to survive the disappointments and the failures that lie ahead? And how long will she allow me to be close to her?

At some point I heard Claudia getting up, then I drifted back to sleep until seven, when the house usually starts to stir to the rhythm of the little explosions of water in the coffee machine and the rattle of crockery in the kitchen.

I got up and went back to the bathroom. The bathroom with its tiles and its towels, like a hearth, a cave with its own mirror, an egotist's paradise. I went through the ritual of shaving, showering, dressing as though I were a Christmas tree being decorated to show off to the clients. Expensive aftershave, exfoliated skin, wine-coloured tie. I find it astonishing, the gap between the poor, sentimental devil, standing soaking wet in his underpants with a splitting headache having his first surreptitious little weep in the bathroom and the man holding forth in meetings, the perfect gentleman in the grey suit and freshly ironed shirt.

I found myself in the dining room holding a cup and a glass of water.

After the girls got off to school, I told Claudia some of the details of my meeting with Chacho and Guayo, explained about them being Papá's lieutenants during the war. 'They told me a lot of things, stories about torture and executions.'

'What things?'

'I don't know, just stories . . . Officers used to throw dead bodies and rubbish into the ravines so wild pigs would eat them and their families wouldn't be able to recognise them. Once three soldiers killed a baby in front of its mother and then raped her next to the dead body of her son.'

'Please, don't tell me any more,' she begged.

'OK. But all that stuff was just retaliation for what Sendero Luminoso were doing, they burned prisoners alive and hung signs on the charred bodies. A widespread Sendero Luminoso practice was to execute the mayor of a town in front of his wife and children. They'd kill them right in front of their families and then force the families to celebrate. They hung dead babies from trees. This is what I was told, what I've heard. I've even seen the photos. You remember when they used to publish photos in the papers?'

'That's vile,' Claudia said in a low voice and kept walking towards the living room. 'I can't believe anyone could do such things.'

At work, my headache came back the minute I stepped into my office. A guy who's not much of a drinker has no business getting together with friends of his father, that was the lesson I'd learned from the previous day's events. Jenny came in to see me, told me I looked like death warmed up and offered to bring me a couple of aspirin or a strong coffee.

I spent the morning talking to Eduardo about the dismissals and the possible candidates to replace them. Everything went smoothly. The people we'd fired had simply asked for references.

Eduardo was a past master at ducking out of the office, so he reacted to my prolonged absence the day before with a suspicious, almost congratulatory smile. It was unusual for me to take the afternoon off, so Eduardo was quietly content that I'd done so. According to him, I needed to have more fun: 'Let your hair down sometimes, get your leg over, you're too bogged down in your work and your marriage, that's your problem.' He asked if I'd been with someone and who the lucky lady was. I told him I'd run into some friends I hadn't seen in a long time and we'd got into a drinking session that went on until late.

'Actually, they weren't really friends of mine, they were friends of my father,' I clarified.

'Yeah, that kind of session can be pretty rough. Right, back to business,' he said, opening a folder. 'Two new clients have signed up, so we've got reason to celebrate, partner.'

At midday, after Jenny had made me a fourth strong coffee, I went for lunch on my own. I stuffed some pending paperwork in my briefcase. Almost out of inertia, I headed for the Larcomar shopping centre and went to Laritza D, a café and ice-cream shop.

I ordered a salad and a papaya juice. Rather than going over the pending contracts, I took out the pad on which I took notes (or pretended to) at meetings. It had been a habit since my years at university, jotting down things that had happened over the past few days. I still have the page that reads:

Things that happened:
1. My mother died.
2. I found a letter by a woman named Vilma Agurto cursing my mother and all her descendants.
3. She called the house.
4. Meeting with my brother Rubén and his revelations about my father's conduct during the war.
5. Meeting with Chacho and Guayo.
6. The story of this girl Miriam whose life my father spared and who escaped from the barracks.

Suddenly, in a rush that surprised even me, I remembered something else. I wasn't sure whether it was something I had actually heard, or something I simply imagined. I dimly remembered that just before his fight with Guayo, Chacho had told me that when she ran away, Miriam was pregnant.
I jotted down:

7. Possibly have another brother/sister.

87

VIII

I N THE DAYS THAT FOLLOWED, I WOKE TO THE FEELING
of a dreadful weight which faded only gradually as the
morning wore on.

I felt as though I were being punished. And the punishment
was unfair, a random punishment, a chance curse. First the
death of my mother out of which a perverse sequence of events
had grown: Rubén's return, the appearance of Chacho and
Guayo, the story of Miriam.

The death of a loved one always fills us with guilt, I
thought. Maybe if you'd done something your mother might
still be alive; was it really too much effort to spend a little
more time with her? And who was your father, this man
who tortured and murdered all those people? And why has
all this come back to haunt you now? It was a constant
nagging worry tacked on to my routine; I felt like a puppet
of myself.

At work, everything seemed normal. I uttered the same
sensible phrases as ever: 'That's something we'll need to look
into,' 'I'll have an answer for you tomorrow,' 'The law on that
point is very clear.' If a professor had filmed me, he could

have shown the footage to his students as the work of a model lawyer. It was pathetic.

I carried on dealing with things at the office, giving my opinion, supervising reports for existing clients, talking to Eduardo, developing strategies to bring in new clients. To take my mind off everything that was going on I was also seeing a lot of my old friend Platón Acha.

Platón and I had been friends for ever. His father had taught philosophy at various schools. Señor Acha's obsession with Plato's dialogues was such that he would sometimes re-enact sections from the *Georgics* or of *Phaedrus* at his house. I remember watching these performances when I was young. Acha's sons would declaim the speeches while Señora Hermelinda Acha, Platón's mother, would serve *chicha* and *empanaditas* to the assembled company. Señor Ancha, with his tie, his gold watch and his pinstriped waistcoat, would occasionally make comments. At the end, there would be questions from us, Platón's friends. Afterwards, we'd all have cake, also made by his mother. Platón, named after the 'great thinker', had quickly given up on the idea of studying philosophy as his father wanted him to. I met him at university when he was studying law, which he gave up for a more pedestrian and profitable career in dentistry.

Platón was plump and good-natured, prone to giving advice and laughing. He invariably wore a red or an orange tie, something that simply accentuated his thick lips and the wiry shock of hair that opened out like a fan. His wire-framed glasses, an attempt to correct his thick-set features, concealed large smiling eyes. We would meet for lunch from time to time. Sometimes Claudia and I would go to the cinema with him and his wife, Gladys, who was a replica of him. The years had adapted her body and soul to her husband. She was chubby and cheerful, had loud blouses and hands stiff as crabs. Claudia could hardly stand Gladys but she put up with her to keep me happy. Platón dismissed the problems of the world in the same cavalier fashion with which he rejected his father's advice. There's no problem, nothing's wrong, there's nothing to worry about.

I told Platón everything that had happened with Rubén, Chacho and Guayo. 'So, that's what your old man got up to? And your mother never told you about any of this?

'And now you want to find this girl Miriam? But what are you going to say to her if you find her?'

It had been almost a month since my mother died. I don't know how to describe what I felt during that month. The world suddenly seemed somehow bigger, objects more remote, there seemed to be no room for me in the chair where I sat every day. The fact that I had found nothing to reproach her for made my grief worse.

In her will, Mamá had divided everything equally between me and Rubén, which seemed fair. I could hardly have expected that, in some arbitrary act of love, she would leave more to me (who had stayed here in Lima with her) than she had my brother. Her sense of fairness prevailed over everything else. She had even left instructions about what to do with her clothes, her shoes and handbags. Any personal effects I did not want to keep were to go to the Carmelite nuns in Sicuani.

I decided to keep a brown leather bag and a pair of shoes that I put in a box in my wardrobe. This bag, these shoes had been hers, they had touched her skin. I thought about that a lot.

The sensation of floating in the universe, the solitude of my body drifting, this strange feeling I could not bring to qualify as 'grief' or 'loss'. The thought of future memories was a consolation to me. In years to come, words and images and fragments of scenes with her would come back to me that I could not imagine now. Those memories would sustain me, perhaps even comfort me. Her calmness, her enthusiasm, her little joys she felt with my daughters.

That Wednesday, a Mass was said on the one-month anniversary of her death.

I've never thought of myself as religious, but Mamá was, and perhaps I still half-believed. For a while, as kids, Rubén and I had gone to Mass with her every Sunday.

'There's no better company than God. When you feel alone, talk to God. It's a great comfort to me. Solitude brings you closer to God.'

'I don't really believe in all that, Mamá.'

'There's a line from Machado – "*Men who talk to themselves hope one day to talk to God.*"'

'That's beautiful,' I said. 'But it's not true.'

'Waiting is futile,' she went on. 'What matters is searching. Searching with others, in communion with others. And those others are in church, they're at Mass, they're among your friends, they're in your city, the poor who have no one to turn to. You have to think about them. We think about them at

Mass. The good thing about Mass is that it gives you time to think about other people, Adrián. These days, who's got half an hour spare to think? Who's got time to think about other people, to say hello to them? I go to church and I think about people. And I think about myself. About me and about you and the people I know and the people who have nothing.'

My mother could always make herself heard, with crystal-clear determination. A Mass, a meeting, an assembly. Wherever people gathered. All these things had been important to her. For me, the problem was that priests and Mass bored me rigid. But this time, for my mother, it would be different.

At some point I considered the possibility that this woman called Vilma Agurto might show up (at the house, or worse still, at the church) and curse us for what my father had done.

But when the Mass came, at 7.30 p.m. on a chill evening at the Carmelite church, everything went smoothly. There were hugs and commiserations and memories. At the entrance to the church, a handful of friends and relations came to meet me. Two or three of the women told me anecdotes about my mother, amusing stories that I had only recently heard: the day she stained her dress and had to have it cleaned, the afternoon she slipped getting out of her chair, holding a cup of tea. 'She slipped on the carpet so gracefully that she didn't even spill her tea. That was your *mamá*, she was so elegant, such a lady.'

I felt reassured, almost flattered to see the little throng crowding the pews, the queue to receive communion, the number of times the priest intoned the words 'our sister Beatriz'. Rubén would later hear about the Mass in a letter I sent him and he sent back a short note, a one-sentence thank-you and a story about his new *gringo* girlfriend.

For a while, I forgot about Vilma Agurto. I had not heard anything from her since. Claudia mentioned her the day after the Mass. 'She's probably some crazy woman who just phones people at random,' she said. 'Let's not talk about her any more.'

But I confess that in my nightmares I heard the phone ring, heard a crackly voice over the receiver: '*Buenos días,* Señor Ormache, my name is Vilma Agurto, I'd like to talk to you about my niece Miriam.'

Around that time, Quique Salas, one of the interns at the office, almost died.

We had just hired Quique on the recommendation of some lawyer friends and in the few short weeks he had been with us, he had proved very impressive. He was a polite, nervous, diligent boy who seemed to have every point of law relevant to any discussion at his fingertips. Seeing him come into a meeting was a relief to those, such as myself, who have memories like sieves.

Like any intern striving to create a place for himself, he came in to work on Saturday mornings. It happened at about 11 a.m. He was sitting at his desk, poring over the civil code. Suddenly he felt a painful pressure in his chest. Jenny called me on my mobile at midday, just as I was about to dive into the heated pool at Club Regatas; she told me he had been taken by ambulance to the Clínica Americana and then transferred to the Hospital Almenara.

I decided to go and see him. The Hospital Almenara is a huge dilapidated building that takes up a whole block facing the old San Fernando University. Traffic was backed up all the way, moving in fits and starts through the grimy, depressing, narrow streets and alleys. Shadowy doorways, latticed windows, dusty walls, potholes, dithering pedestrians, rickety cars belching steam . . . The car lurched along and finally I came to the entrance to the Accident and Emergency department on Calle Cailloma. Inside, the waiting room was teeming with people in serried ranks of chairs. A small, uniform multitude of short-legged people in grimy clothes all craning forward, all waiting to see a doctor.

Their faces were all turned towards the TV screen mounted on the wall. It suddenly occurred to me that what I was seeing looked like an act of worship, like the congregation at the memorial Mass for my mother. A spellbound multitude, gazing heavenward. The TV screen, the only moving object, was a sign from God. All eyes were drawn to it in an instinctive state of trance.

I was informed that our intern Quique, was in the Intensive Care unit which I managed to gain admittance to after speaking to the security guard. A long tiled corridor. A succession of iron beds, a wooden table with a doctor writing something. In the beds, gaunt men, their cheeks sunken, their bodies barely moving beneath the sheets. Pain simplified their features, made their bodies, their legs seem smaller, restricted the movements of their hands. One lay open-mouthed in a frozen gesture of surprise. There was a bald obscenity to death, I thought. The colour that the

94

eyes of a dying man take on is the only colour that has no name.

I stopped next to a trolley. The face of the man on the stretcher was half consumed by a white beard, his eyes glassy, his hands thin and bony. Life seemed to be a burden to his body, which could barely cope with the physiological process of dying. A woman went up to the doctor and asked about her husband. The doctor told her that he had just passed away and pointed towards something. I saw the woman lean against the wall, speechless, her eyes wet with tears. A nurse went over to her.

'*Señora*, would you like me to put your husband's things in a bag for you?'

The woman looked up.

'Things? What things?'

'His wallet, his watch, his ring. If you like I can put them in a bag for you.'

The woman stood, motionless.

I moved down the narrow ward. Bed after bed after bed. A small team of nurses moved from one side to the other, pushing trolleys, attaching IV drips to arms, questioning newly arrived patients.

I kept walking until eventually I found Quique. His father was with him. I talked to one of the doctors who confirmed the boy had had a heart attack.

'We couldn't afford private health insurance for a clinic,' his father told me. 'We had to bring him here, they tell me they have good cardiologists here.'

Quique on the other hand seemed calm, almost happy.

'From now on, you're not to smoke, and I'll be keeping a close eye on your diet.'

I told him, 'We'll help you in any way we can, don't worry about any treatment not covered by your insurance.'

I felt happy and satisfied in my role.

Quique's father told me that at the Clínica Americana they had done some X-rays and two ECGs, but that in all the confusion they'd been left behind. The doctor was asking for them. I didn't say a word. It was an unusual role for me to play, the noble soul (I'd always thought that generosity was a profession in itself), but after a moment's hesitation, I offered to go and collect the ECGs from the Clínica Americana.

It was Saturday night. As I drove to San Isidro all the cars I passed had couples in them.

Eventually I arrived at the clinic. I went into the Accident and Emergency unit and asked for Enrique Salas's records. Unlike the Hospital Almenara, the Clínica Americana was like a vast, empty mansion, a luxury hotel with all the doors closed, some with brightly coloured balloons ('It's a boy!') or sprays of flowers tied to the door-handles. I had entered via a hushed, spotless corridor and found myself in a circular room. I saw a sign for the X-ray department.

The place was immaculate, solemn and in a certain sense more desolate than the hospital I had just come from. Next to me was a little girl with a bandage on her foot. The doctor was explaining to her that she'd sprained it; the girl whimpered and squealed in pain. Her father stroked her face and told her it would all be over soon.

I went back to the Hospital Almenara, to the Intensive Care

unit, and was once again shocked by the silence of all these people. A rich little girl with a sprained ankle made more noise than a dozen poor men dying; there was something blackly funny about it, I thought.

In the corridor, I ran into the woman who had just been told her husband had died. Her clothes were mournful, her hair frazzled, her eyes sunken, her dark skin seemed to prefigure her grief, her whole body appeared marked by death. Two women were talking to her in hushed voices.

That night, I told Claudia what had happened and she suggested we forget about it, go for a drink, see a film.

'OK then, let's go,' I said.

'Don't be like that, darling,' Claudia said. 'Don't let it get to you. They'll take good care of him at the hospital. He'll be fine, you'll see.'

Sunday. We spent the day reading the papers, having breakfast at Los Delfines, visiting my in-laws. Claudia and her sisters fought over spending Sunday with my in-laws. The daughter who took them to lunch won the first moral victory of the week. Sometimes, it was simply a question of who phoned first. By an edict of my mother-in-law, there were certain Sundays when we all had to eat together.

On Monday, I got to work early. A number of lawyers had been to see Quique in hospital. He would be fine once he had his operation.

Jenny gave me a rundown of my appointments for the day. And for that night. I was invited to a dinner organised by one

97

of my clients, Tito Terán. Tito had just had confirmation of the merger between his bank and an Italian corporation (our practice had handled all the papcrwork), and he'd decided to celebrate at San Ceferino, a restaurant on the Avenida Dos de Mayo. Tito was a garrulous guy who got up at seven, spent an hour working out and lifting weights and was at his desk every morning by eight thirty. He worked with the same passion that he talked with. Going to dinner with him meant a sea of blue jokes, garlic bread, ravioli, dirt-dishing, loud toasts, pizza, brandy and espressos, a wild night that wouldn't be over before two in the morning. Entertaining with clients like Tito was a lawyer's duty.

The following day, I came into my office to find the window covered in something wet and dirty. It looked as though some passing pigeon had had diarrhoea. I sat down. A faint light streamed into the office. On my desk was an envelope with an address scrawled in pencil. I opened it:

Señor Ormache,
    My name is Vilma Agurto. I will be at 388 Calle Manco Cápac, La Victoria, at four o'clock. Don't bring anyone, come alone, just you. It's very important for you, Señor Ormache. For the memory of your mother.
    Sincerely,
    Vilma Agurto

It was a feint-ruled piece of paper torn from a school exercise book. It had been folded in four. Whoever had written it had struggled over every word.

I called Jenny in.

'Who delivered this?'

'I don't know. I think someone handed it to the security guard outside.'

'Can you go and ask him?'

'What's up?'

'I'll tell you later. Just go and find out who delivered it.'

I stood there holding the envelope as though somehow I might find out something more just by staring at it. Jenny reappeared.

'He said some old banger pulled up outside the office around half seven and a kid gave it to him to give to you. He handed it through the car window, he didn't even get out. What is it?'

'Have you ever heard of Vilma Agurto?'

'No. Who's Vilma Agurto?'

'Here, take a look.'

At that moment, the phone rang. Someone who wanted to talk to Eduardo but had been put through to my office by mistake. Jenny pressed some buttons, the envelope dangling from her trembling hand.

I leaned back in my chair and started leafing through the papers. Jenny hung up the phone.

'What did they want?' she asked, still staring at the letter.

'I think they want to blackmail me.'

'Why?'

'Because they know about something my father did in Ayacucho when he was in the army up there.'

'So what are you going to do?'

'I'm going to go and find out what's what.'

'You'd be better off going with a driver. Let Nelson take you.'

'You think?'

'Absolutely. So who is this woman?'

I had lunch in the office – lettuce and tomato salad, cheesecake and a bottle of mineral water. Afterwards I got a coffee and smoked a couple of cigarettes. I paced up and down the rug.

At three thirty my driver turned up.

Nelson was a retired policeman who bragged about having shot a couple of criminals during a pursuit ten years earlier. He'd tell the story in the office kitchen to anyone who would listen.

'I didn't even aim, really,' he'd say, raising his right arm. 'I just fired.'

He'd happened on the crooks on the Avenida San Borja Norte as they were making a getaway after a bank raid. As Nelson talked he waved his hands and shook his head, as though he was standing in the middle of a public plaza. He had hard black eyes and hair like straw plastered to his head. He earned more as a driver these days than he ever had as a policeman, but he missed his years with the Policía Nacional and sometimes he'd remind me that he wasn't just a driver, he was my bodyguard. He was tough though polite and he talked more than he should, but I felt safe with him.

I got in the car and told him to find the third block on Calle Manco Cápac. I assumed this was the main avenue in the La Victoria district of Lima. Sitting behind the steering wheel, Nelson put the map to one side and looked up.

'Excuse me for asking, *señor*, but what would a gentleman like you want in that kind of neighbourhood?'

We got to the Plaza Manco Cápac. In the centre, the statue of the Inca warrior stared forlornly, pointing towards the horizon.

In the harsh midday sun, a series of shadows – vague figures, sometimes in groups of two or three – wandered between the broken benches, the leafless trees, the patchy yellow grass of the plaza. Signs for pharmacies in greenish lettering, walls unrecognisable through the layers of caked grime, metal blinds on the windows, bus conductors shouting, the hoarse whining of the buses themselves. On one corner rose a church the colour of cement. An elderly couple were peacefully eating a bowl of nuts.

I told Nelson to park the car by the church and wait for me there.

As I walked a shoeshine boy followed, alternately begging and threatening. I came to the Calle Manco Cápac and turned left. I saw the number marked on the door. A hole-in-the-wall restaurant, with plastic tables and planks of wood as benches; the floor of pale yellowish tiles was strewn with sawdust. Next to the door, the menu was chalked on a blackboard: *Arroz cubano S/.3, Chicken and fries S/.4, Bread and olives S/.1.* Through a window lined with bottles of coke, a woman was staring at me from behind a wooden counter.

Her face was small and misshapen, distorted by her huge mouth. Suddenly she pointed to me: 'Señor Ormache? In here, Señor Ormache.'

A boy appeared from behind her and sat down, never

taking his eyes off me. He was wearing a black Batman T-shirt.

I guessed he was the woman's son and that he was here to protect her and to intimidate me. I leaned against the cracked plastic partition. I can still hear the words Vilma Agurto said next, her voice clipped and hoarse like a cough.

'*Buenas tardes, señor*. First of all, thank you for coming. I have to tell you something, *señor*. Your father was a very wicked man who hurt my niece Miriam many times, many times. She has things, letters, little things of his. We have photos too. I contacted your mother about this before. Many times she gives me money so I don't talk to the papers, so I don't tell some journalist about your *papá* and my niece. But now that the *señora* has passed away now – my deepest condolences, *señor*, your mother was a good woman, a decent woman – but now, well, you see now, we'll have to deal with you, that's all there is to it. Your *mamá* always did her duty by me, and now, well, you'll do your duty too, just like her.'

She fluttered her hands as she talked. Her fingernails were short, almost non-existent. She toyed with the spoon in the sugar bowl and the metallic sound soothed me.

A policeman came in and asked for a mineral water; the boy got up and served him.

I was trying to stay calm. I sat down, clasped my hands together on the table and looked her in the eye.

'*Señora*, listen to me,' I said. 'This is the first I've heard about any of this. My parents divorced when I was a baby. I didn't see very much of my father. It's true I was close to my mother, but she never said anything to me about this, *señora*, and I'm sorry, but I don't believe that she gave you money to keep quiet. Can I ask whether you have any proof of these allegations you're making?'

At that point the boy came over and muttered something I couldn't understand. She silenced him with a look.

'I only saw your *mamá* once, that's all. A tall, distinguished woman, very elegant, she was, I remember that. She saw me at her house, at your house on – what was it called – ah, the Calle Jorge Basadre, over in San Isidro, that's where I saw her. I went there and I saw her, saw her in her own house. I went there and I talked to her. There was a big clock in the living room, wasn't there? I was there. She said she would send a man with the money. Every month he came here, every month he brought the money. Oscar, his name was, Chacho Osorio they called him. Well, he came here and he brought a thousand dollars on the first of every month, *señor*. He did that for your *mamá*. And I talked to him the other day and he told me that your *mamá* had passed away and that he had nowhere to get the money from any more. As a favour to your *mamá*, he used to come, that's why I called you, so you could come here and do your duty by me. You don't have to come here. Just ring Señor Chacho. You give the money to Señor Chacho. That's all you have to do, *señor*.'

I pictured Chacho's face, pictured him in the restaurant by the seafront telling me my mother was a good woman.

'So you said you have photos and things that belonged to my father,' I murmured.

'Photos. We have photos. Your father will be disgraced. We'll go to the papers, tell them everything, if you don't pay what you owe, *señor*. If you don't believe me, *señor*,' she added slowly, 'if you don't believe me, I can show you the photos. Three photos, we have, I can show them to you. You want to see them? Your *papá* had a camera up there in the barracks, a Polaroid camera. He gave the photos to Miriam as a present.'

She went on staring at me with a faint smile.

'Sure, bring me the photos. I'd like to see them.'

The woman didn't move but the boy got to his feet and went behind the counter and came back with a crumpled envelope. He handed it to me and, holding it away from me, I opened it slowly.

Three photos slid out into my hand.

The images were a little blurred, but clear enough so I could recognise my father's face and part of his body. He was naked, next to a young girl. It was him. Was it him?

Her mane of long hair almost completely covered his face. But I could still make out his profile, his nose, his forehead, the gleam of his lips.

In the first photograph they were standing, turned sideways to the camera. He was kissing her, one leg wrapped around her waist, she barely touching him. There was a trace of wetness on her cheek.

The other photos were more blurred. They were in bed, you could see the folds of a blanket; in both, he was on top of her.

It was almost impossible to make out their faces. It was the sort of thing my father probably showed his friends for a laugh, as a badge of honour.

'It would be bad for you if these photos appeared on the

news or in the papers. Nobody talks much about your *papá* these days, but if these got out, a lot of people would talk. That's what you need to worry about, *señor*. And there are more photos, and we have copies of them too. So then, what happens next is down to you.'

Outside the door, the noise of passing buses had not stopped. There was a constant din of conductors shouting, horns honking, buses rattling. The noise came in waves, rising and falling, sometimes merging with the voice of Vilma Agurto.

'So you're blackmailing me, Señora Agurto?'

'Well, if that's what you want to call it, *señor*, call it that. But you have to pay up. What I will tell you is that if anything happens to me, someone will send these photos straight to the television and the newspapers. Straight away. They'll send copies to a judge too. And to your friends. And your *mamá's* friends will see these photos, Señor Ormache.'

I leaned against the back of the chair. The wood creaked.

'So, that's what this is, Señora Agurto. Blackmail, pure and simple.'

'I'm just telling you how it is, Señor Adrián. You'll see.'

At that point I realised that the boy was staring anxiously at the woman.

'Well, Señora Agurto, I'll need more proof. Tell me where I can find this girl Miriam. I'd like to talk to her.'

She glared at me, her beady eyes glittering.

'You're not going to see her. You're never going to see her, *señor*. Never, ever, ever.'

'The thing is, I need her to tell me whether these things are true.'

'You can't see her, and I don't ever want to see you again either, *señor*. Tomorrow is the first of the month. Get Señor Chacho to bring the money here at the usual time. We'll be waiting here. Make sure to send Señor Chacho, I won't deal with anyone else. This is his address. Thank you and goodbye, *señor*. That's all I have to say.'

She handed me a piece of lined paper. Chacho's address was scrawled on it in capital letters.

The woman stood up; the boy let her pass, then followed her back behind the counter.

She disappeared. The boy sat behind the counter. He was reading a newspaper.

The noise of the traffic boomed and thundered round me.

I stepped into the street just as a bus stopped with a squeal of brakes. The conductor, a kid with a rag tied round his head, shouted something to the driver. I found Nelson.

'Drive to San Borja. And step on it.'

During the journey I barely moved. I felt my anger seep through every pore, I could hear the woman's voice hammering in my chest, I could see Chacho's face. *'Get Señor Chacho to bring the money. I won't deal with anyone else.'*

It didn't take long to reach Chacho's house. Nelson got out and went to the door.

A woman came out.

'Señor Chacho isn't here. I don't know what time he'll be back.'

I called Chacho's mobile and got his voicemail. *'Please leave your name and number after the tone.'* It was funny. The haughty politeness of a torturer and a blackmailer.

'Call me as soon as you get this.' I heard my faltering voice. 'I've got something I need to ask you. Call me, Chacho.'

I went back to the office and went through a list of the documents I needed to go over. A surge of white-hot rage paralysed me for a minute, then I grabbed the pile of folders and threw them on the floor, watched as pieces of paper fluttered everywhere and I lashed out with my foot again and again as paper rained down around me.

'What's going on, Adrián?' Jenny asked. 'What are you doing? You're behaving like a child.'

I started picking up the papers.

That night I stayed behind after everyone had left. The objects in the office – the computer, the books, the picture on the wall – all seemed like living creatures just waiting for their moment to leap out at me. I went down to the park, wandered around for a bit and came back. I poured myself a shot of vodka.

Señora Agurto, her son.

The photos of my father, the woman's voice. '*Your* mamá *always did her duty by me, and now, well, you'll do your duty too, just like her.*' The hypothetical image of my mother putting a thousand dollars in an envelope and giving it to Chacho . . .

But there was another presence, not a body or a face this time, it was like the shadow of a woman. That woman, Miriam. A grey shadow, blurred lines that could not quite define her features. I couldn't see her clearly, but it was her. I wanted to see her. Wanted to talk to her. But what exactly would happen if I managed to track her down? Wouldn't she just remind me of the unspeakable things my father had done to her, maybe even ask for more money than her aunt had? Why exactly had my father spared her life? And was it true, this dim memory I had of Chacho saying she was pregnant? Obviously this was something I hadn't dared ask Vilma Agurto.

Did I have a little brother or sister growing up with her in that hovel where I'd seen her?

IX

I SPENT ALL NIGHT CALLING CHACHO'S MOBILE. EVERY time I got the voicemail, I hung up and pressed redial. I made several attempts, each time dialling five or six times. In between these bouts I sat at my desk, working on a report, with a vodka bottle to hand.

Eventually, after a series of frenzied attempts, in which I pressed redial over and over, as if feeding an addiction, I suddenly heard Chacho's voice on the other end of the line and salsa music playing in the background.

'Hey, I've been calling you.'

'I know, what's up?'

'I can't really hear you, where are you?'

'El Maximo.'

'Where?'

'It's a club on the Avenida de la Marina.'

'I have to talk to you urgently.'

'OK, sure, call me tomorrow morning.'

'Listen, it'll only take a few minutes.' I started shouting over the noise of the music. 'Just tell me where you are.'

'I'm not on my own, I'm with this girl.'

'Yeah, so you just ditch her for a minute, we talk, then I leave.'

The security guard came into my office.

'Your wife is on the phone, *señor*.'

'Tell her I'll call her back.'

'It would be easier to talk tomorrow.' I heard Chacho's voice from the phone.

'I'm heading over right now, Chacho. Wait there for me.'

The music in the background roared.

'OK, all right. Come if you want to.'

The club was a huge concrete barn of a place with gold columns and a couple of spotlights playing on the dry ice and dust.

I walked past two or three languid couples and stood on the dance floor, peering through the lighting rig towards the back of the club. I spotted Chacho dancing with a girl with wild curly hair. I went over to them.

'I need to talk to you right now, Chacho.'

'Then wait till I'm done, don't fucking hassle me.'

'This can't wait, I have to go. We talk, I'll go, you can get back to what you were doing. I'm sorry for interrupting, *señorita*, this won't take a minute.'

'Go on, Chacho,' the girl with the curly hair said.

'What's so urgent you had to come down here? What's the matter with you, Adrián?'

'Nothing,' I said. 'Nothing's the matter.'

We sat on a couple of plastic cushions by the picture window. The dirty glow of a street lamp dissolved on the glass.

'How long have you been running money to the Agurto family?' I said.

'What?'

'How long have you been taking money to the Agurtos, you arsehole?'

He looked down. The floor was spangled with blue and red lights.

'What are you on about? I don't know what the fuck you're talking about . . .'

'I know, Chacho. They told me. I talked to Vilma Agurto. So, tell me, how long was my mother paying them off?'

He clasped his hands behind his neck.

'I don't know.'

'Tell me, Chacho, how long have you been taking them money? If you don't I'll get a court order and have you arrested. I can have you all comfy and cosy in your own little cell by morning, you understand me?'

The music suddenly changed to a treacly ballad, a throaty voice crooning; a few couples had taken to the dance floor again. The girl with the curly hair was standing, arms folded, staring at us.

Chacho's lips quivered. He wiped his mouth with the back of his hand.

'This one time your *mamá* called me. Asked me to help her out . . .'

'How long was she giving them money?'

'Fuck, I don't know how long it went on for . . . three, four years, it must have been. She asked me not to say anything about it to anyone. I just brought them the money, that's all.'

'A thousand a month?'

'Yeah. They called you?'

'They want me to pay the same, they want you to act as go-between.'

'Jesus. Your *mamá* wouldn't have wanted you to know anything about this.'

'Maybe. But now they want me to pay them off.'

The shadow of the girl with curly hair appeared beside us.

'Chachito, honey, how long you going to be with this guy? I'm getting bored here all on my own.'

'I'll just be a minute. Go on. Go and buy me a beer and get one for yourself. Here.' He pulled a banknote from his pocket and gave it to her. The girl wandered off.

'So what else did this woman tell you, Adrián?'

'Nothing else. She said you were to bring the money round tomorrow.'

'She showed you the photos?'

'Yes.'

'Yeah. Of course.'

I looked out across the dance floor, then back at him. I clapped him on the back.

'And how much did you take for acting as go-between, Chacho?'

'Me?'

The girl arrived back with a bottle of beer.

'Chachito, you coming?'

'How much, Chacho?' I said again.

'That's fucking disrespectful, *compadre*. What are you

thinking asking me shit like that? It's disrespectful, Adrián. You know what? I'm out of here. I'm just going to walk away and pretend this conversation never happened. I'm going back with my girl, *compadre*.'

'Yeah, come on, leave this guy to it.' The girl took his arm.

Chacho looked at me, his eyes blank, his arms tensed as though he was about to hit me.

'Your *mamá* wouldn't have wanted you to know any of this shit. She was grateful, you know? And, yeah, sometimes she'd give me a tip for helping her out. She was a great woman, your mother, a great woman.'

'Do you have any idea where we could find this woman, this Miriam?'

'Are you coming, or am I going to dance on my own?'

'Let it go. You're never going to find Miriam, *compadre*. You can't find her.'

He brought a hand up to his head and let it fall, then folded his arms as though somehow impregnable.

'Is it true she was pregnant when she escaped?'

'Who told you?'

'I think you or Guayo mentioned it the other day. You told me.'

'Fuck, I don't know.'

'But that's what you said, isn't it?'

'I don't remember.'

'So was she or wasn't she?'

'I don't know,' Chacho roared.

Some of the dancers had turned to look now.

'Come on, Chachito, that's enough now, come and dance with me . . .'

'You don't even remember her surname?'

'OK, then, I'm going, Chachito, I'm tired of waiting around. What you gotta talk to this guy for?'

The girl disappears onto the dance floor.

Chacho sips his beer.

'Miriam died years ago, least that's what I heard. That's all I know about her.'

He disappears into the smoke on the dance floor. There are more people in the club now. A little later Chacho reappears, dancing and laughing in the flickering light.

When I came out I could hardly see my car. I opened the door, got in, and sat motionless for a while behind the wheel in the murky silence. A shaft of light slid across the windscreen.

For a moment, I thought about going back inside to look for Chacho, but what would I say to him?

I keyed the ignition. The drive home seemed incredibly long. The pounding music from the club seemed to boom from every pothole. I'd been driving for a while before I came to myself again. I was on the Avenida Javier Prado. I was almost home.

I wandered into the living room. The whole house seemed deserted. Still the music from the club echoed in my head. The place was silent. It wasn't particularly late, but Claudia always went to bed at eleven so she could be fresh for her gym class in the morning. I slumped into a chair. The room was dominated by the solemn, venerable grandfather clock that had belonged to my mother. It seemed to stare down as if passing judgement on what had just happened. I had betrayed this clock which had always been a tall, tangible symbol of the house, almost like a shrine, a sentry, standing by the door watching us leave, welcoming us home.

As a boy, every morning after breakfast before heading off to school or to university, I'd glanced up at that circle of numbers and lines, the white clock face now yellowed with age. I'd looked at it so many times.

My mother had always checked the clock several times a day. Had seen the slim, sharp hands, the pale skin of the face etched with roman numerals, the thick lines marking twelve and six. She had looked up at it and perhaps she had thought about the moment when Chacho would ring the bell and she would have to open the door and hand him an envelope containing a thousand dollars for Señora Agurto.

The clock was like a crystal ball in which I could glimpse the past. My mother arriving back from the bank, counting the notes one by one, placing them in Chacho's filthy hands. Every banknote slipped across her skin, then slid into the envelope before she carefully sealed it. My mother's strong, good-natured face, and the voice which had comforted me on so many nights, were the face and the voice of the woman who had made these monthly trips to the bank; the hands that had held me were those that had held the envelope that would bring a smile to Señora Agurto's face.

And yet . . . this flaw that now appeared in my mental image of her did not make it crumble. In a way, it simply made it stronger. She had done precisely what I would have done, what I would have to do, in fact. And though I felt angry and a little sad, I didn't blame her for keeping it from me. My whole life had run perfectly smoothly on roads that paved over any memory of who my father had been. She had mapped out those roads, built and maintained them. Now that I had finally found her out, it was as though she had come back to defend herself. *What could I do, son? That woman threatened to reveal that story about your father. Tell me, what choice did I have? I had to give in, I had to.*

The minute hand of the clock clicked again and a brief peal rang out: three notes, 3 a.m., a time when I would always be at home, in bed. Mamá would come and give me a goodnight kiss at 10 p.m. I'd say my prayers with her. *'I had to protect your papá, I had to protect my sons. I had no choice, you have to understand.'*

I was happy to be alone here, in almost total darkness. The lingering humidity. The images of the past, of my mother sitting on the sofa, tight-lipped in the silence of the room. *'I have to get the money, a scandal like this could ruin Adrián, what else can I do, best not to say anything to anyone, certainly not to him. All I have to do is get the money, put it in an envelope, give it to the young man when he comes and forget the whole thing until next month.'* Was that how it had been?

I went upstairs and lay down next to Claudia, ran my fingers across her shoulder and kissed her.

*   *   *

I was woken by a noise at the window. It was nine o'clock – shockingly late by my usual standards. I found a note from Claudia by the bed:

> Morning, sleepyhead. I'm going to my mother's place from the gym this morning. The girls are at school.

I was still in my pyjamas, sitting on the bed. Get up, shower, dress, make the leap. This was the feat I performed every day: steeling myself, standing up, showering, getting dressed, making the leap. The bathroom was the frontier, the place where feats were possible; a man could step in a tattered rag and emerge as a gentleman.

In the car on the way to work, I took a couple of calls on my mobile. The radio droned on, the voices of ministers and members of parliament.

In the office, I had a quick meeting with a client, then buzzed Jenny to come in.

'So, what happened yesterday?'

She listened, eyes wide as I told her.

'I can't believe it,' she said.

'I want to meet this woman, this Miriam.'

'But I thought you said she was dead?'

'I don't know, I think Chacho was just saying that because he had to say something.'

'But he told you she was dead.'

'I don't know. He said that's what he'd heard, but I don't believe him.'

'So why do you want to track her down?'

'I want to see her face to face.'

At that moment, the phone rang.

Jenny picked it up. She adopted her placid office voice.

'It's Chacho Osorio,' she said, putting a hand over the mouthpiece.

'Oh, OK. Tell him he can call in at twelve.'

'OK.'

She hung up, looked at me, her head resting on one hand, nails pointed towards me.

'Well, I suppose I have to give him the money, I don't know what else I can do.'

'Are you sure?'

'No, I'm not sure. But right now, I have to go and get a thousand dollars and give it to him. I'll try to work out how to get the photos back later. At least this way we gain some time.'

Jenny got to her feet, leaned on the desk.

'There's one thing I don't get about all this, Adrián.'

'What's that?'

'OK, let's say this girl, Miriam, let's say she was angry about what happened in the barracks, about being held prisoner, about everything that happened to her . . .'

'Yeah?'

'Well, why would she keep the photos and why would she give them to her aunt? The girl was really that hard-headed? You see, that's what I don't get. Most decent women wouldn't hang onto things that bring back terrible memories, don't you think?'

'What makes you think she's a decent woman?'

'I don't know. But even though I don't know her, I think she is . . .'

She looked me in the eye. I sat down.

'I think you're right.'

'Whatever you do, you should get Nelson to keep an eye on this Señor Osorio, and on the old woman too . . .'

I called Nelson into my office.

'Yes, sir.'

'There's a guy who's going to come here to collect an envelope,' I told him. 'Jenny here will point him out to you. I'd like you to follow him and tell me where he goes, got it? Follow him for as long as it takes. I want to know everything he does. And don't let him know you're tailing him.'

His eyes lit up.

'Yes, sir.'

At twelve, Chacho turned up. He had a black bag and he was wearing a pink shirt and a grey tie. He'd brushed his hair and was smiling at me.

'I wanted to say sorry for last night . . .' he said. 'I'm really sorry. It's just I was with this girl and I'd been drinking so I don't really remember what happened, but I'm really sorry if I offended you, Adrián. And sorry for the other day with Guayo, too. I don't know what's got into that guy.'

'It's OK, don't worry about it. But I want you to tell me everything you know about Miriam.'

'The *chola*? Nothing.'

'You told me she was dead.'

'No, honestly, I don't know why I would have said that, I don't know anything.'

* * *

119

He sat opposite me and crossed his legs.

'Thank you,' I said, 'for doing this for me.'

'No, don't thank me, don't thank me, I'm just trying to help.'

'How much are you going to charge for acting as a go-between?'

'Nothing . . . shit, don't say that. I'm not going to charge you anything. I'm doing this for your father, to protect your father's memory. I'd like to think you're my friend, Adrián, you know how much I respected your father.'

I proffered the envelope and he took it.

'Best to count it,' I said.

He thumbed the notes, his fat fingers like worms wriggling.

I watched him get to his feet, shake my hand.

'Go on,' I said, 'I don't want to see you again until next month.'

He smiled in reply, closed the door.

Jenny looked at me, her eyes shining.

'Wow, that guy's ugly,' she said.

'The first thing you've got to do is go to the Public Registry Office. You need to check any land sales on the Avenida Dos de Mayo.'

'Why there?'

'Guayo saw Miriam working in a bodega there near the headquarters of Banco Wiese.'

'A bodega?'

'Yeah, but there are no shops there now, only offices. That's why I want you to find out who owned the land

120

and whether they sold it or built on it themselves. Maybe one of the previous owners can tell us where we can find her.'

'You're really desperate to find her, aren't you?'

'Yes.'

'Why?'

'I don't know.'

Jenny looked at me, then I looked away, stared at her computer screen.

'OK, well, it's lunchtime, so I'll head over to the Public Registry Office.'

I went home for lunch. Getting out of the car, I looked at the waxy leafed creeper on the facade. I thought about telling Claudia the whole story.

When I went into the house, she was on the phone and raised a hand to greet me. The girls had already had lunch and were sitting in front of their computers. I went to say hi, gave them a kiss, asked them how things were at school. 'I'm bored, I'm sick to death of school,' said Alicia. 'I can't wait to go to university next year.'

As I sat down at the table, Claudia hung up the phone and came to sit with me. She started telling me about the problems she was having with her cousins, Marita and Pocha. I vaguely followed the story.

Claudia spoke clearly and confidently as though teaching in front of a class of children. 'Pocha was always Papá's little girl. Even when they were children. Thankfully, Marita was never bitter about it. But then one day . . .' My mobile rang in my pocket. I took it out, gingerly opened it as though holding an amulet, and heard Nelson's voice.

'This guy Chacho is having lunch with the old woman, *señor*. I just saw them together. Seemed to be on very friendly terms, from what I could tell. I took a couple of photos. She handed over some of the money, I saw her give it to him.'

'I'm heading over there now.'

Claudia broke off and asked me what was going on. I told her I had to go, that I'd call her as soon as I could and explain everything. I headed for the door.

I heard a screech of tyres as I set off.

While I was driving, Claudia called me on my mobile.

'What's going on with you?' she said.

'Somebody's been trying to con me, I'll tell you about it later.'

I hung up and phoned Nelson. He told me Chacho had just left the café in La Victoria.

'He's in tight with that old woman. She handed over a wad of cash. Saw it with my own eyes. I pretended I just came in to buy a drink. The whole thing was done and dusted pretty quickly, but I managed to get a couple of photos with my little camera.'

As I drove to Chacho's house, the story began to fall into place. Every time I stopped at a red light, a new piece of the puzzle clicked.

My version of events was a series of plausible scenes. Scene one had my father showing the photos to his army buddies while he was drunk and bragging about how he'd fucked the little *chola*. Scene two had Chacho finding the photos in my father's apartment, probably after he died. Scene three, Chacho went and found some woman – didn't matter who – and together they blackmailed my mother. Last scene, he persuaded the woman to phone me so they could keep the thing going. Was that how it had happened?

I drove with my foot to the floor. I reckoned I could catch up with Chacho at his house, assuming he was going to stash his share of the money first.

I got to the Calle Liszt in San Borja and just as I was getting out of the car, I saw him pull up. He parked next to me and got out of his car with a tense smile.

There was no time to lose.

I strode over and shoved him as hard as I could, roaring at him, 'You and the fucking woman are in on this blackmail together, all these years you've been blackmailing my mother, you fucking shit, and I'm guessing you provided the photos – stole them from my father's place after he died. You're a first-class motherfucker.'

I had obviously got carried away, because no sooner had I lashed out at him than I realised that I was not going to come out of this well. His fists were like hammers. I felt the first blows and then everything disappeared in an explosion of pain. I felt my face smash against the pavement. He dragged me to my feet, jerked me towards him. I managed to knock him down and he fell into the garden yelling abuse at me. He'd hardly got back on his feet when I felt a blow that shattered my jaw. Everything went dark, I was dazed, fumbling on the ground, choking on blood. I struggled to my feet only to stagger and fall again onto a patch of grass. He was shouting something at me.

By the time I got up again, Chacho had gone into the house. I was spitting blood. My shirt was spattered and stained and I was dripping with sweat. I rushed to the door and started kicking it, then picked up stones and started throwing them at the windows, stopping only when I needed more stones. There wasn't a pane of glass left unbroken. Even after all the windows were smashed, I went on throwing.

I slumped to the ground, wiped the tears from my face and managed to drag myself into the driver's seat. My arms were shaking, but I got the car started. I drove home sobbing as streets slowly dissolved into one another. Finally I pulled up in front of my house.

When she saw me, Justina, the maid, clapped a hand over her mouth. '*Señora, señora,*' she screamed.

Claudia appeared. 'Oh my God, what happened?' she asked. She followed me as I went up the stairs, stumbled into the bathroom, took off my clothes and dropped them into the laundry basket. Claudia was knocking on the bathroom door.

'It's OK, I'm just going to wash myself off,' I said. I turned on the shower, called to Claudia and asked her to bring me clean clothes. When I came out of the bathroom, the pain made me double over on the bed.

'What happened to you?' Her voice sounded distant. 'Should I call an ambulance?' She sat down next to me.

'No, don't call anyone.'

'Adrián, can you please just tell me what happened?'

'I got into a fight with some bastard.'

'With who?'

'One of the guys who served with Papá.'

When I'd finally explained everything to her, Claudia pursed her lips and said it would be best if no one found out about this, then asked me to show her the bruises and scratches.

'Call your cousin Enrique, you need to see a doctor.'

I said I didn't think I was seriously hurt.

'If I'd broken anything I wouldn't have been able to drive, I wouldn't be talking to you now.'

Claudia disappeared into the bathroom and came back with ointments, bandages and plasters.

I made a phone call, then lay back on the bed. Claudia sat next to me.

Eventually, Nelson came and picked me up.

'Why didn't you tell me, *señor*? I would have got a bunch of mates together and we'd have sorted that bastard out.'

I left the house in spite of Claudia's pleas. I promised I'd be back soon. I was still sweating when I got to the office. Only the brutal rage inside me kept me upright, gave me the strength to climb the stairs, distracted me from the stabbing pain in my stomach, in my head.

When I arrived, Jenny was holding the photos Nelson had taken.

'What happened to you?' she asked.

'Nothing, I got in a fight.'

'Have you seen a doctor?'

'It's nothing, just a couple of bruises,' I said. 'Let me see the photos.'

In one of the photos, Señora Agurto was handing money

to Chacho. In the others, they were drinking a beer together. I don't know why I hadn't worked it out earlier. I told Jenny to go and get a hundred dollars and slipped the photos into my wallet.

'Are you all right?' she asked.

'Yeah, I'm fine. I'm just going to see the doctor. I'll be right back.'

When I stepped into the restaurant, Señora Agurto seemed surprised to see me. Clearly Chacho hadn't told her about our little run-in.

I sat down next to her. Nelson stood beside me. I showed her the photos of her and Chacho. I told her it was enough evidence to put her behind bars for the rest of her life.

'You know what?' I said. 'I'll tell you something else. The mayor of La Victoria is a good friend of mine and I can have this shithole restaurant of yours closed down overnight, the whole thing gone, your blackboard and your bottles and that moron in the black T-shirt back there. But because I'm a good man,' I said, 'I'm prepared to give you a hundred dollars right now in exchange for the photos and any copies.'

She looked at me stone-faced. When she spoke, her lips barely moved. 'If you do that, then I'll tell everything,' she said.

'Don't you get it?' I countered. 'I've got friends in every TV channel in the country, and in every newspaper too. You don't really think they're going to publish this? Your little scam is over . . . So if you mention this to anyone ever again, I'll take the photos that prove you've been blackmailing me and I'll happily have you arrested and banged up for life. As you've probably guessed, Chacho's already confessed. You want me to call the police right now?'

She didn't move. She stared at me, her eyes hard and wrinkled.

'I can come back tomorrow with the local police and have this place shut down, and you'll end up in Chorrillos prison and your boy will end up in Lurigancho. What do you think?'

'But how can you do that, Señor Ormache? You can't have me arrested, because I'll talk to the press, I'll talk to your friends, I'll tell them everything.'

'You don't seem to understand. Who could you talk to? You can't touch me. But if I take these photos to the police, they'll shut this place down tomorrow. Who do you think people will believe, you or me?'

There was a long pause broken only by the sound of traffic. Then suddenly she stirred. Suddenly she was shouting.

'Pepo, Pepo.'

The boy appeared.

'Bring me the envelope,' she said.

'Huh?'

'I said, bring me the envelope.'

She couldn't make herself look at me. When the boy came back she told him to give the envelope to me. He stared at it with his sad cow eyes, then did as he was told.

Inside were the photos. I gave her the hundred-dollar note, stuffed the envelope in my pocket and got to my feet.

Nelson walked beside me. Out on the street, I felt the fresh breeze. Walking as quickly as I could, I was trembling. I felt scared and a little ashamed of what I had just done. But I felt happy too, even proud.

When we got to the car, I remembered I had a pair of scissors in the glove compartment. Claudia kept them there in case she needed to snip off a loose thread on her dress on the way to a reception. Nelson started the car. We drove quickly. I took out the scissors and the photos.

There it was, completely clear this time, my father's face. The tangle of bodies, barely visible yet utterly clear.

I felt disgusted and dimly fascinated. All I wanted was to be rid of them. There were three photos, each from a different angle. In them my father's face was much closer to the camera than hers, a dragon devouring a deer in the darkness.

I took the scissors and carefully cut her face out of all three photographs. A moment later, in the palm of my hand, I had three blurred, passport-size photographs of Miriam. I picked up the scissors again and cut what remained – particularly my father's body – to shreds.

Nelson was already turning out of the Avenida Iquitos onto the motorway into the city centre. I rolled down the window and threw the scraps of paper into the river of cars behind us. I looked out the window. The pieces briefly fluttered and whirled, then settled on the motorway.

X

I WENT HOME AND SLOWLY CLAMBERED OUT OF THE car, terrified that the stabbing pains I had felt all afternoon were getting worse. I had to see a doctor, to call Enrique, but how was I going to explain this away?

Claudia opened the door. She hugged me.

'Are you OK? Does it still hurt?'

'It's a lot better.'

'Where did you get to?'

'I went and got the photos back.'

'What did you do with them?'

'I cut them up and chucked them out the window on the motorway.'

'So that's it? It's over?'

'Yes, it's over.'

'Here, take this for the pain, it's just ibuprofen. But we need to call the doctor.'

'No, no, don't call the doctor, I'll just go and lie down for a bit. I'll give Enrique a call later. Could you phone the office and tell them I won't be coming back in this afternoon?'

I sat down in front of the TV, flicking through the channels while Claudia phoned Jenny – the news, some film with Robert de Niro, a European Cup match. The shooting pains were less intense now; my legs still ached, but it was bearable.

Enrique came round and checked me over. I told him I'd got into a fight because of a legal fuck-up with a client and we both joked about my wasted talents as a boxer. He reassured Claudia that I was fine and refused her offer of a coffee, a tea, a beer.

'I never drink when I'm working.'

'But you're not working, you're visiting family.'

Enrique's phone rang and he took the call, an emergency he had to deal with. He hugged us both and rushed off.

10 p.m. 'How's the pain?' Claudia asked.

I watched her go to the bathroom, then she came back, gave me a kiss and went to bed.

I felt paralysed in my chair as the films and football matches flickered on the screen.

I went to bed shortly before midnight. I slept fitfully, kept awake for long periods by the throbbing bruises on my arms and chest, and woken various times in the early hours by thirst, the urge to piss and a burning sensation under my skin. At one point, I got up and took the photos out of the envelope. Three faces. In the clearest picture, she was in profile, caught in the camera flash. Her hair tumbled down one side like a plume of smoke.

I had cut away my father's body, but I could still see his fingers curled over her shoulder.

I slipped the photos back into the envelope and lay down again.

I woke up.

I stumbled into the bathroom. I barely glimpsed myself in the mirror.

When I got to the office the following day, Jenny told me that a Señor Gualberto Martínez – Guayo – was waiting for me.

'He's been here for some time.'

I watched him come in. He smiled at me. He was wearing a jacket and tie. He was doing his best to seem polite, even cheerful.

'Were you in on it too, Guayo?'

'No. But Chacho's told me everything. How did you find out?'

'She told me herself.'

'The old woman?'

'Vilma Agurto herself, she told me.'

'Weird . . .'

'Why?'

'Because she's Chacho's aunt. She's his aunt.'

He was smiling at me.

'So I'm guessing she's not related to the girl, Miriam?'

'No.'

'And Chacho stole the photos after my father died?'

'How did you get her to tell you?'

I tried to think of an answer while I pretended to tidy some papers on my desk.

'I offered her five thousand dollars and she gave me the photos. Ask her yourself.'

'Five thousand dollars?'

'Yeah, that way she can live comfortably. Now you'd better go, I've got a lot of work on, *compadre*. And I never want to see your face again, Guayito.'

He came over to me, his eyes blazing.

'You're lying to me, aren't you?'

'You can believe what you like.'

'I didn't know anything about this, Adrián. I would never have done something like this to your *papá*. It was Chacho, it was all Chacho.'

'It doesn't matter now.'

He sat down and stretched his legs out, his hands in his pockets.

'Are you really going to turn them in?'

'I don't know yet.'

'Chacho is a bastard, I'm not defending him, don't think I want to defend him. But if you grass on them, you could end up fucking things up for yourself.'

'Like I said, I don't know what I'm going to do. Truth is, this whole thing has really screwed me up. Now do me a favour and leave.'

'You think you're a big shot, don't you?'

'If you want the truth, I think I'm an idiot.'

'You going to turn them in or not? Tell me.'

At that point something inside me snapped. I got up and started shouting like a lunatic. I was right up in his face, waving my arms and screaming a whole litany of insults and accusations, how he'd tortured and killed all those people, how he'd blackmailed my mother.

'If Papá were still alive he'd kill you both. You're a pair of fucking scumbags, that's what you are, I'd like to see both of you banged up, you fucking shits.' I don't know what I said to him.

At some point, he started trying to explain.

'Look, Chacho was broke, I mean back then he didn't have enough money to eat.'

But I just kept shouting and as I did Guayo's face became frozen, motionless, like a huge toad; his wide-eyed stare the only sign of life. Eventually, Nelson came into my office and I asked him to show Guayo out. Guayo looked at him, shrugged and walked down the corridor.

Jenny was standing in the doorway. She asked if I needed anything, brought me a glass of water and closed the door.

Sitting at my desk, my heart hammering in my chest, I realised that my father was not like them, like Chacho and Guayo. Faced with death, my father had repented. '*There's a woman up in Huanta, you have to find her.*' That day he had charged me with a duty. What could I call it? A duty of guilt, of memory, of remorse? '*There's a woman up in Huanta. There's a woman, you have to find her.*' Now I held that woman's face in my hands, her face, her body in the shadows of the photograph. Fulfil that duty . . . I felt my father's shadow pass over me, he had asked something of me and now he was asking again . . .

That night, I told Claudia about the incident with Guayo. She tried to reassure me, told me I'd be alright.

'There's no talking to people like that,' she said. 'I hope you never hear from them again.'

We were in the kitchen, about to go round to the Sanchez Leóns for one of Marcia's delicious *asados* when I told her that I was planning to look for Miriam.

'For who?'

'The woman my father had an affair with. The one who escaped. Her name's Miriam.'

'Look for her? What do you mean, look for her?'

'I want to find out where she is.'

'Oh, Adrián, what do you want to do that for?'

'I don't want people to find out about this some day. I have to stop her talking.'

'No one will find out if you don't push her. You've no reason to find her.'

'My father asked me to.'

'What?'

'Just before he died, he asked me to. It's just that at the time, I didn't realise.'

'You didn't realise?'

'I thought he was raving. He was talking to me about some woman in Huanta.'

'So now you want to find her?'

'Yes. I have to. It's what he wanted.'

'But I thought you said your father was delirious?'

'He was, but what he was raving about was true.'

'But even if you find her, what then?'

'I don't know who else knows about this. I can't afford any sort of scandal, you know that.'

'But how are you going to find her?'

'I don't know yet.'

'Look, why don't we talk this through calmly. Some other time . . .'

She stalked out of the room.

We talked it through calmly the next day, and the day after that. She was fascinated by the subject because I seemed so determined. Eventually, in a conversation in the kitchen, Claudia raised a series of objections: You're wasting your time; you'll get yourself in trouble; you and your fantasies, always off in your head somewhere when we need you here; you don't owe anything to some random girl your *papá* once knew. If no one knows about this now, they're never going to find out. If she hasn't said anything, why would she say something now? Why do you need to look for her? What put the idea in your head? The real reason is you're trying to get away from your family, isn't it? That's the real reason, you think I don't know that?

In the middle of the argument, Lucía came into the kitchen and started to cry.

One morning, before heading for the office, I opened my wallet and looked at the photos again. At Miriam's face. Somewhere in these shadows, surely, were the reasons my father had been seduced by her – had fallen in love with her? The long, slender face, the chiselled features, the glossy lips, the fiery gaze, I could make out her smoky body in the darkness. I was sitting on the bed, the fragments of the photos in my hand. I put them away again.

'Adrián,' Claudia came into the bedroom with a big smile, 'it's all settled. I told you weeks ago Papá invited us to Isla Margarita for the holidays. This is exactly what you need right now. We're leaving on Monday.'

'What?'

'Papá's taking us on holiday, you remember. Oh, don't tell me you don't want to go now.'

'To Isla Margarita?'

'Yes. Isn't it wonderful?'

'What are we going to do there?'

'Look, Adrián, this will be good for you. A little holiday is just what you need right now. I told you that a couple of days ago.'

'You go, take the girls,' I said, putting on my jacket. 'I've got a lot of work on next week. With all the shit I've had to deal with, I've been neglecting my work.'

'Darling, just leave all that for a week, can't you? File your problems away in a drawer, you can open it again next Monday. You really want to miss this? It was so good of Papá and Mamá to invite us, and it's all been paid for, the hotel, the meals, the flights, everything. Besides, they really want us to come. They told me they'd be really lonely without us. We just pack a couple of books and spend the days on the beach reading, what do you say?'

'You're right. It's too good to miss. You and the girls should go.'

'No, Adrián, don't be like this. What's the matter with you?'

'I can't go. We've got new client meetings scheduled all week.'

Claudia made a disgruntled sound.

'The real reason is you can't stand my family,' she muttered. 'Or maybe you're pissed off about Papá paying for everything?' She threw her hands up. 'But if it makes him happy to pay, what does it matter, darling? We could do with a holiday together now . . . especially since the girls are on holiday from school all week.'

'I can't, Claudia, but you and the girls should go.'

I went into the bathroom and straightened my tie in front of the mirror.

I heard Claudia whispering something into her phone.

Monday came, the day my family were to leave. I had breakfast with Alicia and Lucía. I told them I'd miss them.

'Will you be here when we get back?' Lucía asked.

'It's only for a couple of days,' I reassured her. 'Anyway, we can still talk on the phone.'

I suggested we all go to a pizzeria for lunch.

'Wow, cool,' said Lucía. 'Can I have a Margherita?'

'Of course, *hija*, whatever you want.'

'But we're not going to see each other for a whole week,' she said to me. 'It's so sad. What are you going to do without us, Papá?'

XI

THAT NIGHT, AFTER I DROVE BACK FROM THE airport, I thought about going out. I found it difficult to be in the house alone. I could take a long walk, maybe even a run before going to bed. Maybe I should have gone with them, I thought. After all, I had no real reason to stay here.

I put on my tracksuit and headed out; the road seemed vast, like a huge tunnel with no walls.

I started running.

A breeze stirred the trees.

I stared down at my trainers as they pounded the concrete. They seemed very far away. The streets that ringed the park, the houses, the white glow of the street lights, everything was swathed in an eerie mist. This was my neighbourhood, I knew it like the back of my hand, yet it felt as though I had never seen this place before – this hazy dreamlike landscape of trees and buildings.

The frantic barking of a dog came from one of the houses. I quickened my pace. I stopped. I thought about taking off my T-shirt but knew that I would end up shivering with cold. The small cloud of my breath appeared and disappeared.

A vague feeling of euphoria started my feet pounding again. I had lived my whole life in this neighbourhood. These streets brought back happy memories.

Just over there was my mother's house. Further along was where one of my uncles lived. A little further still, the school I had gone to. The network of streets that comprised San Isidro and Miraflores, this warren of neat little houses . . . Now, here I was, on my own, without Claudia and the girls, running for no other reason than that I liked to exercise, to keep in shape.

I came to the Avenida del Golfe and ran along the verge. The traffic boomed past me like gunshots. I decided to head north. I crossed Libertadores and Conquistadores and cut through Bosque del Olivar park, the wind whipping at the trees. I heard a distant sound, like a car horn somewhere out on the avenue.

A taxi pulled up beside me. Suddenly I had the mad idea – one that seemed completely normal to me at that moment – of visiting El Ángel cemetery in Barrios Altos. I asked the driver to take me as far as the Hospital Almenara. He stared at me, seeming surprised that I was wearing a tracksuit. He drove down the Paseo de la República and turned onto Grau. I was panting hard. Before long, we came to the hospital, in the dirty ghostly thoroughfare of deserted offices and houses, the silence broken only by the roar of a bus. I told him to turn right. Up ahead, vast and filthy, the Avenida Grau stretched away: the shadows of buildings, points of light and the smell of rubber and exhaust fumes.

I climbed out of the taxi, determined to run the rest of the way to El Ángel cemetery, it seemed the most natural thing in the world to me. Here I was, a white guy in a tracksuit on these streets, a stranger, a mad jogger; passers-by must have thought I was a ghost.

I kept moving, keeping close to the wall. The trail of dirty lights stretched into the distance. From time to time I heard the slow, sputtering noise of a car. I jogged on and turned left towards the cemetery. The road was completely deserted. In the distance, I could see a lone street light. I was coming up to the church.

From the far end of the street I saw the figure of a short man, arms swinging in an almost military fashion, coming towards me. I quickened my pace. Someone had probably spotted me – a white man in this neighbourhood at this time of night would be conspicuous – and decided to rob me. The figure became clearer. He was walking faster too. There were only fifty metres between us now.

I could almost make him out. I stopped, held my breath. Suddenly he appeared under the street light. He had a round face and eyes that were small and hard like a doll's. He didn't look at me, didn't stop. As he passed I felt a breath of air.

I stood there watching him disappear.

I carried on past the church and took the path leading to Presbíterio Maestro cemetery. I felt as though I was floating. Everything felt unreal: the dry ground, the cracked concrete, a few dead leaves, the railings, the shadows of the gravestones. Suddenly I heard a noise; the door of one of the nearby houses was ajar. A group of men was sitting around a forest of beer bottles. They barely turned to look.

I came to the cemetery gate, the stone angels with their trumpets, the traces of crushed petals on the path. I sat down. I don't know how long I was there, staring at my trainers, staring at the concrete. A tree swayed gently. Everything was deserted. There was an immense hush, as though silence itself had marshalled its troops here.

I waited for a while, sitting on the kerb, my head resting on my knees.

The police van came around the corner, stopped in front of me and a policeman got out. I told him I was fine. I took out my mobile and asked if there was somewhere I could get a taxi.

A taxi came.

I arrived home.

I sought sanctuary in a long shower and when I got out, I slumped into an armchair. I fell asleep. When I woke up at 4 a.m., the TV was showing a documentary about some Caribbean island. Was this where Claudia and the girls were?

In the morning, I had some black coffee and some toast and honey. The kitchen was filled with a bright web of sunlight. From the garden came a chorus of birdsong.

In the office, Jenny was waiting for me waving a sheet of paper.

'I went to the Public Registry Office yesterday,' she said. 'This is a list of all the owners who sold property on the block of the Avenida Dos de Mayo where Miriam was seen. Seventeen names.'

Seventeen was a manageable number for the purposes of

our search. By late morning, she'd tried calling every single one. Those who answered claimed they had never owned or rented a bodega in the area.

'But there were three people who didn't answer,' said Jenny. 'I think the best thing to do is for you to go and see them.'

'OK.'

'I've written down the addresses.'

There was a pause.

'I don't know if I've said how grateful I am to you for helping me with this stuff,' I said.

'I'm not doing it for you,' she smiled. 'I'm curious to find out who this girl was myself.'

The first name on the list was Herberto Cortínez who lived on Avenida Gregorio Escobedo in Jesús María. The second was a woman named Ana María Miranda, on the Avenida de Las Artes in San Borja. The third was someone called Vittorino Anco with an address on Calle Emancipación in El Cercado.

At eight o'clock the following morning, I was driving through the warren of huge square office blocks in Residencial San Felipe. I found Herberto Cortínez's house. I knocked at the door and, a moment later, Señor Cortínez was standing in front of me. He was bald and thickset, with sleepy, somewhat cruel eyes and a face like a brontosaurus. His lips were pursed in an unconscious rictus of contempt.

'Sorry to bother you, *señor*,' I said. 'My name is Adrián Ormache, I'm a lawyer.'

'Yeah, and . . . ?'

'I'm conducting an investigation. It's a personal matter,

nothing to do with my practice as a lawyer. Did you ever own or rent a shop on the Avenida Dos de Mayo?'

The guy was chewing something. His fat beer belly was sticking out. A crucifix hung round his neck.

'I don't know nothing about no shop,' he said, 'and I don't know nothing about you or what you're doing here.'

'You don't know of any shop near your property on the Dos de Mayo?'

'No,' he said in a low voice. 'Look, you seem like a decent guy, I don't know what you're doing going round knocking on people's doors and asking stupid questions.'

He closed the door.

My next stop was in one of the motley, deserted streets of San Borja. Ana María Miranda greeted me herself. She was wearing a pale blue blouse and a long skirt over her stork-like legs. Her face was completely spattered with angry bright red acne. Her beady eyes glittered with an icy sympathy.

I asked her the same question. She shook her head without a word. She was closing the door when suddenly she opened it again. In a bird-like voice she said, 'I sold my house. I don't know anything about a bodega, *señor*. No, sir, I don't know anything about that.'

I got back in my car, glanced at the clock. Eleven o'clock. I still hadn't had breakfast. I bought a newspaper, then went into a café, ordered a coffee and a roast beef sandwich and sat down to read. On the editorial page was an article by Arturo Gaona:

I am very concerned about the situation because as you know, dear reader, I too am grieved by what is happening in Peru.

I leafed through to the arts section and saw an article by a woman called Mona Marazzo who was based in Paris:

I am writing this from Paris as I gaze out over the Place Vendôme. Yesterday, I had lunch with some of the most eminent people in France. It was a magnificent event and such a select group of guests that at no point did anyone get up to go to the bathroom.

I looked for the financial supplement. I had always found numbers and statistics calming.

Suddenly a shadow appeared in the doorway. A giant of a man with broad shoulders and a head that looked as if it had been carved from stone. Next to him was a tiny woman wearing a fringed jacket and too much make-up. Between the woman's bright trousers and red hair and the guy's electric-blue T-shirt and black jeans, they looked like a couple of debauched clowns. They took a table near mine. They looked at me. As I went on reading the paper, I realised they were laughing and whispering. I took out my mobile and called Platón.

'Fancy having lunch today?' I said.

'Sure, if you like.'

'Let's go to Fiesta, my treat. I'll meet you there at 2 p.m.'

I hung up and set off to find Vittorino Anco's house – or possibly office – on the Calle Emancipación in El Cercado. If he couldn't tell me anything, I'd have to go through the whole list again.

I drove to Plaza Grau, passed the impressive flight of steps up to the Palacio de Justicia and then turned onto Lampa. Every now and then I was forced to stop. A procession of microbuses belching smoke, jugglers at the traffic lights, people selling bottles of water and fizzy drinks. I parked on Lampa and walked past a line of taxi drivers so comatose they barely seemed to be breathing.

I found the address. It was a large office building with aluminium railings and walls laminated in cream-coloured plastic. On the ground floor was a small kiosk. Behind the glass was a large pile of oranges, a metal juicer and a sign reading *JUICE S/.1*. Beyond that was a lift. I decided to take the stairs. On the fifth floor, I made my way down a greenish corridor and found the number I was looking for. I knocked several times and waited. I slipped my card under the door only to wonder, as I was headed downstairs again, whether that had been a mistake.

Back at the office, Jenny informed me that she had made some enquiries of her own. In recent years, two plots on the Avenida Dos de Mayo – on blocks 14 and 15 – had been bought and redeveloped as offices. One had belonged to Señora Miranda, who had insisted she knew nothing about a bodega, the other to Señor Anco.

Jenny and I spent the morning trying to get Señor Anco on the phone. At lunchtime, I decided to go back to the address listed for him and ask some of the neighbours if they knew him. A guy with long hair was manning the juice bar. He stared at me inquisitively. I bought a glass of orange juice.

'I don't suppose you've seen Vittorino Anco around?' I asked.

'That's him there,' the guy replied, pointing behind me.

I turned and watched him coming towards me, a man of about forty, maybe fifty, with olive skin and big liquid eyes. He was wearing a dark suit and a blue tie with a gold tie-pin. He had a courteous air about him, with a certain tension that kept his head held high.

'Señor Anco?' I said.

He nodded.

'I'm sorry, you don't know me, *señor*. My name is Adrián Ormache. I am a lawyer, and I would like to speak to you for a moment if I may.'

I held out my hand. He hesitated before shaking it.

'Of course, Señor Ormache,' he said, looking at me mildly. 'There's no problem, I hope?'

'No, no. It's a personal matter. I promise I won't take up much of your time.'

I gave him my card. He looked at me again. He raised his hand and waved towards the door.

'Please, follow me.'

We climbed the stairs and came into a corridor dimly lit by a small window. He took a bunch of keys from his pocket, turned the lock and pushed the door with his shoulder.

The office had a wooden desk covered with green baize; on it was a sturdy telephone, a pennant and a plaque bearing the name of some university. Two filing cabinets stood at the far end of the room. A bloody crucifix hung on one wall. The window looked out over the neighbouring rooftops: washing lines, piles of planks and mounds of dirty sand. The distant sounds of the avenue.

He asked me to wait a moment while he filed some papers. He opened the drawers, examined each document carefully and put it into one of the cardboard files. I sat on the other side of the desk.

Eventually he turned towards me, hands clasped in front of him. I thanked him for agreeing to see me, then began.

'I'm a lawyer and I'm looking for someone who owned or leased a small shop on the Avenida Dos de Mayo – a bodega – it would have been on block fourteen or possibly fifteen. I don't suppose you might know, Señor Anco?'

'I do, actually, there was a shop on the property I had there,' he said. 'One of my cousins leased it from me.'

'Your cousin? Could you give me your cousin's name?'

'I'm sorry, sir, but if I might just ask first . . . why are you looking for this person?'

'I'm trying to track down a girl,' I said. 'A girl called Miriam.'

His face froze. He brushed his hand across the desk as though wiping dust away.

'Miriam?' he murmured.

'Yes. You know her?'

He clasped his hands again and sat motionless.

'I do, but I'm afraid I don't know what's become of her.'

There was a pause. I smiled.

'You knew Miriam?'

'Yes, but it's been a long time since I last saw her.'

'I believe she worked in the shop.'

'Can I ask why you're looking for her?'

Just then there was a noise from what sounded like a water tank somewhere in the building. It was like some great machine panting into life. It rose to a high-pitched whine, then quickly faded.

'It's, well, it's a personal matter, Señor Anco.'

'A personal matter?'

'A family matter . . . I believe this girl knew my father.'

'I see.'

'Can you help me?'

'Well, I rented out the bodega to my cousin, but I'm afraid there's not much more I can tell you, I'm sorry.'

I leaned back in the chair.

'That's OK, don't worry, but could you perhaps tell me where I might find your cousin?'

I saw him hesitate, his lips moving as though gulping air.

'I have no idea where he might be now. I haven't seen my cousin. But if you'll forgive me, you still haven't said why you're looking for him.'

'I'm looking for her, for Miriam.'

'But why?'

'As I explained, I believe she knew my father . . .' I paused. I saw him glance at me, then look away.

'You say she knew your father? Where would that have been?'

'In Ayacucho, possibly. Or maybe Huanta.'

He was tapping the desk lightly with his finger.

'Well, it's no business of mine,' he said, 'but in any case, I can't help you.'

'You don't know anything about her? Or anyone who might be able to help me?'

His eyes flashed for a second.

'Why don't you give me your address, *señor*? If I think of anything, I'll get in touch.' He opened a drawer and took out a leather address book, licked his thumb and leafed through several pages.

He took my card. He wrote slowly, drawing each letter meticulously and putting little circles over the 'i's.

I stood up and shook his hand again. As I turned, I heard his voice.

'One question, Señor Ormache.'

'Of course.'

'Was your father in the military?'

My hand was on the doorknob.

'Yes, he was.'

He looked at me evenly.

'The navy?'

'Yes, the navy.'

'OK.'

He looked away; closed the drawer.

'If I think of anything, I'll contact you.'

'Thank you.'

A moment later I was running down the stairs.

The restaurant Fiesta looked like someone's house suddenly overrun by strangers: a three-piece suite, deep-pile carpets, and a tiny courtyard. It specialised in traditional Peruvian dishes, duck with rice, steak with rice and beans and *espesado*. But the restaurant had other attractions – the fact that it looked like a deserted house, for example. The furniture and the carpets in Fiesta gave customers the feeling that they had seized the house of a family that had fled, or who were locked up and awaiting execution while we sat in their chairs. It's easy to feel completely comfortable in someone else's house, in someone else's life.

When I arrived, Platón was already at a table drinking a pisco sour, and there was another sitting in front of him. 'I saw you pull up, so I ordered you a drink,' he said.

I took a seat next to him.

'How've you been, Adrián?'

I told Platón that all I'd wanted the past few days was to be on my own to think about my mother. 'I've been round to her house a couple of times. It's exactly like when I used to go round to visit her . . .'

'Look, death's a bitch, you just have to deal with it and then get on with your life, and you remember her, you hang onto that memory . . . the thing you have to forget is death itself. There's so much out there, so much to do. You can't spend your whole life in mourning – sure, you grieve for a while, but not for ever.'

'You're turning into a philosopher,' I said. 'Must be the pisco talking.'

'Must be. So, did you come straight from the office?'

I took a sip of the pisco sour.

'No, I was in central Lima. I'm trying to find someone.'

'Who?'

'I've been trying to track down that girl.'

'What girl?'

'Miriam – the girl Papá had a thing with.'

'You're still on that?'

'He asked me . . . before he died, Papá asked me.'

I finished my drink.

'So have you managed to find out anything?'

'I've talked to a number of people, but no one seems to know her. At least, that's what they say.'

I told him about the three people I'd spoken to. Platón listened, working away at his drink. He ordered another and then glanced at me.

'This guy Anco obviously knows something, don't you think?'

'I hope so.'

'But even if you do find this Miriam, what are you going to say to her?'

'I haven't the faintest idea.'

The waiter came over.

'Would you like to order lunch now, *señores*?'

We both ordered the steak and a glass of beer.

'So listen,' Platón said. 'The other day, I ran into my cousin on the street. Haven't seen him in years. Back then I used to see him every day at my aunt's house, now he's just this guy I bump into sometimes, we say hi and we keep walking. It's weird, isn't it? How people change. You start out loving them, you see them all the time and then suddenly something happens – or nothing happens – and you don't see them any more and you don't know why and then later you come across them in the street and you say hello and you keep walking. We used to always hug when we met, now we say hi and keep walking. That's the way it goes. Your own brother can end up being a stranger. Or your father. And here you are worrying about some woman you've never even met. So what are you going to say to this woman?'

'I told you, I don't know.'

'You going to ask her to fucking forgive you? What are you going to say?'

Platón's voice was like a dull roar.

'Forgive me for what?'

'For having a sleazeball for a father.'

'I'm not responsible for the sins of my father.'

'Course you are, you're partly responsible at least.'

'Why?'

'We're all responsible for our parents' sins, and our children's too.'

'I don't see why.'

'Because, just because.'

'That's bullshit.'

'I don't know. The way I see it, we are responsible. They're our parents, our children, they're not just random people. They're part of us. We can never be free of them.'

'But we're not to blame for what they do.'

He smiled, propped his elbows on the table and clasped his hands.

'So what are you going to say to this girl?'

'Well . . . I want her to tell me whether Papá really was the shit people are saying he was. But it's not just that. Honestly, I don't know. I just want to meet her. I don't want to have to justify what he did. Worst comes to the worst, the story might get out, and that would be bad for me. But to tell the truth, I feel like shit.'

'What's the matter?'

'Last night I went out running, and I decided to jog all the way to the cemetery, can you believe that?'

'Why did you do that?'

'I don't know, because I felt like it.'

'Is someone you know buried there?'

A noise from his chest startled Platón; he took out his mobile and answered it.

'I can't talk right now, I'm in a meeting,' he said. 'Stop pestering me.'

Then he raised his glass.

'Cheers, *compadre*. To your *mamá*, and to your *papá* too. And to this girl, wherever she is.'

As I arrived back in the office I heard Jenny's voice.

'How are you, *señora*? Such a pleasure to hear from you.'

It was Claudia. I took the phone.

'We got here safely. The weather's magnificent, the girls are having a ball. Aren't you jealous? Why don't you come out, you could take the first flight tomorrow?'

I chatted with her for a while, had a quick word with Alicia and Lucía.

'It's amazing out here, Papi, it's so beautiful.'

Later that afternoon, Jenny came into my office.

'I've got it,' she said.

'What?'

'Vittorino Anco had a shop on the Avenida Dos de Mayo.'

'I know that.'

'He paid social security for an employee at that address.'

'Who?'

'A man called Paulino Valle.'

'Have you got an address?'

Jenny took out her notebook.

'Paulino Valle lives in the northern suburbs of Lima, an area called Huanta Dos.'

'Huanta Dos?'

'That's what it says. From what I could find out, the area has a lot of immigrants from Ayacucho. Huanta Dos is a subdistrict of San Juan de Lurigancho, I've written the address down for you.'

I tapped the details into my phone.

'Who knows, maybe this guy is Miriam's husband,' said Jenny.

'No, I don't think so.'

'Oh, Adrián . . .'

'What? What is it?'

'I can't believe you've fallen head over heels for this woman Miriam without even setting eyes on her.'

'I haven't fallen for anyone.' I flirted jokingly, 'Except you . . .'

'Very funny.'

Just then, the phone rang.

XII

I TOOK OUT A STREET ATLAS OF LIMA WHILE JENNY answered the phone. It had some information on the area: San Juan de Lurigancho, a vast swathe to the north of the city, was the most densely inhabited part of Lima, with more than a million inhabitants. A broad sweeping avenue – the Avenida de las Galaxias – cut through the neighbourhood to become the Avenida Fernando Weisse. I'd never heard of them; as far as I was concerned this place might as well have been the moon. It would never have occurred to me to go there. I was only familiar with the name San Juan de Lurigancho because it was one of Lima's election constituencies.

'Who was that on the phone?' I asked Jenny as she hung up.

'The American Embassy. They're sending round invites to a jazz night. Gabriel Alegría is playing.'

'Great. Listen, I need to go out for a while – is there anything in my diary for this afternoon?'

'You've got a meeting with Señor Ortiz.'

'Can you cancel it? Or postpone it till tomorrow.'

'Sure.'

'Thanks. And don't put any calls through unless it's an

emergency. Could you buzz through to Nelson and ask him to pick me up downstairs?'

By the time I got down to the ground floor, Nelson was standing by the car waiting for me.

'Have you got a street atlas?' I asked as I closed the car door.

'Of course, *señor*.'

'Good, we need to work out how we get to San Juan de Lurigancho.'

'That's easy – straight down Javier Prado, then turn onto the ring road. Forgive me for asking, but what would a man like yourself be doing in San Juan de Lurigancho?'

As we drove along the expressway, I imagined cars were huge insects carrying a deadly virus swarming through the streets. The infected cars were constantly looking for others to infect, veering and swerving in search of new victims while the others tried to avoid being hit. It seemed funny.

We took the exit off the ring road and ended up in a narrow street with yellow walls, and signs advertising cheap hotels and places offering to exchange dollars. It was like the entrance to a cave. We turned onto a dual carriageway, the telegraph posts whipped past, the road melted into a whitish blur, everything seemed remote, unreal.

As he drove, Nelson chatted away about the match he'd been watching last night, the goal Waldir Sáenz scored.

We stopped to ask a policeman for directions and he told us to keep going straight until we came to the statue of Mariátegui, then turn left and we'd get to Huanta Dos.

'And what exactly are we looking for when we get there?' Nelson asked me.

'We're looking for a guy called Paulino Valle.'

'Oh, OK. But why are we looking for him, you need him to sign papers?'

'I need him because I'm trying to find someone else.'

We drove along the Avenida Weisse, past Huiracocha park with its posters for volleyball and five-a-side football, past a sign for the Metro and a petrol station. Along the central reservation were young palm trees, but the hard shoulder was nothing but rocks and dust and patches of concrete. All along the avenue were shops, piles of tyres, street sellers with handcarts laden with fruit, a queue of mototaxis, schools, dentists, a line of purple microbuses. We passed a nightclub called Hawaiian Music with a banner announcing a party on Friday.

At some point I asked Nelson to pull over. We both got out. I walked over to a small bodega with grimy windows and bought two bottles of juice, handed one to Nelson and started walking up the block past the Colegio Bertolt Brecht and a sign for the National Engineering University. I wandered towards the university building. From the second floor I heard a professor's voice explaining some mathematical problem. It felt strange, hearing someone's voice in this wasteland.

We went back to the car and drove on, past a couple of churches with posters advertising Religious Studies, and found ourselves in an area we were told was called Jicamarca. We drove up a hill and I saw a bus depot and, next to it, a restaurant called El Misky. We stopped and talked to the owner, a chubby-faced man called Max with a high forehead and wide-set eyes. He talked quickly, his 'r's clipped.

'We're looking for a place called Huanta Dos . . .' I explained.

'Ah . . . it's back a little way – those houses down there. People from Ayacucho, mostly, they set up there. Huanta Uno is a bit further, next to the prison. It was the prisoners who built Huanta Dos, you can see it there, see, just past the petrol station.'

'Shall we head back?' said Nelson.

We drove to the expressway, this time turning right at the statue of Mariátegui onto a dirt road, past a patch of waste ground, then turned right again and found ourselves face to face with a pack of dogs, brick walls, barred windows. The car rattled and jolted. We stopped in front of a blue house with a grille over the window and a scrawny plant held up by a cane. A black plaque with gold letters spelled out the address Jenny had given me. This was where Paulino Valle lived, the man who worked in the bodega with Miriam.

I got out of the car and just stood there, unable to move. After all, what did I know about this man? And what was I going to say to him? 'Did you work with Miriam, did you know her well, did she ever mention a Comandante Ormache who kept her prisoner? Well, I'm his son and I'm looking for her, I don't know why, but I'm here.'

Sure. That would be a brilliant little speech.

I may have been a lawyer of some standing but now here I was, knocking on the door of some stranger called Paulino Valle who, though he lived a few kilometres from my house, was light years from my world. I came from a different universe, from a different dimension where people ride around in cars, sleep in kingsize beds, have walk-in wardrobes filled with designer clothes. What did I have to say to him?

I stood, paralysed by a strange sensation. For a split second, I thought Miriam herself would answer the door.

'You want me to come with you, *señor*?'

'No. No, it's OK, Nelson, you can leave me here.'

I rang the doorbell. Took a step back. A dog barked somewhere nearby. The door opened.

The man had a chiselled, angular face that emphasised his cheekbones. He was wearing a pair of black trousers, a white shirt and a gold medallion round his neck. There was a fearful deference in his movements that reassured me.

'Señor Paulino Valle?'

'Yes, yes, that's me.'

'I'm sorry, you don't know me, Señor Valle, my name is Adrián Ormache.'

'Yes, sir.'

'Would you have a minute to talk, Señor Valle?'

'Talk about what, sir?'

'Some years ago, you worked in a bodega on the Avenida Dos de Mayo?'

He didn't move. He stared at me, his beady eyes glimmering dimly with fear.

'Why . . . why do you want to know?'

'I'm looking for a girl. Miriam, I think her name is. She worked in the shop with you, didn't she?'

'What did you say your name was?'

'Adrián Ormache.'

I stood there, lost for words.

'Is she in some sort of trouble? Has she done something wrong?'

'No, she hasn't done anything wrong. The truth is, I want to help her.'

A wisp of hair fell over his forehead.

'Help her? Help her how?'

His voice was barely audible. He brought a hand up to his face and slicked back his hair.

'I'm a lawyer, there's something I want to do for her.' I stared at him.

'Do what?'

'I want to see if she's all right, help her if I can.' I paused and then added, 'That's all I want to do, Señor Valle.'

He stepped aside.

'Come in,' he said.

I stepped into a living room with plaster walls, black floor tiles, two overstuffed sofas. We sat down. Next to me hung a calendar bearing a portrait of a blond Christ.

'Are you related to Miriam?' I asked.

'No.'

'But you know her?'

'Why do you want to know? I'm sorry, I don't understand.'

'I know that she had a difficult life when she was younger, that there was trouble in the village she came from. I heard about her case and thought maybe there was something I could do for her. That's all.'

He looked down.

'Well, she worked in the bodega in Lima, but then the shop

was sold by the guy who owned it. They were going to build an office block so we had to give up the shop.'

'And how long have you been living here?'

'Thing is, I came here, well, I came because there was a group of people who set up here, built this neighbourhood, we're all from Huanta, *señor*.'

'You're all from Huanta?'

'That's right, sir, all from Huanta.'

'So you work locally?'

'I work shifts driving the microbuses on the Montenegro –Manchay route, the station's just down there.'

'Do you know where I can find Miriam, Señor Valle?'

He brought his hand up to his mouth. Rubbed his face.

'I don't know what became of Miriam. After we closed the bodega I think she went back to Huanta. She was from Luricocha, her family had a little shop, so she went back there. That was years ago, I haven't heard from her since.'

'Excuse me, Señor Valle, but how do you know Miriam?'

'We all come from round there, we're all from Huanta.'

He looked away. For a moment I thought he was going to tell me Miriam lived here in the *barrio*, maybe even in this very house. I smiled to think I had fantasised about finally coming face to face with her here.

'Do you think there's anyone around here who might know anything more about her?'

'I don't know, *señor*. You'd have to ask them.'

'What was Miriam's surname?'

'Ah, that I don't know either. In the bodega we just called her Miriam. I never knew her surname.'

I got up, jotted down my phone number and asked him to call me if he remembered anything else about her.

'Thank you,' I said.

As I walked back to the car, it occurred to me that he had recognised my surname the moment I first mentioned it.

'*Ormache, the son of Comandante Ormache, the bastard Miriam told us about in the bodega. It was his son who came here. Came here looking for you. Tracked down your cousin Vittorino Anco and then came here to the house looking for you. Why is this man so desperate to find you, Miriam? Why does he want to see you? Does he want to kill you, to persuade you not to talk, to give you money so you don't talk about what happened? What does he want?*'

Perhaps this was what he would say to her later. Perhaps Miriam had told him about her ordeal during the companionable hours spent working in the little shop.

'How did it go?' asked Nelson. 'Any trouble?'

'No, no trouble. Let's drive round for a bit.'

'Around here?'

'Yeah, just for a look.'

I got him to drive through the unpaved streets. We passed houses of cement block and iron bars, a beauty salon and in the window a hairdresser setting a woman's hair in rollers, a pack of drowsy dogs, children squatting in the dirt playing marbles. Eventually, I told Nelson to head back to the main avenue.

When we came to the tarmacked road I said, 'I'm really tired, Nelson, I think maybe I'll take a break, go to Ayacucho for a day or two.'

'Ayacucho, sir? Why there?'

'I don't know. I've always been curious to see it. Now my family's away for a bit, I can afford to take a little time off.'

Nelson accelerated.

'But why Ayacucho, *señor*? Is something wrong?'

'No, Nelson, there's nothing wrong. There's nothing wrong at all.'

That afternoon I went to the bookshop on the Calle Miguel Dasso. The shop assistant recommended a number of books about the war against Sendero Luminoso. I found a thin volume, no more than a hundred pages, published by the Defensoría del Pueblo entitled *Voices of the Disappeared*. Fifteen stories, all of them anonymous, by people who had been in Ayacucho in the 1980s.

I bought it, and went into the café next door. The waiter brought me a coffee.

Each of the pieces had a heading with the initials of the writer and their date and place of birth. Almost all the contributors were women. All the stories began in much the same way:

One night soldiers came into our house and took my husband away, we had just finished eating when they burst in; we went to the barracks to find out what had happened to him and they said they didn't know anything, so we went to the next barracks. I don't want those who murdered him tracked down. All I want now is for them to give me back his body. I want to know where they took his body, where it is, so I can visit his grave.

I went on reading. I came upon the story of a forty-year-old woman from Ayacucho:

One night, while we were asleep, a group of soldiers with a torch burst into the house in the early hours, five or six of them there were, and they took my son. Just to question him, they said, they just wanted to question him but then when we went to the barracks they told us they'd never heard of him. Days passed and still we didn't find him. No one could tell us anything about what had happened to him. We never saw him again. We went back again and again and we asked but the soldiers always said the same thing, we don't know anything, come back tomorrow, that's what they said. And life is too big now, too empty without my son.

I read by the light of one of the backlit panels. A white glow that shimmered on the plates and the tablecloth.

I glanced around, ordered another coffee and went back to my reading. Around me in the café I vaguely heard groups of people coming and going. Eventually I put down the book and leaned back in my seat.

It was a long time before I got to my feet.

One night, we heard trucks outside, a gang of eight or ten soldiers kicked the door in, they smashed through the metal door, they charged in, the whole lot of them and my husband Luis was there, and they grabbed him by the hair and dragged him away, said you fucking terrorist you're coming with us and I told them he wasn't a terrorist, but they dragged him away anyway, and my children were crying and screaming and crying. I hung onto him, to my husband, and I said to the soldiers even if you kill me I'm not going to let go, you're not taking him, but they hit me with a rifle butt and shouted, 'Shut up you terrorist bitch, we'll take you with us too. If he holds up under torture, we'll let him go,' that's what they told me. That night they took him and I didn't sleep and the next day was Sunday and I went to the barracks at Los Cabitos and they told me they didn't know anything, that he was taken to the police station, that I'd find him there, I spent the whole day crying and I went to the police station and they told me he wasn't there, and then on Monday some man came and told me he'd been taken with my husband. 'There were several of us, and they let the rest of us go. But they didn't let him go, they tortured him.' So I went back to the barracks but they wouldn't let me in, so I went to a lawyer but I had no money to pay him, there was nothing I could do, at the barracks this officer called Barzola told me that if I brought him some food he'd help me, so I brought him some food but he didn't know anything, so then we went to Ayahuarcuna, this place out on the road to Huanta called Ayahuarcuna where they dumped the bodies, and what I wanted was to find my husband, even if he was dead, so at least I'd have his body. That's all I wanted. It was out in Ayahuarcuna that the army and Sendero

Luminoso dumped their bodies. I went with two other women who were looking for their husbands too, we found piles of bodies, they'd been horribly tortured, tongues, penises, fingernails, eyes ripped out, fingers cut off. Afterwards I talked to a soldier, I begged him to let me have Luis' body, that's all I wanted. Then I talked to a general, I even talked to a general because the soldier let me into the barracks. He told me he didn't know anything but asked me if I could find someone to work for him as a maid in his house in Lima.

'How are we going to live without Papá?' my son asked me later.

Sometimes my elder son would go out looking for his *papá*. He was always drinking. If at least we had his body we could have visited his grave. If we only had that, but we had nothing. Nothing. All that racking our brains, it gave us all a headache. We still don't know anything to this day. Everyone in my family ended up alone. All of us were left alone with his death.

By the time I'd finished reading, the café was heaving. Most of the tables were full. At one of them, a group of people was bellowing 'Happy Birthday'. The racket was deafening. I called the waiter but when he came over I didn't know what to say to him. Still the voices carried on.

XIII

NEXT MORNING AT THE OFFICE, EDUARDO AND I had a meeting to discuss our new clients. There were three: one of them a bank. Eduardo was very happy, and so was I.

At five or six that afternoon I was doing something I hardly ever did, pacing up and down my office. It felt so cramped, so claustrophobic that it occurred to me it might not be a bad idea to buy a sledgehammer at the nearest hardware shop and knock down the walls to give myself some room to move. It would have been fun. The whole floor in ruins, Eduardo screaming and shouting, me running up and down in the debris. Then Jenny came in with a plane ticket to Ayacucho.

'Are you really going?'

'Of course. What makes you ask?'

'I don't know, but I won't believe it until I see you get on the plane.'

I called Eduardo to tell him I was going, and he was happy to let me take a couple of days' leave from the office, though he had a few questions.

'I sort of thought you might take a break,' he said. 'Your mother's death has been a terrible shock. But why Ayacucho?'

'Someone told me there was a fabulous hotel there with a pool.'

'A pool?'

'Besides, I want to buy some handicrafts for the new patio.'

I slipped the plane ticket into my pocket.

I had dinner with Señor Cano and got home at about eleven. Señor Cano was easy to deal with, as his favourite subject of conversation was himself: his houses, his trips abroad, his wives. It was easy to keep him happy, all it took to win his approval was to ask the same questions: How's the new house? How was your holiday? How are the kids? Didn't I see a photo of you in the paper the other day? The questions were like music from a barrel organ; the monkey that was his ego started dancing as soon as he heard them.

When I got home, I slumped in front of the TV. As soon as I pressed the remote control I knew what was going to happen. I zapped from channel to channel, an explosion, people talking, people singing, changing bodies, the succession of monotonous images merging to form a movie with an infinite parade of characters, or the same character infinitely shape shifting. It was sort of funny in a way.

I felt lost in the house without Claudia and the girls. I went into my daughters' rooms. It felt a little mawkish, but I even lay down on their beds.

That night I tossed and turned, sleeping only fitfully. Finally 4.30 a.m. came. My plane was scheduled to leave at six.

*　　*　　*

At the airport, I elbowed my way through a group of tourists heading for Cuzco. At the boarding gate for the flight to Ayacucho were about five or six people. We were led out onto the runway. The plane was a Fokker with twelve tiny seats, the pilot a lanky, listless guy who looked as though he wore his sunglasses even when he went to bed at night. Finally the plane took off, effortlessly climbing almost vertically and then settling into the air.

Every time I board a plane I feel the same excitement, the same fear. It's as though I'm flying for the first time. The carpet of cloud, the wind whipping around the wings, the sun glaring through the window, it feels as though I am seeing them for the first time. The five or six other passengers barely spoke during the flight; a cargo of corpses would have been more fun.

An hour later the pressure beneath us dropped as the plane wheeled and headed towards the narrow runway between the mountains and we landed in Ayacucho, brakes screeching on the tarmac. As I stumbled down the steps, I felt as though the sky was falling on me. The vibrant blue of the sky and the outline of the mountain peaks made me quicken my pace. Simply walking in the icy purity of this air felt strange.

I told the taxi driver he could take me to whichever hotel he recommended. He reeled off a list of options; I settled on La Tres Máscaras simply because I liked the name – the Three Masks. We passed through the main square, the Plaza de Armas, past Ayacucho cathedral and San Cristobal University. I was reminded of a holiday I'd taken here as a teenager during Easter Week. I was at university at the time and my mother was still a young woman. I'd come with a group of friends. We'd stayed up all night drinking beer and playing guitar.

I got out of the taxi, and went into the hotel reception where I was greeted by a boy with a droning voice and beady eyes. I filled out the registration forms and followed the boy down a corridor to a room that looked out onto a terrace. He handed me the key and asked how long I would be staying. A couple of days, I told him, maybe three. The room had high ceilings and a large window that opened onto the terrace and the garden. I lay down, thinking I might catch up on some sleep.

When I woke up, it was 11 a.m. I left the room, taking the key with me. I realised that I was rushing.

The Huamanga–Huanta bus station was at a crossroads. Outside, it was a line of microbuses and trucks, their drivers looking around, scouting for passengers.

A group of kids in flip-flops was sitting in the back of a truck. I noticed a girl with plaits, her feet hanging over the side of the truck. She was a pretty girl with hard, dark eyes and delicate features, dressed in rags that covered her almost completely. She was, I thought, an example of how nature resists the plans of history.

Two or three drivers crowded round me, jingling their keys, touting for a fare. Behind the group stood a man with a Chevrolet that had large fins. 'Thirty *soles*, good price,' he said. 'There and back.'

He had curly hair, a glint in his eye and a red T-shirt that hugged his beer belly like a watermelon. 'Anselmo Ramos, *señor*,' he said, 'at your service.'

We took the main road out of town and headed for Huanta. I asked Anselmo whether he'd been living in Ayacucho during the war. 'Horrific,' he said, in a gruff, booming voice, spraying himself with spittle as he talked. 'Just going down the street here was terrifying. Walking around the area meant taking your life in your hands. If Sendero Luminoso didn't snatch you off the street the military did. But Sendero Luminoso were worse, I'm fucking telling you.'

The landscape was all hills and hollows, scattered shrubs, hairpin bends, rocky clefts, sharply defined clouds. We drove along a paved road between the peaks, a topography of stone and earth with patches of vegetation. The air was clear, the clouds in sharp focus, the cold was biting. We met a few microbuses and trucks loaded with baskets coming the other way.

'So are you from Huanta?' I asked Anselmo.

'Yup, born and raised there.'

'What did you do during the war?'

'I barely set foot outside the town. If you left the town Sendero Luminoso would kidnap you, steal your car and if you were lucky they might leave you alive to walk back home. If they didn't butcher you, they took your car. That's how it was. That's how they were, the *senderistas*. They'd take everything you had. But there were some people who didn't give in so easily. I had a friend, Hugo Matta his name was, he was stopped by Sendero Luminoso and they were going to burn his car, but he wasn't about to let them just torch his car, so he started screaming and shouting and they got a big rock and they smashed his head in. Same thing happened to another guy, Leonidas Cisneros, a lieutenant governor. Leonidas stood up to them, told them he wasn't having them coming into his village so they put a bullet in his head right there. Why are you interested in all this, *señor*?'

'I'm thinking of doing an investigation.'

'Journalist, are you?'

'No. No, I'm not a journalist.'

'So, what then?'

'Did you ever hear of Comandante Ormache?'

'Oh, the guy up in the barracks in Huanta? Yeah, I heard about him. Can't say I remember much. But they were the same, the whole lot of them. Well, the navy were worse than the army, I suppose – when the army came up here the district was a bit better. The army didn't round up people the way the navy did.'

'So what about Comandante Ormache? Did people know he had a woman at the barracks?'

'A woman? No, I never heard anything about that, *señor*. See there,' he said, pointing out the window of the car, 'just up there is where they used to find the dead bodies. And over there, that bridge, they call that the Puente Infiernillo – Hell's Bridge. They used to find piles of corpses round here. Sendero Luminoso would dump the bodies right here by the roadside. The army used to dump bodies here too, just leave the dead lying here.'

I asked him to stop the car. We were in a small dip between two hills next to a bridge. There were some rocks lined up along the grass. I took a couple of photos. I don't know why. I headed towards the hill, turned right after the line of rocks and sat on the grass.

'Right here is where they used to dump them,' Anselmo said.

This natural hollow between the hills was the perfect place to hide corpses, I thought, it was close to the main road, the ditch made it easy to pile one body on top of another to save space. The gorge was like an open-air coffin created by nature.

'Right there . . . just dumped them,' I heard Anselmo say. 'Anyone driving past would see them. Most of them were dead by the time they were brought here, tortured, limbs cut off. They'd be here for days sometimes and then the troops would come and take them away. Sometimes they just dumped them a bit further from the road.'

Just then, a thought occurred to me. It seemed funny but it reassured me. This magnificent sky, I thought, was death's last, unspoken joke on those still alive when they were brought here, those who lay here dying looking up at the vast expanse of blue sky.

The rest of the trip took no time at all and we quickly arrived in Huanta. Narrow streets, squat adobe houses, a line of mototaxis, cars lumbering slowly belching smoke, a soaring mountain peak in the distance.

'Where do you want to go, *señor*?' Anselmo asked.

'To the barracks.'

'Ah, well, to get there you'd have to take a mototaxi. The car wouldn't make it up there. Just tell me what time you'll be back and I'll meet you here on the main square.'

I got out of the car. A mototaxi was parked on the corner, its tyres worn, the pillion seat ripped and tattered, but the engine still growled. The driver was a skinny kid with close-cropped hair. I asked him to take me to the barracks and, seeing him hesitate, I offered him double the fare.

We rode along a dirt track, skirted around the mountain and slowly began to climb. I was thinking I should take a picture of this place where my father had lived for a while. A photo, a backdrop against which I could picture him. His uniform, his moustache, his drooping eyelids, the mole next to his nose, his rasping voice barking orders at his men. That uniform I remembered from my childhood, the sleeves piped with green and black, the way my father looked when he came to pick me and Rubén up from Mamá's one time. I could picture him here, the beret, the bulletproof glasses, the boots caked in mud, coming up this dirt track in his jeep.

Eventually we arrived. All I could see of the barracks was a high wall, a lookout tower with a sentry and a tall wooden door. The guard glared down at me, gripping his rifle, head cocked like a dog.

To buy time, I asked him if I could go inside.

'It's against regulations, *señor*, you're not allowed to be here.'

I pressed the entryphone.

'Go away, go away,' he said, then suddenly disappeared. Maybe he was coming down to open the door. I managed to peer inside.

Maybe that window I could see across the parade ground . . . I wanted to get closer to take a photo of that window, maybe that had been Papá's room. But I had to get out of here before the guard confiscated my camera.

I clambered back onto the mototaxi but, suddenly, without knowing why, asked the boy to wait a minute, although I was convinced that any moment now the sentry would come through the front door looking for me.

I pictured this place on a starlit night. Pictured this woman called Miriam, her hands shaking, buttoning Guayo's uniform and walking out onto this dirt track, barely glancing up at the squat tower from which the guard was watching. She had lit the cigarette, was focusing on every movement of her muscles, carefully imitating Guayo's voice, 'I'm just going for a walk,' her shoulders seeking a way to move forward without alerting suspicion, finding the narrow strip of air separating her from the sentry, 'I'm just going for a walk,' she said and then passed under the watchtower and stepped out into the fresh air. Perhaps she witnessed a miracle, a hand raised in salute acknowledging she was leaving, and then found herself outside in the vast expanse of darkness. Perhaps on the very spot where I was now standing. She must have walked past these rocks, careful not to give in to the desperate urge to run; she kept walking, smoke rising from her cigarette, exposed to the heavens, never hurrying, never turning back, controlling the temptation to make herself invisible until she reached the road. I tried to imagine her here, on this dirt track, embracing the cold, stepping into the darkness, into the paralysis of speed. Was that how it had happened?

The barracks door swung open and a soldier pointed at me. He came closer, shouting, 'Get out of here before I turn you in. Nobody takes photos here, got it?'

I went back to the mototaxi and asked the driver to take me to Huanta stadium. He started the motorcycle.

'Huanta stadium?'

'Yeah, let's head there.'

I had read about Huanta stadium, the football pitch, the stands, the dressing rooms and the offices that been converted by the navy into a concentration camp, a place of torture. How many people had died here – hundreds, thousands, tens of thousands? This was where Chacho and Guayo had worked. Guayo's voice: *'You know, just by looking at a prisoner, Chacho here could tell how long they'd hold out underwater. Fuck, you were a vicious bastard with those terrorists, compadre, a fucking thug. We worked up there with Comandante Álvaro Artaza – the Truck, we called him – a brutal fucker when it came to torture, didn't believe in anyone, even shot a journalist who came to interview him one time. You remember those two women, schoolteachers they were. They were definitely involved with Sendero Luminoso, they seemed nice enough, we wasted a bullet each on them. Sometimes, instead of filling the bucket with water, we'd fill it with insects or animals, rats or giant ants from out in the jungle. It was like an appetiser, watching them struggle, before we hooked them up to the electric cables.'*

I don't know how long I stood there, staring. It seemed so small when you thought of all the prisoners who had died here. I'd read in a newspaper that if you lined up their corpses they would circle the stadium a hundred times, given that the people round here aren't exactly tall (some journalist's idea of a joke). For a while, I stared up at the windows. A series of rectangles, holes punched into the concrete, the broken panes in pairs. Yet from inside, where prisoners were tortured and killed, these windows must have seemed like a chain of lights illuminating the grounds, the sunlit remnants of the outside world.

Another curious idea came to me. Perhaps this window – seeing this window, staring through this piece of broken glass, gazing at the sunlight – had helped someone hold out longer than usual, the glimmer of hope in that glow had probably prolonged his dying moments, making it more bearable at first, needlessly drawing the moment out. Perhaps hope is the worst that can befall someone, uselessly prolonging their suffering. Or perhaps not, perhaps these windows had served no purpose other than to fuel the speculations of someone on the far side of the glass.

What had the routine been like in this place? Chacho and Guayo had told me that the torture session could easily go on all night if they were in a bad mood. I remembered reading something about it. A lot of torturers became addicted to the screaming, the convulsions, the pleading, the signs of distress. Can causing another human being pain trigger delusions of grandeur? Is it a comfort, a defence? Did torturing and killing people make them feel the same thing could not happen to them? The single most frustrating thing for the torturers was seeing the prisoners die; the worst, surely, was to see them die smiling or shouting terrorist slogans. A smiling corpse would goad the soldiers and make them more eager to drag in the next victim. It was impossible not to imagine them. The group of prisoners being brought for torture, the shared glances as they stepped into the room, the ones who kept their spirits up, the ones who screamed, the ones who stared into the void. The coffee, the water, the sandwiches the torturers made during their rest periods. They had to have enjoyed it, it was like turning on a switch – '*Come on, time to get back to work, let's see who's first up.*' And then the sound of fist hitting face, of wires attached to testicles or breasts (an almost inaudible click, Guayo had said), the howls from the other side of the wall, the queues waiting to rape, the stench of your own flesh, blood spattering your face, the bitter taste, making you slightly queasy. A victim with a gun pressed to his temple as the group of soldiers laughed. For the prisoners, simply facing death was a feat, the ashen skin, plunging into the endless hours of abuse, a table, a couple of chairs, these brick walls, a white spotlight, '*Keep screaming, you fucking terrorist bastard, scream louder, scream louder.*'

But the torturers also felt fear, they too could be killed or captured. The soldiers laughed over their morning meal.

'*They laughed because they were scared shitless,*' this was what Guayo Martínez had told me that afternoon. '*They laughed at breakfast because they knew that this day might be their last – an ambush, a grenade, an attack, a sniper shot while you're out on patrol. Any second it could happen: a blast, a pool of blood, a mangled corpse – and that was that – maybe a coffin draped with the Peruvian flag if you were lucky. You became another statistic. No one would remember. But you get used to fear,*' Guayo said, '*fear is something hard and black, it's like it has its own shape – like your stomach or your heart, fear is a thing, a hairy thing deep inside your body that spreads out, becomes hard and long and broad, it's fear that makes you the way you are.*

You have to kill them, you have to just keep the fear at bay, to make it go away. What else can you do?'

I took a last glance round the place, ran my fingers along the railing, then decided to go for a walk through the streets of Huanta.

It was impossible not to wonder what this town was like in the 1980s. The people I could see now, for example, the people of Huanta walking past, that man in the hat, the woman with the short hair . . . it suddenly seemed to me strange that they had survived the war. That they were walking through these streets. Maybe heading home, maybe going to visit friends or family. They had watched people around them die. And now here they were walking casually through the streets.

I went into a cafeteria with plastic chairs and had a beer. On the street, passers-by sometimes turned to stare at me; slow, hazy shadows giving me a sidelong glace, a tight grimace from beneath a black hat. They saw me as a human object, an oddly familiar animal that somehow wound up here by chance. Not that I could understand them, I would never really know them. Nor could I understand the soldiers, not my father, not Guayo or Chacho. Obviously they didn't run away. Soldiers aren't allowed to run away, they are doomed to carry on.

I walked around a while longer and then took the same moto-taxi to the neighbouring town of Luricocha. There I found a bodega, a timber-framed door, adobe walls; inside was a counter stacked with bread, bottles of lemonade, a few avocados and *lúcumas*.

A girl with plaited hair was staring at me. I posed my question.

'I don't know anyone called Miriam, *señor*, I don't know who you mean.'

I asked if I could speak to her mother and the girl disappeared and came back with a woman in a traditional *montera* hat.

'I don't know anyone by that name, *señor*. Miriam? Never heard of her.'

'How long have you worked here, *señora*?'

'A year ago it must be that we came here.'

I thought about taking a walk around the town. I went to the church which the mototaxi driver told me was called San Antonio de Padua. There was a large piazza in front of the church with stone benches. I stopped a boy to enquire whether there was a priest around only for one to suddenly appear.

The priest was Father Marco. He had a rather angular face with big eyes and olive skin. He was from Cuzco, he told me. 'I don't know any Miriam, but I promise I'll ask my older parishioners. I'm meeting with some of them at midday. Why are you looking for her? Was she from here?' I told him she was and he said he would see what he could find out.

I took another mototaxi on a tour around Huanta. We stopped on the Plaza de Armas. Palm trees, street lights with round glass shades, wooden benches, a scattering of red flowers. The plaza was painted green – a nod to Huanta's nickname, the Emerald of the Andes. I went into a *cebichería* called Lobo del Mar. At the back of the restaurant, by a door, I saw a sunflower. On the wall hung a picture of Christ with a ribbon around his shoulders, next to it hung a television.

I slumped in a chair from which I had a view of the Palacio Municipal and a nightclub – where, according to the waiter, soldiers used to take local girls from Huanta during the war. It was there too that the only cinema had been. A flight of steps ran from the pavement down to the plaza. A tall, thick tree cast a hazy shadow like a stain across the concrete. Opposite was a shop with a yellow facade, some tiled roofs and the church with a statue of the Assumption of the Virgin wreathed in blue and white between the twin spires. Sagrado Corazón cathedral was a large stone building which, the waiter told me, was the monastery of the Redemptorist Fathers. I sat gazing at the building as the beer bubbled in the glass . . . a building of brick and stone with crucifixes on the doors . . . I took some more photos. I felt a vague fascination for this place, as though I had been here before.

Back in Luricocha, I passed the sign for the José Félix Iguaín school and met up with Father Marco again. With him were two older people, a man and a woman, dressed in black and wearing hats. They spoke no Spanish. I asked the priest to ask if they had known Miriam. At the mention of her name, the woman's eyes flashed and she began speaking rapidly in Quechua.

'Yes, she remembers Miriam,' the priest told me. 'She says one day soldiers came and took her away and no one ever heard from her again. She asks if you know something.'

'Did she have any relatives in Luricocha, in Huanta or in Ayacucho?'

The man shook his head.

'They say her mother and father are dead, they refused to serve members of Sendero Luminoso in the bodega. They say that Sendero Luminoso took her brother and forced him to fight with them. Later the *senderistas* launched an attack on the police station here and Miriam's other brother was killed. After that, no one heard anything. They don't know where Miriam is. The house is still boarded up. People believe it's haunted. They don't know anything about Miriam's family either.'

Father Marco walked with me back to the road where the mototaxi was waiting. The priest had the air of a retired soldier. His hands were remarkably large for his slight frame; he wore a large crucifix over his cassock.

'What can you do to comfort these people, father?'

'They don't want comfort, my son, but they want to talk, to tell me their stories, so I simply listen. I listen and they talk and I go on listening and when they leave, I sit alone and cry until I have no more tears. I go to my room, lie down on my bed and pray for a while and then I start to cry and I turn onto my side. I don't do anything, the tears just come and I find myself weeping, and it's better that way, and I feel better afterwards, I tell them to pray, tell them not to forget – that above all things – not to forget their dead but to remember them with gladness, that's what I say, and so they go on remembering them, and so do I. This is how we manage to go on living, though always weeping.'

XIV

I FOUND ANSELMO AND HIS CHEVROLET ON THE MAIN square in Huanta. Several times on the drive back to Ayacucho, I asked him to stop so I could take more photos. Squat trees framed against the mountains at dusk, the road winding through the hills, to my right a rocky area scattered with small plants.

'Is it possible to walk from Huanta to Ayacucho?' I asked.

'It's a steep climb, but there are people who've done it, who still do it.'

'Even at night, in the dead of winter, you think it would be possible?'

'Everything's possible, *señor*, everything's possible.'

Anselmo dropped me back at the Plaza de Armas. It was dark now. I wandered down one of the streets and happened on a little restaurant advertising barbecued chicken and chips. I went in and sat at a table with a red-and-white checked table-cloth. The room was airy, there was a radio and a sideboard filled with bottles. In the dim light, through the bars of the window I could just make out a garden. Behind the counter a thin guy with a bushy moustache and glazed eyes stood, slowly washing glasses.

Chicken, chips and salad was the only dish on offer. The place was like a postcard from the past. Papá used to take Rubén and me to El Rancho in Miraflores all the time for chicken and chips. I called the waiter over and ordered a beer. He disappeared quickly as though running away from me. I put a cigarette between my lips – probably a mistake on my first day at high altitude. Only then did I notice there was a woman sitting at the next table.

I assumed she was from Lima, or from some other city because of her clothes – a white blouse with a collar of silver thread, black trousers, pearl earrings, rings on several fingers. She was eating with judicious voracity, cutting small pieces of chicken and sipping her beer. Every now and then she glanced at me.

I wanted to go over and sit with her. I could resort to something banal, go over and say, 'Don't I know you from somewhere?' but it sounded too much like a cliché. Instead, I went over and simply asked if I might join her (after all, the worst she could do was refuse). She didn't answer, but did not seem bothered when I sat down. We chatted. She told me she had been born in Ayacucho but didn't live here any more. She was back for a couple of days and would be leaving tomorrow.

She had such a deep voice, her every word was like a brick in the wall she was building around herself. I was astonished by her large, limpid eyes which looked at me as though from afar. She had a mean, thin-lipped mouth.

I told her I'd just arrived and that I was all on my own in the city. She clearly thought this worthy of her pity.

'Are you from Lima?'

'Yes.'

'Here on business?'

'No, I came here to find a girl.'

'What girl?'

'A girl from round here.'

'Who is she?'

'Someone my father knew when he was living round here. It's a long story. What's your name?'

She opened her handbag and took out a notepad, as though to check something. She said she was leaving the following morning.

A man walked over and turned up the volume on the radio. There was the sound of a saxophone, a violin and guitars. A group of customers laughed softly. She slipped the notebook back into her handbag.

'So, what's your name?' I insisted.

'Guiomar,' she said. 'My name's Guiomar.'

She rummaged through her bag for something.

'Guiomar?'

'It's an Arabic name. My father was a professor of literature. There was a poem by Antonio Machado he liked a lot, it was about a woman called Guiomar, so that's what he called me.'

She sounded bored. She'd probably had to give the same explanation over and over.

The waiter brought my bottle of beer.

'You got family here?'

'No. Not any more.'

'So who did you come to see?'

'I came to visit my parents, they're in the cemetery. And to see the the Danza de las Tijeras.'

I slowly poured the beer into my glass. An Andean folk song was playing on the radio, a voice repeating the words *madre querida* – darling mother.

'You're interested in the traditional dancing?'

She drummed the table with her fingers.

'It's not that I'm interested,' she said, 'it's my life.'

'Your life?'

'Yes.'

She took out a cigarette and lit it as though trying to dismiss me. She didn't look at me. There was a protracted silence. A family bustled into the restaurant, walked past us and sat at a nearby table. The two children, who had sweet, diabolical smiles, ordered lemonade.

I leaned back in my chair.

'So you're really interested in the Danza de las Tijeras?'

She didn't answer.

On occasion I'd taken foreign friends to clubs in Lima where I'd seen Scissors Dancers. It was basically a group of guys in multicoloured suits and another guy with a violin playing something that seemed to go on for ever.

'It's not the same as what you might see in the clubs in Lima,' she said as though she could read my thoughts. 'Here they dance for a reason.'

'What reason?'

I was feeling calm and expectant as I watched her.

'Because the dance is a way of facing up to pain.'

'What has pain got to do with it?'

'The whole dance is a confrontation with pain. The dancers perform for hours, stick needles into their lips, flay their skin. It is about overcoming pain.'

'But why do they do it?'

'Their pain is a gift to life. When they dance, the dancers are defying death.'

'I don't understand.'

'The dance is a distraction from death. Around here, people have always known death. If they have not always been able to defy it in reality, they have defied it through music, through tableaux, through dance. That is why this area has always produced great artists.'

She spoke with wilful slowness, her voice barely rising above a whisper. She was talking to herself, looking backward, hardly aware of my existence.

'That's always the way. People say that about all forms of art,' I said. 'Death is a pretext to make something seem momentous, isn't it?'

She smiled. Her teeth were large and very white.

'Tell me, have you ever gone up the mountain roads, onto the plateau to the south of Ayacucho at night?'

'No, why?'

The radio crackled. From the kitchen came the sound of running water and dishes being washed.

'Because when you stand there, the cold mingles with a wind that seeps into the pores, stops up the blood and if you stand there long enough, it will freeze your heart. If you die, no one will ever find your body because the wind will carry it up to the mountaintop and you will remain there for ever.'

'I don't understand you, really I don't.'

'The people round here aren't like people elsewhere,' she went on slowly. 'Nobody here believes that life is a normal state. Here, they know that life is a shadow. A friend said that to me once. Death is a good mistress.'

In the kitchen, the waiter stopped washing dishes. The two kids at the next table were both talking at once.

'In Lima, we'll never understand these things,' I said, thinking it seemed the most appropriate thing I could say.

'People from Lima, people like you, all they know about this place is that they think the handicrafts are pretty. Then they forget all about us and go back to their cars and their trips. See that boy over there washing dishes?'

The young man had a narrow face. His hands worked quickly in the sink; the rest of his body was utterly still.

'What about him?'

'He might only be a few feet from you, but right now the distance between you is greater than the distance between the earth and the sun.'

I made a face, almost a smile.

'Look, I suppose you're trying to make me feel guilty. But I've got no reason to feel bad about myself. It's not my fault I don't know anything about him, is it?'

Under the table, I stretched my legs. There was something pathetic about sitting here with a perfect stranger who was trying to lecture me. But to my surprise, it wasn't an unpleasant feeling. In fact, I think at that moment I felt happy.

'Have you ever thought about what humility means, about what it means to be ordinary, to be poor, to be humble simply to stay alive – can you even begin to imagine that?'

For the first time, she had raised her voice. Her dark eyes stared at me.

'Sometimes.'

'But can you really know what it means to be ignored, to be treated like a dog, forced to be polite, to grovel to your master merely to survive?'

'That's something everyone has to do, here or anywhere.'

'Maybe, but the people who have to suffer in silence are worse off than those who get to complain, you know. To be able to complain, God, what a luxury. Silence, on the other hand . . . I don't know . . . it's like a cave.'

I looked at her. There wasn't a trace of emotion in her face. Her coldness was almost cruel.

'Yeah, I suppose I can understand that.'

Suddenly, she smiled. In that moment she looked extraordinarily beautiful. The muscles of her neck were tensed but her limpid eyes were still distant – she was a spirit who had taken on a human form.

'You don't seem like a bad guy,' she said, looking at me.

'Thank you,' I smiled.

'I'm heading somewhere else now, but if you want, you can come with me.'

'Somewhere else?'

Picturing her as I write this, I wonder if some day, somewhere, Guiomar will read this book. I need to say that I still hear her voice at the most unexpected moments, in the uproar of a work meeting or in the emptiness of my bedroom.

'You coming?'

'Why do you think I'd be interested?'

'I don't know if you'd be interested.' She took a drag of her cigarette. 'Come if you want to come.'

She tapped ash onto her plate.

The waiter brought the bill. I raised my glass as though to cover my face. I took out my wallet. She didn't move. She knew I'd pay.

We walked past a long adobe wall beneath the shadows of the mountain peaks, our footsteps barely audible. Above, the moon shone, streaked with cloud.

Guiomar stopped in front of a large wooden door, its thick planks partly covered in moss. She knocked once. The door opened and a young man ushered us through a garden of grass and stone into an adobe house with a corrugated-iron roof. We passed through a small courtyard, down a long corridor and into a round walled garden whose edges melted into the shadows.

Sitting next to us were men and women in sombreros, jackets and black trousers, some wearing flip-flops. Guiomar passed me a handful of coca leaves to chew. I savoured the pungent taste. I realised that we had been listening to music for a while now.

The *danzante* wore an elaborately embroidered hat and suit trimmed with white fringes and mirrors, and a pair of trainers, and as he danced he carried a pair of blades: the scissors or *tijeras*. The violinist's bow moved in rapid sweeps. The movements of the *danzante*'s hands, his feet, all these things I had dimly seen before; I felt I was seeing them now for the first time. The fury of the dance forced the air to retreat, like sound before a silence. The *danzante* never seemed to touch the floor. Embracing the void, legs hammering the ground, he seemed to believe he was a messenger from the past charged with perpetuating the movements of centuries which others would take up after him.

I don't know how long we spent there. At some point, Guiomar and I stood up and suddenly found ourselves out on the street again, walking side by side in silence.

On the street, I took her hand.

We came to the Plaza de Armas and sat on one of the benches. We were in a bowl of air ringed by the mountains. The plaza was deserted. The sky, ragged with stars, gave the stone a pale cast.

'The dancer was Sebastián. I think he recognised me.'

'Who is he?'

'A friend. I don't see him any more.'

'Why not?'

'Family stuff.'

'Has he always been a dancer?'

'Like his father and grandfather before him.'

'And you've known him a long time?'

'Since I was a girl. I grew up with him and the others. On Good Fridays they'd dance.'

'On Good Fridays?'

'That's how it works. When God is away, the devils can come out and demand the favours of the earth.'

I could see a silver shape against the facade of the cathedral, a shadow on the far side of the square, a man walking slowly who turned to look at us, then went on his way.

'I don't understand.'

'Because when the *danzante* dances, he is no longer the person he was,' she whispered. 'He leaves behind his name, his memories, his hopes. The dancer is the dance. The costume, the music, the air, these are his body. Nature breathes through him. Through the dancer, the life of a tree, a mountain, a stream is preserved and it belongs to us. That's why, when the world ends, it is our duty to recreate it. Dance creates it, music creates it. The body is each one of us. If the gods no longer have bodies, then we must lend them ours. The *danzantes* were the first to recreate the world. That's why they dance, that's why they are always with us, to weave life, our lives, through dance. The *danzante* is the god. The dance is the god. We are the god.'

She stopped. A flock of clouds moved across the sky, a slow, deliberate, menacing march like a migrating herd.

Around us, pages of newspaper whipped along the plaza towards the wall, for a split second creating a furious eddy.

Guiomar's eyes glittered with a sort of frozen sorrow. Body straight, head held high, she stared at me. 'Who are you?' I said. 'Why are you here?'

I moved closer, hugged her to me. She barely moved. I could feel a fragile warmth, a darkness in my hands, an explosion of frozen stars in my arms. Suddenly she got up and started to walk away. I watched her vanish towards the cathedral. She had disappeared.

That night, I walked for hours. I don't know how many streets I covered.

The following day, I woke up to a rectangle of sunlight on the floor. I showered, dressed and had a cup of black coffee on the terrace. I called the airport. They told me a flight had left five minutes earlier. Then I remembered her checking her notebook in the restaurant and telling me, '*My flight leaves first thing tomorrow morning.*'

I had a second coffee in a courtyard of the university next to the cathedral. I could see Guiomar's face in the flagstones, her clear eyes, her jet-black hair, the white long-sleeved blouse, her hard skin. I got up and left.

I went to the market, bought a souvenir armadillo-shell guitar called a *charango*, pan pipes and a couple of other instruments. I had no idea what I was going to do with them.

At 11 a.m., I took a trip back to Huanta and Luricocha, this time with a driver called Saturnino Sandia who told me his family had lived in Huanta for generations. I asked him if he knew a girl called Miriam who had lived in Luricocha.

'I don't know anything,' he said.

As we passed the Puente Infiernillo I stared out the window, trying to come to terms with what had happened here.

At Luricocha church, I met with Father Marco again. He was chatting with two women, mother and daughter I assumed, who said their goodbyes when they saw me arrive.

'I've got good news for you,' he said. 'A couple of elderly locals have just arrived. They might know this girl you're looking for. They live just round the corner.'

We walked round to the house. The man who opened the door had his head bowed and was wearing a traditional hat.

'Miriam? Yes, I knew her, of course I remember her.'

'You know her?'

'Knew her since she was a little girl.'

'Do you know what happened to her?'

'A gang of soldiers came and took her, *señor*, that's what happened, and we never heard word of her after that, never heard anything more about her, nothing at all. They killed her is what I reckon.'

'They didn't kill her. They didn't kill Miriam,' said a voice from inside the house.

The man turned.

'Is that Señora Teodora in there?' said the priest.

A woman in a hat and overskirt appeared. Her voice was hoarse and cracked, her breathing slow and wheezy, and she looked as though only a thin thread stopped her collapsing to her knees.

'Miriam wrote to my little Carmen. Found a letter among Carmencita's things, I did. Miriam wrote to her, *señor*, she did.'

'A letter?'

'Yes.'

'Could I see it?'

The woman vanished and reappeared with an envelope. The return address was on Calle Pedro Venturo in Lima. I noted it down.

'Would it be OK if I read the letter?'

'No, *señor*, no, I couldn't allow that. The letter was for Carmen, *señor*.'

'When was it sent?'

'Oh, a while ago now, when our Carmen was still alive.'

'And none of her family work still at the bodega?'

'No, no one. All dead they are now.'

I said my goodbyes and Father Marco and I walked back to the church.

'Señor Sillipú's son was murdered too,' he said as we came to the door.

'The man we just met?'

'Yes.'

'Who killed his son?'

'Sendero Luminoso. They poured petrol over him and lashed him to a rock high up in the mountains so he would slowly burn to death in the sun. That's how he died. And Señor Sillipú knows it. He knows how his son died. And there's not a day goes by that he doesn't come to talk to me, to pray with me. Not a single day. And I never tire of talking to him. And his other daughter, Georgina, she used to come here too, Georgina Gamboa she is now, you saw her a little while ago, she was with her daughter. She was raped; seven soldiers took turns raping her in broad daylight and she gave birth to the little girl you met. The girl found out recently that her father was one of those seven soldiers. "I just have to go on living," she said to me. "Just go on living." And they're not the only ones. There's a woman I know, Paula Socca her name is, her six sons were killed and her husband, and now she comes here sometimes, comes here to Ayacucho. It was Señora Socca who introduced me to Quinta Chipana, that boy, over there, see him? He used to live in Vilcashuamán, in a little village called

San Miguel de Rayme. And *senderistas* came to the village and they found out there was an older man, a man called Luis Zárate, and because this man had given food to the army the *senderistas* went to his house, cut his throat and dragged him to the Plaza de San Miguel de Rayme. They hanged Luis Zárate from the only tree on the square. They left him there and they warned the villagers that no one was to take the body down and bury it. But that boy there, Chipana, he felt terrible seeing Señor Zárate hanging there from the tree, so one morning he rounded up a group of friends and they took down Señor Zárate and buried him, you understand? They buried him because they wanted him to rest in peace, and because seeing him hanging there every day saddened them. Chipana and his friends defied Sendero Luminoso, they risked their lives when they took the body down and laid Luis Zárate to rest in peace. After they buried him, they were scared, so they all ran away, they hid out in caves in the mountains. But at least Señor Zárate could rest in peace, he wasn't left hanging there like a rag. Thanks to Chipana he's at peace. And there he is, over there.'

We talked for a long while. He offered me a *quemadito*.

'A local drink – rum burned with sugar,' he explained. We went to his room and I stayed there until it was time for me to leave.

That night, back at the hotel, I started writing. It was there that this book was born. I remember the lampshade shuddering, the scratching sound of pen on paper.

Before going to bed, I went out for a walk. The moon made

the darkness deeper, seemed to create a dimension of black light in which the world was reversed and I had passed over to the other side, had stepped into a photographic negative. I left the town centre and wandered the stony side streets.

Back at the hotel I called Claudia, and told her I'd been to Ayacucho.

'That's what they said when I called your office. What were you thinking of?'

'I'll tell you when you get back.'

'My parents are staying a few more days. But we're back on Monday.'

'I'll pick you up at the airport,' I offered.

'You bet you will.'

That night I slept soundly and the following morning I had my coffee in the Café D'Onofrio on the Plaza de Armas reading the papers.

I felt a terrible sadness. Already Guiomar seemed like a chimera. Not that I had ever expected to see her after that night. And yet . . .

About Miriam, I had gleaned nothing but that address on the Calle Pedro Venturo. Would she still be living there?

I went to the bus station and bought my ticket back to Lima. I had decided to go back by bus. The trip would take all night. I spent the rest of the day roaming the city. I bought a book in which I found out that in colonial times Ayacucho had been a thriving city with thirty-three churches with magnificent altarpieces and religious paintings; it had once been an obligatory stop-off on the route from Cuzco to Lima. The church of Santo Domingo was one of the most beautiful in the world. In the early seventeenth century, the buildings in what was then called Huamanga were famed for being the most beautiful in the kingdom. According to native tradition, in Huamanga Viracocha, the eighth Sapa Inca of the Kingdom of Cuzco, fed a falcon from his own hand giving the city its name.

I went back to the bus station, a sort of long corridor that ended in a small waiting room. Sitting on a plastic chair waiting to board the bus I met a guy who said hello, claimed to know me. We'd been to university together, he insisted. 'We were in the same year. I'm up here for the cochineal beetles, we're studying some of the cochineal farms round Ayacucho.'

On the bus, when I was finally alone, I peered through the window trying to make out some trace of something visible. The engine started up and everything began to shudder. The bus wound upwards in long, slow curves towards the plateau. Suddenly the TV over my head sputtered into life and announced some martial arts film and I decided I should take a pill. We would be driving for hours at high altitude, thousands of metres up, through a landscape of lakes and stones on the long road to Lima.

Squeezed into the cramped seat, slipping into the liquid darkness of the sky, I knew that the images I took with me from this trip were a blessing that would stay with me for ever: Father Marco's face, Señor Sillipú and his wife, Guiomar, the Church of the Redemptorist Fathers, the Plaza de Armas, that single window in the barracks up in Huanta. Together they formed something like a new paradise.

The air was getting thinner. I leaned my head back, tried to sleep against the thick blackness of the window. Unexpectedly, as we skirted around a peak, I opened my eyes and saw the disc of the moon, a fierce, bloody brilliance covered with stains. It would follow me through this long night.

XV

WE CAME TO THE MISTY LINE OF THE COAST. I caught a taxi on the Avenida Javier Prado.

At home, all the furniture seemed somehow cramped, pushed closer together. Justina only ever moved furniture when she used the floor polisher. I took a shower, made myself some coffee and toast, then climbed into my car and headed for the address Señora Sillipú had given me on Calle Pedro Venturo. The door was opened by a girl in a pale blue uniform who told me that the woman who lived there wouldn't be home until late afternoon.

I called on my way to the office and assigned some jobs to Jenny and the other juniors. When I got in, I answered a few questions about my trip.

'How did it go?'

'Good, very good.'

I met up with Platón for lunch at Wa Lok, a Chinese restaurant on Avenida Angamos where we were greeted by our friend Liliana Com. We ordered the speciality *pescado en flor* – whole sea bass delicately carved into a flower and sautéed in butter, with steamed rice and shumai.

'So, how was the trip? Did you find Miriam?'

'I met a couple of people who remembered her. And at least I came away with an address.'

'Where?'

'Here in Lima, over in Surco. I'm going over there later.'

'You look like hell,' Platón said.

'I feel great.'

'Come on, let's order some beer. No – actually, let's get a couple of pisco sours. Like I said, you look like shit.'

'What do you mean shit?'

'I mean shit – you should have a look in the mirror.'

Later that afternoon, I went to the Calle Pedro Venturo. The house was little more than a wall with barred windows and a stone porch. The wall was covered by some sort of flowering ivy. I pressed the buzzer, heard a voice ask something and said my name into the intercom. A woman answered.

She was tall, with a long slender face, and a fringe that fell onto her forehead. She wore a garish multicoloured suit and a leather belt with a large buckle. She looked me up and down.

'Yes?'

'Excuse me, *señora*, we don't know each other, but I was given your name by someone. I'm looking for a girl called Miriam.'

'Why? Who are you anyway?'

'My name is Adrián Ormache, I'm a lawyer.'

'Oh, yes, I think I've seen you somewhere before. We know each other, don't we? I saw you with your sister-in-law Camincha. Who did you say you were looking for?'

'Miriam, I believe she used to live here.'

'Miriam? Oh, yes, of course, Miriam. My name is Paloma Fox, by the way, why don't you come in?'

I followed her through the small rose garden into the house. The living room was a collection of matching white furniture with a large rug and a painting of black orchids. Everywhere there were glass cabinets filled with armies of crystal animals, ashtrays and miniature lamps.

'Miriam lived here for just over a year while she was working,' Paloma said, not looking at me. She crossed her legs, toes poking out of tight-fitting sandals, five of them tugging and pulling at the carpet like bad-tempered children while she swung her other foot gently to and fro in a continuous, almost perverse movement and waved her claw-like fingernails as she spoke.

'What can I tell you? She was a nice girl, clever too, we used to chat sometimes, she'd tell me things.'

'Did she tell you about her time in Ayacucho?'

'In Huanta? Yes, she told me about that. But she never talked about that stuff, about the war, she didn't talk about it.'

'How did she end up here?'

'Someone who worked for a friend of mine recommended her, said she was his cousin. I met up with her and I thought she was special, she had a nice face, you know? The problem was, she had a child with her, but thankfully the little boy never caused any trouble, always kept himself to himself, a little angel he was. Miguel. That was his name, Miguel, I remember now.'

'She had a son?'

'Yes. He would have been a toddler at the time. A quiet little boy but very sweet.'

'Then it's true,' I said.

'What?'

'No. Nothing. Do you mind if I smoke?'

'No, I'm sorry, no one here smokes.'

'That's OK, I apologise. Please, go on . . .'

'Well, as I was saying, when she was staying here we became friends, you know. Thing is, after a while I noticed that sometimes she'd go all weird, at night sometimes I'd hear the door, the sound of the door closing – my children would hear it too, it scared them a couple of times – and then later I realised that sometimes she'd go out in the middle of the night. I'd hear the front door closing and I knew it was her, then a little while later she'd come back. And the next day, the table would be laid for breakfast, the kitchen would be tidied, it was like nothing had happened, so I never talked to her about it. I'd ask her if she'd been out and Miriam would say she'd just gone for a walk. After a while I got used to it.

'But then, this one time, something weird happened. One night I was waiting for her to come back and I found her in the living room. "Miriam, what's wrong with you?" I said to her. "Where are you going at this hour?" "Nowhere, *señora*," she said. "Just out for a walk. I can't sleep," that's what she said to me, but just looking at her I could see she was sweating, she was sweating like a pig, she'd already been walking, and I said, "Why don't you go walking in the morning?" but she didn't say anything. I think she'd been running. Running, not walking.

'Well, that's what Miriam was like – I don't know, a bit strange, maybe, but she was a good person, she'd clean the house, she was a good cook, she'd lay the table, sometimes she'd even come to the cinema with me and the girls, almost like a sister she was. She used to tell me she wanted to be a hairdresser, with her own salon and a sign outside, "Emerald of the Andes". She liked the sound of it. It was the name of the village she came from in Huanta. I encouraged her. Gave her books to read, a few novels, and she told me she enjoyed them. But after that I don't know what happened, one morning she went out, took her son, left the bed made, the house spick and span, went out with her son, left the key on the dining table, a note saying thank you and then nothing. Not a word, not another word we heard from her. It was sad, tell the truth, losing her like that, and a bit ungrateful of her, don't you think? Never did know what became of her. Probably better that she left, in a way, because she was so pretty – the boys round here, the neighbours' sons, they'd follow her in the street and say things. That was the only bad thing, but luckily she never paid them any attention.'

'So one day she just left?'

'Yeah, she went off and I never heard anything after that. Very strange. I felt bad when she left, and my friend's maid never heard from her either. It really was ungrateful of her walking out like that, though I realised I should have known it would happen, but I felt bad for a couple of days and then it passed, but maybe I'm talking too much. Typical of me. Has she done something bad? Why are you looking for her?'

'No, she's done nothing wrong,' I told her. 'It's related to a case I'm working on. I want to help her. Tell me, do you know what her name – what her surname was?'

'Miriam Anco, her name was, sometimes I'd see her writing it on a coupon so she could win a prize.'

Miriam Anco. Could it be? Why hadn't I thought of it before?

I hurriedly thanked Señora Fox. Glanced at my watch. It was time for me to head for the airport.

Traffic on the Avenida de la Marina was like a solid wall around me. Several times, I was hemmed in on all sides by buses and microbuses. By the time the traffic began to move again I could see the airport control tower in the distance. The plane would be landing any moment now. As I walked through the glass doors into the arrivals hall, my family were waving to me from the customs area.

Claudia and the girls came over, smiling, all talking at once about their holiday. I listened to Claudia. The trip had been fabulous.

That night, I put Lucía to bed, said her prayers with her. 'When are you going to come on holidays with us?' she asked. Then I went into Alicia's room for a chat.

'We need to start thinking about finding you a preparatory school for university,' I said to her.

'I know, I've started looking into it, but if I get good grades in my *bachillerato* I can go straight to university.'

I went to my bedroom. The world was in order again. I

was in bed with my wife. My daughters were asleep in their rooms. Everything was fine.

The next morning, I went back to Señor Anco's office. I knocked several times. I talked to the guy at the juice stand who said he hadn't seen him.

At the office, Eduardo was talking about the party he'd been to at the Gómez Sánchezes', asking why I hadn't been there. I explained that Claudia and the girls had flown back last night. Then I went and asked Jenny to dig out all the information she could on Señor Vittorino Anco. The girl's name is Miriam Anco. Could he be her uncle, her brother, her father?

I went back home at lunchtime, took the photos of Miriam from my wallet and put them in the drawer in my study.

In the afternoon, I went back to the office on the Calle Emancipación. Señor Anco had disappeared without trace.

When I came down to breakfast the next day, Justina was just making coffee. Claudia was in the shower. We stood on opposite sides of the table, Justina and I.

'Shall I pour you some coffee, sir?'

'Yes, thank you.'

The fierce, implacable barrier between me and Justina. Me and Justina – the words didn't belong in the same sentence. The master and the servant (is that what they were called these days?). It was slightly absurd. The eyes deferentially lowered, the commonplace distance of fear, the mane of hair, the arms thin as twigs.

One of the mysteries of my house. An ordinary mystery. A

tall, white man spending years sharing the same space with a short, dark-skinned woman, Justina. We saw each other every day, year after year, but in all that time we had barely uttered a handful of polite platitudes. Those niceties were her safe conduct through this house, confirmations of our separate identities. They are stock phrases, empty shells of words: *'Good morning.' 'Can you tell my wife I'll be home late?' 'Would you like me to serve lunch early?' 'Lunch was delicious, thank you, Justina.' 'You're welcome,* señor.' We could live together in the most surreal and tolerable silence, a silence made up of banalities. I knew barely anything about Justina: she was from Cajamarca, she was a good cook, she loved the girls. That was enough for me.

That evening, there was a show on at our daughters' school for Independence Day, music, dancing and recitations and, Claudia reminded me, Alicia was to be master of ceremonies. At 7.30 p.m., Claudia and I were sitting in the school auditorium occasionally greeting other parents also waiting for the pleasure of seeing their children on stage. Then, the lights were dimmed, a spotlight came on, there was a hush and I was surprised and pleased to see my daughter standing in the light facing the packed audience.

Still tanned from the Caribbean sun, she was wearing a figure-hugging white dress that made her look very mature for seventeen. The dress, the high heels, the make-up, the necklace and the earrings gave me a glimpse of the woman she would soon be. She welcomed the audience and gave a rundown of some of the musical numbers for the evening, for all the world like a professional MC addressing an audience of parents, a young woman with precociously adult confidence and gravity.

My daughter suddenly transformed into a woman, I thought, the workings of the bizarre magic that is time. I thought about writing something about this moment. How would I put it?

A little girl steps into a magician's top hat, the magician says a few words and she emerges as a woman. A father is watching his baby crawl around the living-room floor. He steps out of the room for a moment – when he comes back, his daughter is a young woman and the room is filled with strangers, her friends. Some of the friends stop to shake the father's hand, politely murmur, 'Nice to meet you, *señor*'. You step into a room, protected by your three-piece suit, your smile, and shake hands with strangers.

I turned my attention back to the stage.

The show ended with a performance by the youngest pupil, a little girl of five who read a poem she'd written: 'The world is a big garden and we are all gardeners. Every day the flowers need to be watered. Watered with love and fed with cuddles . . .'

When she finished, the auditorium erupted in applause. Alicia thanked everyone who had helped with the production, and the headmaster took the stage to congratulate the students. Alicia did a wonderful job, everyone said later. And Lucía looked so pretty.

When Alicia finally came out, Claudia and I hugged her and I suggested we all go for pizza. At the restaurant, amid the smells of pizza and the taste of wine, they asked me about my trip.

'I went to deal with some problems your grandpa had while he was living in Ayacucho.'

'What problems?' Alicia asked.

'Well, the truth is, I think he hurt a lot of people and I went there to see what I could find out.'

'Did you find out anything?'

'No, not really. I think he ill-treated a lot of the prisoners he was responsible for.'

'Was he really nasty?'

'Yes, I'm afraid I think so. But that's what war is like.'

'And anyway,' Claudia said, looking away, 'we have no right to judge other people.'

In the office the next day, Jenny had news for me.

'Señor Anco and his property holdings. They're all here.'

'What?'

'I've got all the information on Señor Anco, he has a lot of property holdings. Here, look.'

She handed me a document from the Public Registry Office and another from the Borough of San Juan de Lurigancho.

'This is a list of the properties.' She ran a finger down the list. 'A shop, a petrol station and a hairdresser's.'

I noticed the name of the salon. It was the name Paloma Fox had mentioned. 'Emerald of the Andes'.

'All that effort looking for her,' I said, 'and she was here all the time.'

'Where?'

XVI

I GOT TO THE AVENIDA WEISSE AND HEADED FOR San Juan de Lurigancho.

A huge truck roared past, shaking the car. The line of fruit carts, the row of telegraph poles, the mototaxi rank, the piles of tyres along the roadside, the billboards advertising doctors and schools and dentists, the white expanse of sky, the molten stretch of motorway, the statue of Mariátegui where I had to turn left. I was back in Huanta Dos, a stone's throw from the house where I had seen Paulino Valle.

I swung the car around, some children turned to stare at me.

I stopped.

I was here.

An adobe wall with a big door on a packed dirt street. It was a hairdressing salon. The sign in pink lettering read 'The Emerald of the Andes: Beauty and Elegance for Hair'. I remember driving past this place on the day I'd come to visit Paulino Valle.

I sat in the car as though waiting for something to happen,

fingers drumming on the steering wheel, tapping out the rhythm to a song, a song I used to sing as a child. Mary had a little lamb, little lamb, little lamb. I'd always thought there was something sinister about the tune. I felt as though Mary was petting her little lamb and about to sacrifice it.

I got out and leaned against the side of the car. From here, I could see much of the inside of the salon, a counter filled with plastic brushes, shampoo bottles, conditioners, a hairdryer. A pair of scissors poking out of a glass and a box of hairpins. Mounted on the wall was a porcelain washbasin with a sign next to it: *Wash & Blow Dry S/.2*. There were photos of blonde women. *A Pretty Face is the Mirror of the Soul*. The floor was tiled in blue and black and recently polished.

I was standing in the doorway. There were three styling chairs, three little mirrors. A woman stood behind one of the chairs cutting a customer's hair. She looked at me – no more than a glance – then went back to her work. The photos I had got from Vilma Agurto, the photos I kept in my wallet, stood before me in the flesh. It was her. It was Miriam. Was it really her?

Her long slim body was accentuated by her tight white blouse; her skin, the colour of earth, was lit up by her grey-brown eyes. She clipped the woman's hair with meticulous speed, flexing her long legs from time to time. She was wearing blue jeans and black shoes.

She probably thought I was a customer. It was nothing unusual for a man to have his hair cut in a salon. Though my black Volvo and my suit and tie looked out of place in this area.

I managed to sit on the chair closest to the door. She went on clipping, the click of the metal scissors . . . sounded like a little bird singing, I thought, the squawking of a newly hatched chick.

She ran the comb firmly through the woman's hair. After every pass, she smoothed the hair with the palm of her hand. Eventually, she took the blue gown from around the woman's shoulders, turned her towards the mirror and said:

'There you go, Señora Melchorita, all done.'

The woman got to her feet, handed her some money and left.

She looked at me.

'Are you here for a haircut, *señor*?'

I hesitated, then shrugged my shoulders and said yes. Not knowing what else to do, I sat down in the styling chair. She pulled the gown around me, tied it at the back of my neck and picked up the scissors.

'How do you have it cut?'

'Nothing special.'

'Just a trim, then?' she said, running her hand along my neck.

'Just a trim.'

I felt the clack of the scissors in my hair. Noises came from the street: a dog barking, children chattering, a car.

The situation was almost comical. Here I was with my hands trapped beneath the gown and her standing behind me. I looked at her closely. This woman whom my father had imprisoned and humiliated was holding a pair of scissors at my throat, the blades inches from my flesh. If she had known who I was, she might well feel entitled to cut it.

I remember exactly what happened. In fact, as I write this now, I'm sitting in exactly the same position as when I watched her that day.

I stare at her in the mirror. She seems completely focused on the patch of hair she's cutting, as though I'm just another customer. Obviously, she doesn't know who I am. How could she? She's calmly working her way round my head. It's a methodical sound, every snip of the scissors makes a dull click.

'How long have you had the salon?'

'Three years.'

'And how's business?'

She hesitates before replying.

'Good. More or less. Times are tough, but we get by, you know, you do what you can and you get by.'

She has a deep voice, or maybe laconic, I don't know how to describe it. She's checking the sideburns to make sure they match, clipping along the scalp, scissors fluttering next to my ears. Suddenly the sound seems to fade. She stops for a moment, then starts again.

'You have a lot of local customers?'

'There are always people who want to look their best,' she says. 'No one likes to look bad.'

The scissors advance, across the nape of my neck, around to the temples, make short work of the sideburns. I stare at her hands, long slender fingers with nails filed to a point.

There is a long silence.

Is she almost finished?

And I think that will be that.

She'll finish cutting my hair, I'll pay her, I've seen her, I know where she works, that should be enough. I can see that she has survived, that she has come through the past of which my father is a part with her dignity more or less intact. At least she has an income, and from what I can tell the salon is also her home. And she looks as though she's doing fine. Is this the end of my search?

She goes to get something, comes back, sprays water on my hair and combs it. I look at myself in the mirror.

There is a long silence. The noises from the street have died away. The silence is like an extension of something. Then suddenly I hear her voice, soft and clear next to my cheek.

'Señor Ormache,' she says, 'you're exactly like I was told you were.'

I feel a sudden void, as though I were falling.

I jump to my feet and turn to face her. She is standing, stock-still, looking slightly astonished, still holding the scissors. I take off the gown.

'What were you told?'

She sets the scissors down on the counter.

'That you were looking for me.'

She looks down. Takes a broom and begins to sweep the piles of hair into a dustpan, then empties it into a bin.

'And who told you?'

A fleeting smile lights up her face. She takes the dustpan and brush and sets them in a corner. She sits down, crosses her legs; I stare at her black pointed shoes.

Above her are photos of smiling women with perfect hair, rosy complexions and necks like swans, all staring down at

214

me. At that moment, it is as though she is part of a fresco, a dark-skinned goddess surrounded by an entourage of pale warriors.

Then her face comes alive. She looks at me again, a gleam in her eyes.

'You still haven't told me why you came looking for me.'

Her hands are folded in her lap; she looks as though she is struggling to stay calm.

'Because I wanted to meet you.'

'Just to meet me?'

'Yes.'

She gets to her feet, walks slowly towards the door and stands there staring out.

'What do you want? You want me to promise not to tell anyone about what your father did?'

She glances round at me. When she turns back to the street, I see a vein bulging in her neck, a long vein hard as a twig. In that moment she seems extraordinarily beautiful, though there's something cold about her too.

'You're right. I don't want you to tell anyone.'

'Well, you don't have to worry.'

She walks back towards the mirror, slips the scissors into a case. Only then do I notice her long legs, her flat stomach.

'The salon, it belongs to Señor Anco?'

'Why do you ask?'

'Just curious.'

She snaps the case closed and puts it into a drawer.

'Yes. He's my uncle. I rent the place from him, but I'm planning to buy it. Why?'

'How much is the rent?'

She folds her arms.

'None of your business.'

'How much do you pay?'

'You want to give me money?'

'Do you need money?'

'No.'

Silence.

Offering her money. It's a reckless thing to do. And it's stupid. But it's the only thing I can think of. I hear voices. A group of men outside talking about some football match they've just played.

'I went to Ayacucho, you know. I went to Huanta and Luricocha looking for you.'

'Yes, I know.'

Suddenly something moves behind the plastic curtain. A boy appears. He's twelve or thirteen, and he's wearing a white T-shirt, black trousers and shoes. He looks at me.

'Miguel, go on, go back inside.'

The boy vanishes.

'Does he go to school?'

'None of your business.'

There is a silence. She raises a hand, lets it fall.

'You don't want me to tell anyone about your father. That's why you came, isn't it?'

'Yes. I don't want anyone to find out.'

She laughs, she has a throaty laugh, it goes on and on.

'OK, then, well, you don't have to worry, *señor*, nobody is going to find out.'

She looks at me again.

'How did you escape?'

'What?'

'That night, how did you get out of the barracks? How did you get away from my father?'

'Why do you want to know?'

'I don't know. Just curious.'

'Just curious?'

'I was told you were dead.'

'Who told you that?'

'Chacho Osorio.'

'Do they know where I am?'

'No, don't worry, they don't know.'

The phone rings. She answers it. Yes, Señora Carmen, don't worry, I'll be waiting, no, I don't have anyone booked right now.

As she talks, she unties her hair which uncoils and tumbles onto her shoulders. From outside, there is a smell of smoke. She is still sitting there, head bowed.

A woman in a purple dress comes in and asks Miriam if she'll be there later, tells her she's just popping round to her sister's and will be straight back. The woman nods as she passes me and goes out.

'I can see you're not short of work.'

She raises a hand as though to say the meeting is over.

'Look, why don't you just go. I've told you I'm not going to do anything or say anything.'

'What can I do to help you?'

'Help me? Why would you help me?'

'I could help your son.'

She lowers her eyes again. She is crying.

I decide to go. I put some money on the counter. As I get to the door, I hear her call me.

'Señor Ormache,'

'Yes.'

'Don't ever come back here. Please.'

I get in my car.

I take the motorway back. There is a yellowish tinge to the sky. Ahead of me, a filthy lorry inches along, blocking my path. I'm in no hurry.

XVII

THAT NIGHT, I DREAM ABOUT HER. I SEE HER DO the things Chacho and Guayo described to me: drinking a couple of beers, hitting them over the head, putting on Guayo's uniform. I see her more clearly now. Her face in the photo. Her firm brows, her long cheekbones, her lips taut in the light. It's her. As though the Virgin Mary had appeared to me in a grotto, the miracle of a body realised. The white blouse, the apron, the pointed chin. The triangular face, like a half-moon. She is standing, as though hovering above the polished tiles of her salon, but she is there too, on the dirt road in the hills above Huanta, in the hollow known as Infiernillo, standing next to my father in his green-and-black uniform. I try to close my eyes.

In the morning, I have breakfast with Alicia and Lucía. I'm in a hurry. I have an eight-thirty meeting with a client.

Héctor Wakeman was a gentleman with a voice skilled in the subtle nuances of the hushed whisper. At fifty, he had come to only one conclusion in life: that his voice was the surest confirmation of his status as a gentleman of Lima. He complemented his voice by wearing cufflinks, dark suits and patent leather shoes, and on his lapel he wore pins for each of the universities at which he'd taught.

Whenever we talked, he would outline the subjects he planned to discuss, explain that he would list them in order of importance. As he went on to say, 'The first of these concerns . . .' he took special care to gently articulate every syllable. His vowels were like tiny cushions in which one might gently relax. His voice was careful and imposing and he accompanied his words with small hand gestures, now and then bringing his fingertips together to create an archway to shelter his thoughts. He paid me for the costly pleasure of knowing he had another lawyer to add to the four his company regularly consulted.

Don Héctor had a company which exported asparagus; he had inherited it from his father and it was thriving thanks to the hard work of his son-in-law. But he rarely made any mention of the company. The only thing that interested him about money was how it made him look. His suits, his haircuts, even his coughing fits were meticulously planned: hands cupped over his mouth, three coughs, the last almost a whisper. A big nose somewhat warped his features but he attempted to compensate for his facial excesses by marshalling his hair into a small helmet.

Our office drafted reports and analyses for him about customs duties and regulations, but this was simply an addendum. Suffering his interminable drivel was the task that justified the exorbitant fees he paid the practice. I'd listen to him talk about politics, video games, about the 'optimised business market made possible through slow but constant family work'. On this particular morning, Señor Wakeman informed me that he hadn't slept much the night before.

'I couldn't get to sleep. To be precise, I spent the whole night in a state of restlessness with twinges of anxiety. The reason being that my children were playing guitar,' he explained. 'They're very considerate, and they were playing softly, but it woke me anyway because I'm a very light sleeper.'

After my meeting with Wakeman, I got in my car. I quickly realised I was driving at breakneck speed, down Javier Prado and the Panamerican Highway, turning right onto Azcarruz then onto the Avenida Weisse.

I was desperate to see her. I needed to see her.

I only hoped that she would be on her own when I got there. My heart was hammering as I found myself having to stop at every red light, glancing at the line of microbuses behind me. I turned when I came to the statue of Mariátegui, overshot by a couple of streets and did a U-turn, spraying grit and dust. A few people turned and stared as I passed.

I parked in front of the salon and climbed out into a cloud of dust. I found her sitting in one of the styling chairs. She was reading a magazine.

'Could we talk for a minute?' I said.

She said nothing and went on reading. I sat next to her. She was wearing an apron and her hair was loose.

'I've already told you I'm not going to talk about what happened, to the papers or to anyone else . . . so you really don't need to worry, Señor Ormache.'

She stood up, looked at me.

'I want to help you,' I said. 'That's all. The truth is, I'm doing it for myself, too, to make myself feel better.'

'I don't need anything.'

'What about your son?'

'He doesn't need anything either.'

I sounded calmer than I felt.

'There's a little café nearby up in Jicamarca, Misky it's called, why don't we go there and just talk for a while?'

'What for?' She sat down again, still staring at me.

'I don't know. Just to talk.'

She got up and went to the door, looked out onto the street, then came back and started washing some combs and brushes in a basin. The noise of the water filled the whole place.

'Why would I go anywhere with you, *señor*?' she said, not looking at me.

'I just want to talk to you, that's all.'

'We've got nothing to talk about. Now, would you please just go. Get in your car and just drive away and let's leave it at that.'

She dried the combs and brushes and put them away. The silence reflected itself in the mirror.

'I never knew my father,' I said slowly. 'Maybe you could tell me about him.'

'You didn't know your father?'

'I didn't see him for years.'

'So what do you want to know?'

I hesitated.

'I don't know. Anything you can tell me.'

'What is it that you want to know?' she asked again as she turned off the tap. There was another silence. She sat down. I watched her cross her legs. Her black shoes had metal tips. There was a flower embroidered on the thigh of her jeans.

'Could we go somewhere else?'

'Where?'

Her voice was hoarse and slightly menacing. She glared at me.

'Wherever you like. I want you to tell me everything, to tell me what happened up there.'

She bowed her head again and sat for a long moment, motionless, staring at the floor. I could hear the traffic on the motorway. After a while she looked up.

As I saw her face again, she seemed somehow younger. Suddenly, to my surprise, she stood up and took off her apron.

'Let's go. But only for a minute.'

'Is there someone you can leave your son with?'

'He's over at Señora Melchora's house. I'll close up here.'

She got into the car next to me. When I shifted gears, I could feel the warm fabric of her trousers. Nothing was said while we drove.

When we got to Misky's, Max, the owner, seemed to recognise me. I ordered a beer.

'Nothing for me, *señor*,' Miriam said.

We were at the top of the hill overlooking Jicamarca. From here, we could see the hills criss-crossed with brick and adobe walls, low-roofed houses, television aerials. The mountain was framed against a sky the colour of bone.

Miriam ran her fingers through her hair several times.

223

Glanced at me quickly. In that moment I thought she was the most beautiful woman in the world.

'Look, the truth is, I want to help you if you'll let me. I can understand why you don't want my help, but at least take it for your son. How old is he?'

'None of your business.'

'What school does he go to?'

The breeze stirred her hair. She placed one hand on the table; long, slender fingers with delicate nails and silver rings. There was a long silence.

'He goes to Mariátegui school. It's near here.'

'And do you make enough to support him?'

'Yes.'

'To buy his clothes and everything?'

'The salon makes money.'

'OK.'

'Why are you so interested? I already told you I won't say anything about your father.'

I leaned back in my chair.

'I only found out about you and my father recently.'

'What exactly did you find out?'

'That my father kept you prisoner, that he forced you to live with him and that after a while you escaped. Isn't that what happened?'

She started drumming her fingers on the table.

'How did you come to have Miguel?'

'Are you interrogating me?'

'No. I'm sorry. You don't have to answer if you don't want to.'

A couple of men came into the bar. One of them stared at me. They were wearing open-necked shirts, black jeans and sandals. Their faces were covered in dust, they'd probably been working on a building site. They ordered a couple of beers. The one staring at me hesitated a moment before he turned away.

'I gave birth in Lima,' she said after another silence, 'and with my uncle Vittorino's help I finished school. But I couldn't find a job. For a while I worked in people's houses as a maid. Later I went back to my studies and got a job working in hairdressing, and afterwards my uncle gave me the place I have now, the place I'm buying from him, so I work there and I do my best to bring up Miguelito. That's the whole story, since you're so interested.'

She heaved a sigh.

Max brought over the bottle of beer and two glasses.

I poured some for her but she said she didn't want a drink. We sat in silence for a moment.

'Is that all you wanted to know?'

'That, and anything you can tell me about my father.'

She looked down.

'Your father wasn't an evil man,' she whispered.

'Why do you say that?'

She rubbed her hands together, balled them tight and twisted them against each other. She brought them up to her face and it looked as though she was wiping her cheeks.

'I hated your *papá*, I hated him so much, I would have killed him if I could have because he tricked me, he abused me in that little room, I hated him so much. It was because

225

of them – the soldiers, because of *los morocos* – that I lost my family, I couldn't go back to my family, I couldn't face them and now they're dead, they died before I ever got to see them again, and I hated your *papá* so much, but I don't hate him now, in a way I almost love him.'

She leaned back in her chair, never taking her eyes off me. I don't know why, but at that moment I wanted to hold her hand.

'How long were you with him in the barracks?'

'I'm not going to tell you any more. But I want you to know that your father loved you and your brother. He talked about the two of you all the time. That's why I agreed to come here with you. That's the only reason. Now we have to go back, I have work to do.'

We got back in the car. I drove slowly. I stopped outside the door of the salon.

'Give me a phone number or something.'

'What for?'

'So you can tell me more. And I can tell you things too.'

I realised that I was straining my voice. She didn't blink. I opened the glove compartment, found a pen and an old receipt for something. She wrote down the number. 'There,' she said, and got out of the car.

Back at my office there was a meeting to discuss strategies for recruiting new clients.

'There is no strategy,' I said. 'You just have to work.'

'You don't think it would be a good idea to send out letters?'

said Eduardo. 'Why don't we do a mailshot of businesses and embassies?'

'What are we going to do, Eduardo, send out five thousand letters?'

The discussion carried on like this until we got tired and changed the subject.

That night, I told Claudia I had found Miriam.

I slept better than I had the night before. Towards dawn, I slipped closer to Claudia, put my arms around her and we made love the way we used to. She was once again the sexy girl with the long legs and the warm, limber body. For a split second I saw Miriam's face.

I was still thinking about her while I showered.

I needed to hear her voice again. I knew it was a selfish idea, I knew I shouldn't. But I needed to see her, I felt I had to help her in some way. I was convinced she would eventually accept my help, I didn't know why.

In the living room, I picked up my car keys.

At the office, Eduardo reminded me about one of our regular appointments. We were to lunch with the firm's two biggest clients.

'We have to keep in with them,' he whispered. 'Sixty per cent of the revenue of this practice comes from them, you know that.'

Our two biggest clients were Leticia Larrea and Haroldo Gala. I had to meet with them. I couldn't think about Miriam now. I had to focus on them.

* * *

Leticia Larrea. My tongue twists and quivers just pronouncing her name. Leticia was a little over fifty and turned up at the office around mid-morning two or three times a week. Visiting the office was part of her routine, sandwiched between shopping trips and visits to her girlfriends' houses. Before coming in, she would stand in the doorway as though posing for posterity, framed by her red hair which simply exaggerated the garish make-up and the huge multicoloured earrings she invariably wore. She sashayed when she walked, as though dancing a solo mambo. Adorned with ribbons, necklets and bracelets, she looked like an embalmed doll. I thoroughly enjoyed her visits and prepared to receive Leticia the moment I heard her shrill voice at the main door. She stalked through reception, loudly commenting on the fact that the floors were clean and polished thanks to her monthly payments to the firm. Having thus reassured herself, she would climb the stairs, announce herself as she passed Jenny's desk and come into my office. Finding me with a client she would say loudly, 'Oh, I'm sorry, I'll just wait outside,' which was usually enough to persuade whoever I was with to wrap up their meeting. The moment the client left she would stride into the office, though not before stopping on the threshold as though she was inspecting the quality of the door frame.

Her clothes were a testament to her ego: the figure-hugging trousers, the blue and red blouses, the ornate jackets an expression of her haughty plea to be loved. She always had an excuse, some small favour she needed to ask me, though the real reason she sat facing me at my desk was to reassure herself I would listen to her. She believed – quite rightly – that my obligations as her lawyer included having to listen to her telling me about her neck pain ('It's so tense, and there's nothing anyone can do for it, nothing'), the receptions she had attended ('The canapés at the embassy last night were to die for, but you should have seen Tina Brescia – completely overdressed'), and particularly the fantasy worlds in which her children now lived ('Of course you know my daughter Vivian has applied to the London School of Arts').

I would have found Leti's little chats entertaining if only they had been briefer. Usually, Jenny interrupted us with an urgent call ('I've got Señor Cano on the phone, he says it's important') at which point Leti would stub out her cigarette, wish me good luck, tell me she really must call Claudia and have us both over to her house for dinner some night, and dance her solo mambo through reception whose spotlessness she co-funded. Sometimes she would knock on Eduardo's door and inflict the same treatment on him.

Unlike Leti, Haroldo Gala, at forty, our other important client, had adopted all the trappings he believed essential to a distinguished gentleman. He wore a waistcoat and cufflinks and his hair was sculpted into a soft tortoiseshell. When annoyed, he would tilt his head back slightly and his eyes would take on a cold, glassy stare that gave him the fleeting look of an iguana, and utter some phrase he considered deadly: 'I would require that immediately,' or 'I expect this to be actioned post-haste.' A twitching blood vessel. Haroldo always tried to make an impression. He was convinced that he could win over whoever was in front of him by his authority, his sophistication and his good looks. At cocktail parties, he addressed his audience with polished words, pursing his lips and giving a slight bow as though approving and endorsing what he had just said.

Haroldo had once invited Claudia and me to his palatial mansion on the swanky Avenida del Golf. Stepping inside involved an element of ritual. The drawing room of the house had a chandelier, some overstuffed chairs and a sort of shrine whose dazzling centrepiece was a diptych, two oil paintings of Haroldo and his wife Lucha. Over the years, Lucha had come to resemble her husband: the narrow eyes, the soft hair, the hard, thin-lipped mouth. Greeting Lucha, with her tinted hair and her long formal gowns, was a key ritual at these parties. Flanked by her two children, Lucha welcomed guests in the hallway, and they were expected to admire the Gala family first edition of *Don Quixote* in a polished wooden case. From here we were ushered into a large gallery in the colonial style of the Viceroyalty of Peru: opulent furniture, luxuriant rugs, chairs upholstered in green and accented with gold. In the centre, on a huge glass table, was a display of inlaid Bargueño boxes and a candelabra; crossed swords and cutlasses were mounted on the wall.

Haroldo's conversation was also like a museum whose different galleries could be toured. The foyer invariably entailed a little political speculation followed by some thoughts on where the future of society lay. The main gallery was a discourse on male–female relationships and public and private morality. Mini lectures were periodically delivered in hushed tones with much finger wagging. 'I'm all in favour of open relationships,' Haroldo would whisper and go on to offer his thoughts on the subjects of democracy, drug use and birth control. In keeping with the agenda for these meetings, those present would then heap admiration on his possessions in the order they had been presented: his wife, his children, his furniture and his thoughts.

Haroldo's tortuous, oleaginous hypocrisy required a series of ornate screens behind which was hidden the cesspit of his basic needs. From a childhood spent in the mire of destitution he had scaled the dizzy heights of the business world. The next step in this ascent would be a political post in some future government. Our firm, whose coffers he generously filled, was one more instrument in the furtherance of this objective. I regularly received emails from him along the lines of:

> Señor Baroja, the Deputy Minister for Industry, has asked me for a report on the legal framework of our transactions last year. I would be grateful if a copy could be despatched to his office as soon as possible.

Once it had been despatched, he would answer with a one-line email:

> Read and approved. Cordially, Haroldo.

Haroldo's obsession with social class stemmed from his being the youngest son of the indigent manager of a country estate in Cañete. Haroldo had despised his father and his brothers and eagerly ingratiated himself with the González Panta family who owned the estate. Once, as Señor González Panta drove up to the hacienda, little Haroldo had rushed to open the door and offered his hand to help the old man out of the car.

That, at least, was how the story did the rounds of Lima dinner parties: little Haroldo reaching up to guide Señor González, the dance steps of a future couple through which Haroldo hoped to bridge the social divide and consolidate his position as honorary son. Fortunately, through his marriage to Lucha González, he succeeded. He was a happy man, and I contributed to that happiness in any way I could. Read and approved? Absolutely.

XVIII

I N THE DAYS THAT FOLLOWED, I CALLED MIRIAM several times. I left countless messages. Once she actually answered the phone, but I got only a curt rejection.

I couldn't explain it, but I was filled with a sort of emptiness, an infinite sadness when I pictured her standing in front of me. Her hair untied, her grey-brown eyes, the line of bare skin above her belt. I couldn't get her out of my mind. Obviously it was a little strange for a man like me to be thinking this way about a girl like her.

I talked to Platón about it. 'Forget about her, forget about the whole thing,' he told me. 'And if you can't, then marry her, but stop making such a big deal about it.'

I clearly remember the day it all happened. It was a winter afternoon but the weather had unexpectedly cleared up. Jenny and I had just finished talking through some issues when the phone rang. It was Haroldo Gala and he sounded completely panicked.

'I'm very upset, Adrián,' he said in a low voice. 'The thing is, I asked you, asked your office to send a report to Señor Alvites, the Minister for Industry, but I've just been informed that the documents were never delivered. I cannot understand how your office could have been so irresponsible, how *you* could have been so irresponsible. I just can't get my head around it, I am extremely disappointed.' Haroldo's whisper was all sibilant 's's and rolling 'r's. At first I tried to interrupt, then I simply decided to wait until he was finished. Eventually, I told him that I would find out what had happened to the report. I phoned through to Eduardo and asked him. Just then, Jenny came into my office.

'There's a woman on the phone for you. She won't give a name.'

The voice on the other end of the line was clear.

'Sorry to bother you, *señor*. It's Miriam.'

'Miriam?'

'Yes.'

There was a silence.

'Could we meet up, *señor*?'

Why, after so many rejections, had she suddenly phoned me? That afternoon, as I drove down the Avenida Weisse, I was too surprised even to wonder. But later, in the light of what happened, I asked myself that question over and over.

I parked the car outside the salon and went in.

She was alone, sitting reading a magazine. She glanced up, gave me a fleeting smile, then got to her feet. She was wearing a little make-up, which I took as a compliment.

That afternoon, as we drank beer together at Misky's, I told her about my job. The meetings with clients, the reports, the research.

'It can be pretty dull sometimes, but mostly I enjoy it.'

'I once thought about studying law,' she said. 'To get justice.'

It was the first time I'd seen her really smile. A long, slow smile.

She raised one hand. She was wearing a silver bracelet.

It was a short but friendly encounter during which my father wasn't mentioned. I dropped her back at the salon.

On the way home, I stopped at a bar and ordered a whisky. I wanted to be alone; alone with the memory of her, with the feeling of what had just happened. I sat there for a long while, slowly sipping my whisky.

Miriam's crystalline face, the sound of her smile, the sheen of her lips, her teeth parting for the first time, her long hair, her grey-brown eyes, the silver bracelet and the word, thanks. I'll come back next week, I'd said, I'll come back and see you next week, same time.

I was late for work the next day. I spent the morning at home sitting in the living room reading the newspapers. A government crisis, a cabinet reshuffle, the Prime Minister Alan García in Paris, President Fujimori giving a press conference on television. The papers also published a statement by Abimael Guzmán, the leader of Sendero Luminoso. 'I am not a terrorist,' he had announced from his prison cell, according to EFE news agency. 'I am the leader of the People's War.' There was a photo of him next to the article.

In that instant, Guzmán's face was a revelation. An oily face, an evil saint, a silent explosion within a revolting skin. It was not the happy, misshapen face of Mafia bosses who find themselves on the news, that frozen smile dulled by a lifetime of pleasure and risk. Guzmán's features were set in an expression of seriousness, small black eyes like pebbles, a thickset body made limber by rage, by accumulated rage, cold skin stretched over a cauldron of blood. The dark, obscene violence of that face . . . sometimes I tried to connect it with what had happened. Unlike other people, his rage made it possible for him to gaze out on the world with a look of utter emptiness and this cold stare was the gift he had offered his followers, those who had always kept their heads down, kept their mouths shut. Only through him had they managed to . . . give form to their rage, give hope to their fury.

'Are you listening?' Claudia said. 'I'm talking to you.'

In the days that followed, my familiar routine was out of kilter. Claudia berated me for what she called my permanent state of distraction: 'It's like talking to a wall, I don't know what's going on in your head.'

She was so worried that she made the mistake of mentioning it in front of the girls. I made some vague excuse about being tired. But the truth was, I had begun to be exhilarated. Everything I did seemed to me extraordinary; I was convinced that every client meeting, every report directly contributed to the prosperity of the practice and the world market.

I started going to visit Miriam every Tuesday, I don't know why that day in particular, but it became a habit. Maybe because that was the day she had phoned me. It was a rule we established so we could go on seeing each other.

Sometimes when I got there, she would be working. When

she was alone, she always greeted me with a smile. She never once mentioned the gossip that must surely be doing the rounds locally; a man in a Volvo coming to see her every week.

She would get dressed in her finery, put on make-up and we would go out. Her eyes would light up when she talked about her son Miguel. Our meetings were always brief. We'd go for a coffee or a beer or a cold drink at Misky's. Max was an attentive host, always taking her order before mine. I immersed myself in our conversations; being with her was like having a vast land open up before me through which I could wander for hours. She talked to me about her week, about Miguel, about her friend Melchora, about how she missed her parents and her brothers. I talked to her about my family, the law firm, Platón, about my daughters. Every subject seemed wonderful because it was new – strange, but that's how it was. In my conversations with her, I could breathe. Everything she said – the customers she'd had, the things Miguel said to her, stories about neighbours like Melchora and Pascuala – fascinated me. I questioned her about her memories of growing up in Huanta. It was a subject she didn't talk about much.

Before I left, I would give her an envelope with a little money (always sealed) and she would take it without a word, then I would drop her somewhere near the salon. Never directly outside, to avoid stirring up any more gossip.

Over time, I think she got used to me kissing her on the cheek when we said goodbye. I would put an arm round her shoulder as I kissed her, a rather naive gesture on my part. But it excited me to hold her like that. I'd close my eyes as my lips brushed her firm, warm skin. Then I'd suddenly feel terribly embarrassed and scared. Like a teenage boy with his first girlfriend.

Only Platón knew about this arrangement.

'You've been seeing another woman,' Claudia said to me one night as we were going to bed. 'Of course – I've been so stupid, why didn't I realise it before? That's what's been going on. You're seeing someone else, one of the girls at the office probably, some pretty young assistant who threw herself at you, that's what's going on, there's no point trying to say anything, but I'll find out who she is, you'll see.'

I started to deny the accusations, obviously, but then I simply let her talk. I didn't want her to find out about Miriam. I had only told her about our first encounter. Out of fear, probably.

When she finally accepted that I wasn't having an affair with one of the girls at the office, things improved between us. Every morning I was faced by the same headache of shoring up our relationship – what I would say over breakfast, what she would say, what excuses I would give for coming home late. But it was a mundane problem, one that followed predictable paths. I didn't think I was going to have an affair with Miriam (at the time, the idea of it seemed bizarre). But I couldn't explain what was so attractive about her. Not to Claudia, not to myself.

During this period I met up with Platón from time to time. His wife was expecting their fourth child.

'And you can afford to have another kid?' I was incredulous.

'Sure, business at the surgery is great, there's money to be made. I'm just glad most people don't brush their teeth. What about you, still seeing Miriam?'

'Yes, I'm still seeing her.'

'How long is this going to go on?'

One afternoon, I had a meeting with Señor Pozuelo, a client who had been with the practice since we started up. But it was as though I was meeting him for the first time. He had a gaunt face, a cadaverous smile, and dark hair slicked into waves with hair oil. In his youth, he had been a surfing champion at the Waikiki club and still did everything he could to preserve the traces of his gilded youth: open-necked shirt, white trousers, the big-toothed smile of a warmed-up champion. He was a regular client and I'd agreed to meet with him to discuss his routine issues. Jenny called through to tell me he had arrived. 'Everyone out to watch the great Fernando Pozuelo climbing the stairs.'

He came into the office wearing a pale suit and a cotton shirt, his fixed smile never wavering as he took a seat.

'How have you been, Fernando? It's a pleasure to see you.'

'Hey, I heard this great song just now on the radio,' he said. 'The lyrics are brilliant: "I've had sex a thousand times but I've never made love." Story of my life. What do you think? I'm just like that. Brilliant, isn't it?'

At that moment, something strange happened. As soon as Pozuelo paused for a second, I got up, walked to the door and left. I left. I walked straight past him and down the stairs. All he could do was watch me go. Jenny put her pen down and I think she thought about calling to me.

A second later, I was out on the street.

I had left one of our best clients sitting in my office and here I was clutching the steering wheel of my car. My mobile rang and I turned it off. I remember the distant sound of traffic along the motorway. Eventually, I saw the mountains, and turned into Miriam's *barrio*. I parked some way from the door, walked along the dirt path trying not to make any noise and appeared at the salon.

Miriam was there, standing by the basin washing combs and brushes, running her fingers under the stream of water. She was wearing a dark skirt and a blue blouse, her body slightly bent over the basin, framed against the white glow of the window. Her blouse was rucked up, revealing a band of skin above her waist; exposed to the air, the softness of her bronzed skin defying the cold breeze from the doorway. Her back was curved, her dark hair softly falling. There was something implacable in the expression on her lips which might have been the beginnings of a smile, a flash of loneliness as she washed the hairbrushes, one foot forward to support her precarious position. Beneath her the jet of water splashed and sparkled. Behind her the photos of perfectly coiffed women, the crucifix, the white ceiling, the chairs, scattered objects that seemed to have abandoned her.

I decided to leave. I went back to my car and drove to the motorway, locked between the lines of microbuses. Suddenly, I braked, pulled up on the hard shoulder.

I turned the car. I would see her one last time.

* * *

That afternoon, she told me much of the story. There was a carpet of red flowers between us. She spoke in an easy, assured tone, never stopping for a moment, as though reciting a prayer learned by heart.

This, more or less, is what she told me:

'When I escaped, I was wearing Guayo's boots, Guayo's uniform. The first thing I did when I made it back to Luricocha was go home. I knocked on the door, called out to my parents but however much I called no one answered. There was no one there. The whole village seemed deserted. I had to get away. This was the first place they'd come looking for me. I knew I had to get to my uncle Vittorino's house in Ayacucho. I'd have to run all night. My one fear was that I wouldn't make it there before morning, before dawn, because as soon as it was light the army patrols or the *senderistas* would spot me. There wasn't much moonlight, but I still ran as hard as I could and it was so cold I didn't even sweat, I was terrified of being caught by the soldiers or the *senderistas*. I ran all through the night. From Luricocha back through Huanta and on to Ayacucho.

'I started running, I had to run, I had to keep going until dawn, I couldn't stop and at that moment I thought the best thing I could do was visualise a thin red line, a line that didn't follow the road but ran alongside it, through scrubland and grass, through the hills, a line I traced ahead of me, my eyes drawing it out, making it longer, and I followed that line.

'At first, I just ran. I wanted to run faster but the boots were heavy and I couldn't take them off, so I thought I would go through the hills, I wanted to be as far from the road as possible, and suddenly I felt good, I felt incredibly strong, like I had a wild cat inside directing me, running for me. I forgot my legs existed. Fear made me sure-footed, gave me strength too, I could feel it coursing through my whole body, that aching fear that eats at you from inside. My feet began to fly, I couldn't feel anything, couldn't think about anything except running, I even forgot I was heading for Ayacucho, everything was condensed into the simple act of running, the wind whistling past me, I didn't feel the ground or the cold. I felt like I could keep going for ever, for the rest of my life – well, maybe not for ever – what I mean is the body keeps going, desperate to stay alive, you can tell it to stop, tell it you can't go on any more, but it keeps going. At first all I could think was that I wanted to find my *papá*, to see my *mamá*. Where were they? I thought they might be at Uncle Vittorino's place in Ayacucho. But I wasn't sure. By then my feet were hammering the ground saying, Where are they, Where are they. One foot asking, Where are they and the other answering, Where are they. And then I saw them, I'd thought I would see them in Ayacucho, but now they were in everything I saw, sketched in the air, and I was so happy as I ran, I still remember it, thinking they would be there, that I would see my *mamá* and my *papá*. Tears streamed down my face, making it feel cold and the more I cried the colder I felt.

'With my body running for me, I began to worry more and more about what would be waiting for me in Ayacucho. Dawn was about to break. When the sky turned to blue, when it was light, the soldiers would find me, they'd spot me, they'd take me, they'd kill me and if I stumbled on any *senderistas* they would take me, kill me too the way they'd killed my parents and my brothers, my only hope was that the night would hold out. This road I knew so well was dark now, I was running along the verge, over hard ground, weaving past black rocks, sometimes I heard the moon calling to me as it ran on ahead, I felt like it was helping me. Here and there the hills closed in and I was forced to run on the road itself only to dart back into the scrubland when it opened up again beyond the hills. And all the time I was thinking that by morning I'd be dead, the dawn would come and with it would come sound – this was why I had to get to my uncle's house before daybreak. In the darkness, everything was silent, I had been running so long I forgot everything, I just kept running, kept moving forward. Twice, my body gave out, collapsed unconscious on the ground, but the cold woke me and I got up and I kept going. I was very close now, but it was almost morning, dawn would come soon, I could see blue begin to streak the sky. I was so relieved when I saw the walls of Ayacucho in the distance. This was the blue hour, I might be spotted, the soldiers could find me. I had to get to Ayacucho, I was almost there, and just as I saw the blue sky I started to howl from the pain in my thighs, my legs gave out under me and I crawled away to hide. In the distance I spotted an army patrol so I crept through the open fields and reached the streets of Ayacucho and there I ran as fast as I could. I'd reached Ayacucho and ran silently through the deserted streets, the clear air, and came to my uncle Vittorino's house on Jirón Huancavelica, I saw the big wooden door with the grille over it and I pounded on it like a madwoman, I hammered until my uncle opened it. I hugged him and we stood there hugging and crying and he told me what had happened to Mamá and Papá and my brothers. I can still hear him crying to this day. I can still feel his tears. All dead. My older brother had been murdered by Sendero Luminoso because he'd been seen with soldiers, my parents and my younger brother had been killed in a shoot-out one night when Sendero attacked Luricocha. When my uncle told me that my parents and my brother were dead, I collapsed right there, I fainted, and when I woke and saw a window I broke the glass and slashed my wrists, I would have died, if I could have I would have died. My fingers were trembling and my hands were covered with blood. I remember my hands. But my uncle took me to a doctor friend of his and he treated me, and the only reason I'm here now is because of my uncle, he saved my life.

'And that day my uncle Vittorino got me some new clothes. We saw a group of soldiers in the street, but they didn't notice me, so that night my uncle got some money and took me to the bus station – I was crying but I couldn't shed tears in case someone saw me – and I took the bus to Lima. As we pulled out of Ayacucho, the bus was stopped by soldiers, but my uncle had given me my cousin's identity card so they let me go. I fell asleep but I kept waking up and everything was still dark and then I woke up again and I was in Lima, I saw the streets and the cars and the traffic lights and the office blocks and people on the pavement shouting and tall street lights, and nobody looked at me. Everyone just walked straight past me. My cousin Paulino came to the station to collect me. "Come on, *hija*, don't worry, you're going to be fine." That's what he said. I walked with him, I was shaking from all the noise. He took me to his house on the Avenida Alfonso Ugarte, a wide street with several lanes of traffic. I couldn't believe it. Everything I saw made me cry, everything reminded me of my family, I cried and cried for my parents and my brothers.

'I stayed at Paulino's place. Later I worked in his shop for a couple of months and he and his friends arranged for me to see a doctor who sent me to Maternidad de Lima and that's where I gave birth, where Miguel was born – I named him after the archangel Michael. My uncle Vittorino moved to Lima and he helped me out, and luckily I met a woman who knew a Señora Paloma, and I went to her house and she took me on. And so on. And time went by, the years went by and Miguel is growing up. But I still used to talk to them every day, to *mamá* and *papá*, to Antonio and little Jorge. I never stopped talking to them, I talk to them to this day.'

There was a long silence; all I could hear was the hum of traffic in the distance. I said something about how hard life can be, how you have to pull through.

'Time is the only thing that can help, you have to help time do its work,' I said. What I was saying sounded so ridiculous to me that I trailed off in mid-sentence.

Miriam said she needed to go home. I insisted on seeing her again the next day. I would come earlier, at 3 p.m. She smiled and nodded. When she stood up, she looked more beautiful than ever.

Driving home, I was stopped by the police on the Avenida Weisse.

'One of your headlights is broken, *señor*.'

'I'm sorry, officer.'

'There's a fine,' he said.

'Can I pay it directly to you, officer?'

The policeman shone a torch at me, took the money, muttered a thank-you, told me to be more careful in future and disappeared.

I got home and poured myself a drink.

XIX

I N THE DAYS THAT FOLLOWED I REALISED THAT Claudia had been partly right. It was absurd, but I suddenly felt a great distance between us. We still went to bed at the same time, still sat next to each other watching TV, still went round to my in-laws for Sunday lunch. We even made love from time to time and enjoyed it. And yet I only really felt happy when I was with Miriam.

Talking to Miriam made me happier than making love with Claudia. Our encounters were always brief. On Tuesday afternoons, I would pick her up at the salon and we'd go for a beer at Misky's – there was never anyone else there.

Sometimes, Miriam was silent for long periods. We would sit there for a while, not saying anything. There was an indefinable glow in her eyes, a light that seemed to come from far off. But in spite of her eyes, I wouldn't have described her as pretty. In fact, there was almost something ugly about her . . .

She always wore the same clothes: a blue or white blouse, the blue jeans with the yellow flower embroidered on the side, the black shoes. She had a confident air when she moved, yet it always looked to me as though she were about to start shaking. She was uncomfortable in her body, as though it would never truly fit her.

I didn't know her, would never know, I *couldn't* know what she felt for me, hatred maybe, and curiosity and maybe even a certain affection given what she had said about my father.

One afternoon, working in my office, it occurred to me that we should meet up somewhere other than her part of town. The following Tuesday, I suggested she come with me to San Isidro. We were in the salon when I mentioned the idea. She was sweeping the floor.

'Where?' she said.

'I don't know,' I said, 'let's go to San Isidro, that's my neighbourhood.'

As we drove there, she talked to me about how Miguel was doing at school. I parked on a side street and we walked to the large park called the Bosque del Olivar. The weather was bright and clear, the sun disappearing now and then behind a patch of slow-moving cloud, and re-emerging to dapple the chalk-red path. It occurred to me that someone I knew might see me with Miriam, but at that moment, I didn't care.

Neither of us spoke as we walked but I felt as though there was a tacit agreement in this silence.

Around us, the twisted trunks of the olive trees seemed frozen in pain. We sat on a bench by the pond, its dark waters glittering. I felt the sun flare from behind a cloud. I saw Miriam, her shining eyes, the white blouse, her long legs. A breeze stirred her hair.

Giving in to an impulse I had so far resisted, I reached out and took her hand. I slowly brought my face to hers, found her lips already parted, felt her hair tickle my cheek.

A pigeon hopped around in front of us, a grey pigeon performing a little dance. The path stretched out before us, warm and clear. A gaggle of girls just out of school was wandering nearby. Miriam opened her eyes and pulled away. She glanced towards the road and told me we should keep on walking.

We walked back towards the car and, seeing the café of the Hotel el Olivar, I suggested we go over and have a drink.

'I'd better be heading back,' she said, 'it's getting late. Miguel will be home by now.'

'OK.'

'You don't have to drive me, I can get a taxi from here.'

'I'll take you.'

On the drive back, I turned to look at her from time to time.

When we got there, she climbed out of the car as fast as she could.

When I got home that night, I felt as though I had crossed a line. I had given in to a temptation that I only now realised had always been there waiting. That night when I saw Claudia, I had to look away.

The following week, Miriam and I went to a restaurant on the Avenida Weisse. She ordered a mineral water and a coffee. In the car, we kissed and held each other. I let myself be pulled by the slow tide of feelings drawing me towards her. I had a permanent erection. I sank into her arms – it was like stepping into a place filled with light.

'I had a boyfriend once,' she said. 'A good man. But he left me when he found out.'

'Found out?'

'What happened to me.'

'How did he find out?'

'I told him.'

'And since then there's been no one?'

'No, not since. There've been guys who tried to get close, but I wasn't interested, I didn't want to know. I don't know what to do any more, about men. It would be so weird.'

That night when I got back to my car I discovered the headlights and the wing mirrors had been stolen. I had them replaced.

Thinking back now, it seems strange yet somehow natural that in all that time we never talked about our feelings. I don't think I ever told her that I found her attractive, that I needed her, that I loved her. I never even told her that I was always waiting for Tuesday so I could see her again. And she didn't say anything like that to me. We just saw each other.

To my surprise, when I went to the salon to pick her up the following week, she showed me into the back room. An iron bedstead, white walls, a crucifix, a table and a two-ring paraffin stove. Miguel's bed was in one corner. The room was small, simple. There were a few pictures on the wall.

The next Tuesday, I took her to lunch at La Rosa Náutica – a posh restaurant she told me she had never dreamed she would go to. She had walked along the old wooden pier, past the shops, leaned on the railing looking down at the waves shifting on the stony seabed, breaking against the pilings. A flock of seagulls hovered, buoyed up by the wind.

She looked at the menu and ordered sea bass in black butter – something she told me she used to make for Señora Fox when she had guests. I watched her warily use her knife and fork, cutting the fish into little pieces and bringing them slowly to her mouth. She seemed somehow overwhelmed to be sitting at this table, surrounded by these huge windows overlooking the sea, but she didn't say anything.

She was wearing a white blouse, black trousers and a necklace of silver threads which she told me she had bought recently for an occasion like this. I had brought her here for her birthday, albeit a day late.

'How's Miguel?'

'I don't know. I'd feel better if I knew he was happy.'

'What have you told him about his father?'

'That he left us. And that he died.'

'What about the school?'

The waiter poured a little more wine into her glass. She looked up at him, the waiter mumbled something polite and disappeared.

'Nobody at the school ever asked about his father.'

'How is he doing at school?'

'His marks are average, but the problem is he's very isolated, he doesn't have many friends. Miguel doesn't talk much.'

'What do his teachers say?'

'I've talked to them about it, but I don't know if they believe me.'

'Why don't we see if we can do something. Maybe Miguel should see a specialist.'

'You think so?'

'We could talk to a psychologist or someone who might be able to help him.'

'I'm not sure that's a good idea.'

'OK, but let me know if you change your mind.'

She finished eating and took a sip of wine. A group of what looked like businessmen came into the restaurant. I recognised one of them, a lawyer named Renato La Hoz, who waved as he came in. He came over and we chatted for a moment, during which he admitted with a smile that his practice had moved to a new location. I introduced Renato to Miriam and he looked her up and down. '*Encantado*,' he said, then wandered off with a parting shot to me: 'Give my best to the family.'

'Who was your friend?'

'He's not really a friend, just someone I work with. Tell me some more about Miguel.'

'Mostly he's fine. At weekends he helps out around the house. Sometimes we even throw a little party at my house and invite people from the *barrio*, and Miguel helps me cook and organise everything.'

'Are there usually parties at weekends?'

'Someone or other will usually organise a barbecue or something, some of the neighbours will chip in and we have a big meal and there's music and dancing. We turn the radio up loud and have a good time. But I don't know, I don't know how I feel. Sometimes I go over and visit my cousin Paulino

252

and his sisters and we'll chat. We talk about everything, but mostly we talk about our dead, mostly we talk about them.'

'Does the whole *barrio* ever get together?'

'Everyone gets together on the fourteenth of September, for the feast of the Virgin of Maynay. It's a thanksgiving.'

The waiter came over with the dessert trolley. Miriam shook her head but I tried to persuade her to have something.

A little later, we walked back along the pier towards the car park. We didn't say a word until we arrived back at the car. The waves were breaking on the pebbled beach. I opened her door and she looked at me, slightly surprised, then as I slipped behind the wheel she said, 'Thank you.'

From the moment I got into the car, I was kissing her. A lingering kiss in which I could taste the salt softness of her skin, feel her hand on the back of my neck.

What happened next I can only bring myself to mention briefly. I'm deeply ashamed of what I did now, though I don't know if I regret that it happened. We came to a deserted street in Miraflores. She followed me. We went into a hotel. It seemed completely natural – as though we were living there. The moment we closed the door to the room, we kissed again. Through the large window, a faint evening light spilled across the bed. What haunts me now, what my lips cannot forget, is the slow, devastating way she kissed, the warm wetness of her mouth meeting mine. Her eyes were two hard, unfathomable things. Thinking back, it was as though I could see an abyss open up in them. We undressed. And suddenly I felt helpless before her. Overwhelmed by the warmth of her skin. She was surrendering to me and at the same time trying to get away.

Her legs wrapped round me, her belly pressed against mine and still it seemed that her face was far away. I felt a surge of affection well up, enfolding us, convincing me that there would never be anyone for her but me. Just she and I and the long silence that was beginning.

That night as I was coming home, I parked a block from the house and walked the rest of the way. The glow of a street lamp washed the leaves of the trees. I felt paralysed. When I thought about Miriam, it was as though we were living in a fairy tale. It was so ridiculous I began talking to myself aloud, trying to dissuade myself. You're a lawyer, you're a married man, you have two children, what you feel (or what you think you feel) goes against everything you are, it should make you laugh, it should make you angry.

I talked to Platón about it the next day. 'You need to cut this shit out,' he said to me. 'What you're doing is madness. Next time you feel you need to see her, just pour yourself a drink.'

When I called for her the next Tuesday, she stepped out of the salon looking as though she was dressed for a party: hair full and floating, lips defined in a smooth curve, long painted nails. As she climbed into the car, she chatted about how much work she'd had in the salon; there was a christening and a wedding coming up so everyone locally wanted to look their best.

'How long do you think is a good life?' she asked suddenly.

'I'm sorry . . . how long . . . ?'

'Thirty years? Forty? Fifty? How long do you think people should live?'

'I don't know. As long as they can.'

We stopped at a traffic light. A truck rumbled next to us. We were very close.

'But if you had to put a figure on it, how long is good?'

'A figure?'

'Thirty years, forty?'

'I've never thought about it.'

'I think about it all the time. All the time.'

'Why?'

'I don't know,' she said, stretching her legs.

'Why would you want to think about something like that?'

I turned off the engine.

She looked at me, stroked my hand, put her arms around me. I kissed her neck. She let her head fall on my shoulder.

I got home later than usual that night. Claudia barely glanced at me, then went back to sleep. I tried to cover up, trotted out the usual excuses: meetings and more meetings, dinners with clients. The truth was I'd begun to feel horribly guilty.

Something happened a week later. Miriam and I were having lunch in a garishly painted restaurant on the Avenida Weisse. We both ordered pizza. From the moment we arrived, I'd sensed something strange was happening. Miriam looked drawn and haggard and she seemed distracted.

She hadn't said a word since getting into the car. Now, she sat facing me, hardly touching her food, barely answering my questions about what she'd been doing. By the time we had almost finished eating, I fell silent. It was pointless asking her any more questions.

'If you're not going to talk to me, I don't know why you came,' I said, suddenly, inexplicably furious. 'You should have stayed at home. Next time, I'll find myself a girl who's at least prepared to talk to me.'

She didn't move, and I don't know how, but I knew exactly what was about to happen. Her hands were resting on the table. What happened took only four or five seconds. She suddenly let out a scream, grabbed a knife and held it to my throat. I tried to jerk my head away, but she managed to scratch me and a little blood dripped onto my shirt. She lashed out again, but by now I had grabbed her arm. I forced her to drop the knife which fell on the floor. She got up, glared at me, her blazing eyes framed by her long hair and I watched as she dashed out, across the road, and disappeared.

I went out to look for her, but there was no trace. I went back to my car. I'd stopped bleeding by now, but I could see the bloodstains on my shirt. I drove slowly back to my office. I kept a clean shirt there. The cut throbbed a little, but not much. I was shaking.

When I arrived, I dashed past Jenny, washed myself, changed my shirt and sat down at my desk. Claudia was at her mother's place, it was her sister Camincha's birthday. I was supposed to go over later.

I thought about phoning Miriam, but I didn't.

I drove back down the Avenida Weisse, past the restaurant where we had just been. I turned off the motorway onto the dirt road. The salon was closer, the whole *barrio* deathly silent.

I knocked on the door. No one answered. Everything seemed calm.

Suddenly, I turned round and there she was, only inches from me. She stared at me, about to burst into tears. She stepped closer and put her arms around me. She was sobbing now.

'Please, you have to forgive me,' she said. 'I don't know what came over me.'

We got into the car, drove back on to the motorway and I looked for a hotel somewhere on the avenue.

That afternoon, standing by the hotel window wrapped in a bed sheet, we watched a small boy flying a kite that seemed to hover just outside our window. It was strange, I'd never seen a kite this close up. The boy held the makeshift reel with both hands. The kite soared quickly and then disappeared from view.

'I used to have one like that,' she said, smiling suddenly. 'We used to make them for ourselves back in Huanta, mine had a long tail made from scraps of old clothes.'

'A kite?'

'Yes. You don't like kites? They don't make you feel like you could touch the sky?'

'To tell the truth I never had a kite, never wanted one.'

She turned back and watched the boy.

'He's about the same age as Miguel,' she said.

'Yes.'

'You know I'm teaching Miguel to look after a vegetable garden, we had one in Huanta when I was a little girl, this

257

one is just like it. Sometimes when he's drawing, he draws pictures of the garden.'

We said nothing for a while.

Surely now was the time to ask her.

To say it.

What would I say?

Tell me, Miriam, tell me the truth. It would have to be something like that, tell me once and for all, Miguel is my brother, isn't he, he's my father's son, am I part of your family too?

I heard the dull roar of traffic, like waves crashing on a beach; an engine whined. Suddenly I heard birds chirping somewhere very near us. I couldn't see the birds but I could hear them. They might be in the hotel attic.

The dirty off-white sky, a vast, pale sheet of glass about to engulf us. Her eyes blazed suddenly.

'Do you believe in God? Do you believe in God and the Virgin Mary?'

'Not always.'

'I do,' she said, 'I believe. I never stopped believing. Even when I tried to kill myself, before I slashed my wrists, I said Jesus's name. I know he's always with me, whatever happens, I'm sure of it.'

'Do you ever talk to Miguel about this?'

'Yes, I talk to him.'

'And what about him? Does he believe?'

'He prays with me sometimes.'

'But you don't talk to him about his father?'

'No, we don't talk about that.'

There was another silence. Again I asked myself if this was

the moment. The truth was that there would never be the right moment. In my desperation, I had formulated the words so often that they came naturally, spontaneously.

I tried to look at her, tried to smile.

'Miriam, tell me . . .'

'What?'

I was sitting on the mattress, I realised I looked faintly ridiculous, like a judge presiding over a trial. I gave up.

'Miguel, your son . . . is he my brother?'

She stared out the window, a faltering smile lit up her face, then she composed herself.

'No,' she said softly.

'Well, then . . .'

'Well then, what?'

'Nothing . . . nothing.'

'You want to know who Miguel's father is?'

'No. I have no right.'

She fell silent.

'In the end, it doesn't matter, does it,' she said at last. 'It doesn't matter. Miguel is here, he's my son, he's a boy. I don't know what's going to happen . . . but I wish, I don't know, the one thing I wish is that he wasn't sad, that he didn't constantly suffer from this sadness, this terrible silence of his. That's what I want.'

She sat on the bed and smoothed the sheet.

'The most important thing for any parent is to know their child will be fine,' I said, feeling utterly ridiculous.

'I'm scared, if you want to know the truth, all this time has passed and I'm scared that he's growing up.'

Her voice came like an invisible thread.

'But why?'

'Because as Miguel grows, the silence will grow, I've always known that. He hardly ever talks to other children. He talks to me and to Señora Melchora, and to his uncle sometimes. But he doesn't say much. And as he grows up, I'm afraid the silence will develop into something angrier or sadder, something worse than it is now. Sometimes it's like he lives in a world of his own, I don't know what's wrong with him . . . Do you think there might be something wrong with him?'

'I told you, maybe we should take him to a psychologist.'

'But if a psychologist starts asking him questions, he'll start to remember things, things about me, all the times he's seen me crying, all those things will come back to him and I think that would be worse. Worse for him.'

'And he doesn't talk to you?'

'He talks to me sometimes. He goes to school and he comes home, but he's so lonely, he hasn't got many friends, and he's so angry with me. And he's only thirteen. I don't know what goes on in his head.'

'You should take him to see someone who can help him.'

She shook her head.

She got dressed and I did likewise. We stood there, facing each other. She moved to the door and paused, her hand on the doorknob. Suddenly, she turned back. Her voice was flat, completely stripped of emotion, but her eyes flashed angrily.

'I wish he didn't remember me, I wish I wasn't here to have to tell him what happened to his grandparents. He shouldn't have to think about that. He shouldn't have to know that his uncles and his grandparents were murdered, what happened to me in Huanta during the war, what happened to my parents. He should be somewhere else. He should feel that he has the right to live. Don't you think that's something a mother can give her child? – to convince him that life is worth living, persuade him that good things happen, that good things might happen to him? At night, when I pray, I ask God for him to be happy. He needs to feel that he can be happy, even if we live where we live, even if he can't expect much from life. That's all I want, and that's why I don't want him to know what happened. I want him to have a job some day, to have friends, a family, to be healthy. I want him to have enough to buy food and clothes, I want him to have his own family, his own house, somewhere to come home to every day. But sometimes I wonder if he will ever be free of this crushing silence? And what do I give him except pain, the pain he sees in me every day? I need hope, I need to believe things are possible, I need to make him believe he can succeed, but I don't know if I can, I just don't know. Hope is hard when you have so many dead who talk to you.'

She went over to the bedside table and drank some water.

'You can't lose hope,' I ventured.

'You know what Miguel said to me the other day? He said, "I love you very much."'

'He knows he'll always have you.'

We fell silent.

'Looking at you now, you look like your father,' she said.

'Really?'

'A little, something in your eyes, in your face, something.

261

And you're like him too, in a way. He was a brutal and a cruel man, but with me he was so gentle.'

I looked down. I could hear a TV somewhere in another room. Then silence.

'And you don't hate him any more?'

'At first I hated him, but later I loved him. I had to leave him but I still love him. Your father was the worst of men, but with me he was the best of men too. He kept me locked up, but he stopped them from killing me. You know the soldiers could have raped and killed me? I also saw him at his weakest, when he begged me over and over to forgive him, told me how terrible he felt, but still he kept me prisoner. Later he told me he loved me, told me about his life and sometimes he'd talk about you, talk about his sons. He was good to me, but I . . .'

'If you hadn't escaped, you would have died there . . .'

'He would have had to leave me or kill me. I even saw him cry once, and I tried to make him feel better because . . . I heard him talking about you, crying and talking about you and Rubén. I think he was afraid of you. And now I can see he was right, you are a good man, a better man than he was, but you're like him.'

'You seem to know more than I do.'

'Your father did terrible things, he had so many people killed, and he was so afraid that the *senderistas* would come and kill him too and, I don't know, sometimes I would see that he was afraid and I'd hold him, and we'd hold each other so we could forget, forget I was his prisoner and that they were going to kill us. All I wanted was to go back to my family, but he had seen my house, he knew there was no one left. But I didn't know. Once, he said to me, I wish we could be together for ever, but obviously we can't. He went off to Huanta one day and that's why I had to get out of there, I had to escape any way I could. I was so young, I was seventeen. I had to get away or die. I escaped then, but I haven't got the strength to run any more, or maybe I haven't got the heart, I don't know. I feel so tired, a tiredness that's inside me, deep in my bones. My body doesn't have the strength to get up, to move, to walk, to work, to talk to people, because I miss my family so much. I miss tending the vegetable garden with Papá every morning, I miss helping Mamá to cook things in a big pot, and my brothers Antonio and little Jorge who was so small and had such big eyes and who used to ask me if I thought we'd ever escape from Huanta. That's what he used to say. "Do you think we'll leave here some day?" But Jorge never got away. My mother and father didn't escape . . . They're all still up there somewhere, I don't even know where their bodies are, where they are. Sometimes I think I see them, I see them in the doorway of my house and I don't know where they are.'

Her voice had trailed to a whisper. There was a long silence.

'You just have to let them go,' I said. 'There's nothing you can do.'

'How does Miguel seem to you?'

She looked worried. She was sitting on the bed now, her legs crossed, swinging her foot slightly.

'I'd like to get to know him, I'd like to help him, I've told you that.'

'But what do you think of him?'

'He's a good boy.'

The frown faded. She said nothing for a moment, stared at the floor.

'Recently I've been praying a lot, I've been making up my own prayers. I just talk to God, I tell him what I've been doing, I've told him about you, too.'

'Do you pray every night?'

'Every night I make up a new prayer. It's like a dress for me to wear.'

'And you really believe in God?'

'Of course. And I always put on a nice dress when I pray to him.'

'Do you like wearing nice clothes?'

'Yes, but not for other people to see, I do it for myself, so I can see, I like to dress well, to do my hair, and I like making other women look good.'

At that moment, someone in the street turned on a radio. It was a salsa tune by Oscar de Léon.

'Tell me how much money you need to pay off the salon.'

She looked away. I sensed I'd embarrassed her with my question. The Oscar de Léon song faded out and a low voice growled, 'You're listening to the Pharaoh of Salsa, broadcasting just for you.'

'It doesn't matter. The only thing I really care about is Miguel. Do you care what happens to Miguel?'

'Yes.'

She stood up again.

'Tell me, that first day when I came to the salon, the day we met, how did you know I'd been looking for you?'

'My uncle Vittorino told me. And Paulino Valle. I told them I didn't want to see you. But you found me anyway.'

'Are you sorry I did?'

'No.'

I leaned down and kissed her hands, her skin felt warm and damp.

'I can't stop seeing you,' I said. 'I have to see you.'

'But we're from different worlds,' she replied. 'You know that, don't you.'

'Why?'

A slow smile came to her, a smile of fine sharp teeth like a wound opening for the first time. A curtain of dark hair covered her cheek. I considered telling her I thought I was in love with her but I didn't, it sounded ridiculous.

'OK, I think maybe we should go now,' she whispered. 'It must be late.'

I drove her back to her place. Before getting out of the car, she looked at me for a moment, and kissed me on the lips. Then, suddenly, she was gone.

I glanced at my watch. I still had time to get to my mother-in-law's house and wish my sister-in-law a happy birthday.

XX

BACK ON THE MOTORWAY, I FELT AS THOUGH I WAS in a sort of trance. Miriam's eyes staring at me, the dark tunnel between the cars, the procession of shadows, what do you think of Miguel? At a traffic light I stopped behind a bus only to be pestered by the usual crowd of beggars. Generally I barely gave them a second glance, but that night I couldn't help staring at a girl with plaits. I gave her some loose change.

I arrived at my mother-in-law's house just in time for the birthday cake. The next morning, I got up early and went over Lucía's coursework with her because she was due to sit an exam. She was studying the planets.

'On Pluto, the temperature can drop to minus 120 degrees C and Neptune has winds that can get up to 2,000 kilometres an hour. Do you really think it's possible for wind to blow that fast, Papi?'

At the office, Eduardo informed me that he had spent the previous afternoon in bed with Pocha Guerra, the wife of one of our clients.

'There I was in bed with her and her phone rang and it was the school to say her daughter had diarrhoea, and she told the school nurse to give her a pill and she'd send someone to pick her daughter up. I tell you, it was hilarious – frustrating, obviously, but hilarious.'

On Saturday Lucía and I went to the cinema to see the latest *Batman* film. Her friends had already seen it. On the way to the cinema and on the way out, I took her hand and she let me hold it for a minute, then pulled away as we stepped onto Avenida Diagonal.

There were crowds of people milling around, so we sat on a park bench. Lucía was telling me about some boy at school called Ramiro.

'At break time, Ramiro always comes over to us and hangs around so we'll give him something to eat.'

'And do you give him something?'

'Yeah, because he makes us sad. Sometimes he brings biscuits for us.'

'But you don't eat them, do you, Lucía? Who is this boy anyway?'

'He's just some nerd, Papá, don't worry. You're always so jealous.'

We spent Sunday with Claudia's parents at their house. My father-in-law always liked to talk about anything and everything. Right now he was raving about some amazing seafood restaurant in Miami he'd been to.

On Monday I had lunch with a client at La Eñe. I was enjoying paella with squid ink when my phone rang.

'Hello, Señor Ormache?'

The voice was nasal and somewhat familiar.

'Yes?'

'This is Paulino Valle, *señor*, you remember me?'

The man I had met at his house in Huanta Dos.

'Paulino, yes, I remember. How are you?'

'Miriam is dead, *señor*.'

I sat, frozen, staring at the grains of rice on my plate, the half-filled glass. I looked up, got to my feet, staggered out into the hallway.

'Miriam?'

'Yes. She just died. We're here at the wake in her salon, *señor*.'

'OK. Thanks, Paulino. I'll be right there.'

I closed my mobile and went back to my client, Tato Harrison, a red-faced man with a bulbous nose and freckles.

'Problem?'

'Yeah. Listen, Tato, do you mind if we talk tomorrow? I've got an emergency.'

'Of course. I'll send the paperwork over to your office.'

'Send it to Jenny,' I said. 'I'll look through it this afternoon.'

I dropped enough money on the table to cover the bill and rushed out.

I got in my car. There was a tailback down the street and I cut out in front of another driver who yelled something.

I floored the accelerator and drove at breakneck speed as though somehow if I hurried I might get there before she died. The great, grey sky rose up in the distance, the multicoloured microbuses chugged along, the Avenida Weisse seemed never-ending. I found it impossible to believe that the body I had held, had made love to, was down here, spellbound by death, lips cold, eyes rolled back, a stranger's body laid out in a coffin. Every time I had taken this road before, she had been waiting for me; now she would never wait for me again. And still I raced past a line of microbuses, foot to the floor, honking my horn, murmuring her name over and over. As I came to the statue of Mariátegui and turned left, I realised I was sweating and could barely grip the steering wheel. I loosened my tie. When I saw the statue, my body's reflexes, as they so often had before, anticipated my arriving outside the salon, watching her get into the car next to me. Now that I was close, Paulino's words – Miriam's dead, *señor* – finally began to sink in. Miriam had just died, Miriam had finally died, Miriam was dead. It was the end of a process. Just as one day she had begun to live, then had finally died: an end she had foreseen so often in her life.

On the corner, before turning into her street, I stopped the car. An idea occurred to me. I didn't have to go in. I could go back, it would be easy, I could go home and never know anything more about her, about Miguel, about my father. Her death had concluded the story in my name, I owed no one an explanation, it would have been easy to leave it at that. Go back to my office, go over Tato Harrison's papers, send him a bill, hang up the phone if any of her family called. My fingers drummed on the steering wheel. I remembered the song running through my head that first day as I'd stood in the doorway of the salon. Mary had a little lamb, little lamb, little lamb. Mary had a little lamb but one day she killed it and made lamb stew.

I switched off the engine. Turned it on again. Drove on. I was so close.

When I came to the street, I saw a group of people dressed in black. I felt almost ashamed: here, my Volvo looked like some strange ship on a sea of dust and stones. I was surrounded by the people of the *barrio*. Some stared at me and whispered to each other. For an instant, I felt as though they all hated me. Fortunately, after a moment, they simply ignored me.

It was the same salon I had seen that first day. The mirrors and the ornaments had been taken away, the chairs were lined up against the wall. The wooden coffin was set on a pile of bricks. Sitting on a long bench at the back was a group of women; two or three had their hands clasped in front of them, praying.

I moved towards the coffin. Sheets of thin plywood, a few nails, a crucifix. Some of the people were watching me. Then suddenly I heard someone call my name. I turned. It was Paulino. We went out into the street.

'How did she die?' I asked.

'It was her heart,' he said, bringing a hand up to his chest, 'She had a heart attack. That's what Don Vittorino told me.'

'Where did it happen?'

'In her house, last night. Poor Miguelito wasn't there. It was Don Vittorino who found her.'

'But why didn't she get help, if she had heart trouble?'

'I don't think she knew. I don't think she knew she was ill. She left just enough money to pay for the salon and for her funeral. She paid the last instalment to Don Vittorino yesterday, the salon was hers. She went to Mass and to confession. She was in a state of grace when she died.'

'But why didn't she tell me she had a heart problem? I could have helped her.'

Paulino's eyes flashed.

'I don't know, *señor*, I don't know. I'm sure she didn't know herself.'

A group of women began praying aloud. Paulino and I walked towards the main road. A purple Hyundai pulled up and I saw Vittorino Anco get out.

He was wearing the same suit he'd been wearing the day I saw him at his office on the Calle Emancipación. He didn't seem surprised to see me. He gave me a wave and walked on.

'Señor Valle,' I said, turning back to Paulino.

'Yes?'

'That first day when I came looking for Miriam, why didn't you tell me she lived here?'

Paulino looked at me. His eyes were bloodshot.

'She didn't want to see you, *señor*. She already knew you were looking for her, Don Vittorino told her.'

'She didn't want to see me?'

'In the beginning she didn't want anything to do with you. Then later, she told me she wanted to meet you. I thought about phoning you but she told me not to. Don't call, she said, he'll come, he'll come . . . that's what she said.'

'So why did you tell me she might be living in Luricocha? Why didn't you just tell me she lived round here?'

'So you'd stop looking for her. So you wouldn't come back. But later she told me you were good to her. She said that to me recently.'

A new group of people arrived and went into the salon, hands clasped, heads bowed, some clutching rosaries. By the wall, I saw Miguel wearing a black suit. He walked along holding Señora Melchora's hand. She had dressed him for the wake. A black jacket, a tie and black shoes. Señor Anco went over to the boy and hugged him. Miguel barely moved.

Just then, a van bearing a taxi sign stopped outside the door. A slim, grey-haired priest stepped out and went into the salon. The small congregation gathered around him. The priest said a few prayers.

It was an almost silent service. A murmur of voices reciting the rosary. There was a smell of sweat and earth. The priest raised a hand, blessed the congregation and left.

I leaned in the doorway, hands behind my back, my jacket covered with dust. I felt terribly intimidated by these people. I was a stranger whose history some of them knew or perhaps suspected. Miriam's coffin had exposed me. It was almost as though she had set a trap. Getting to know me, telling me about herself, then dying and leaving me to face this mute jury at her wake . . .

A number of young men in suits went in and stood flanking the coffin. They raised it and it floated on their shoulders as they carried it out and placed it in the white van with the taxi sign.

272

I went with the rest of the group along the dirt road, walking next to Paulino Valle – I don't know why, but I felt safe with him. We followed the van all the way to the top of the hill and then down towards the flatlands, towards a field of white crosses with patches of grass, a few headstones with inscriptions written in chalk. The procession took about half an hour and with every step the air seemed to grow brighter. My trousers and my shoes were covered in dust.

We came to a small patch of level ground. Someone had dug a grave. The men lowered the coffin into the earth with two ropes. The priest said a few words, a number of people answered him, 'Lord, hear our prayer,' and then the gravedigger began to shovel earth on the coffin as a wail arose from the women.

Back at the salon, people split into small groups. I saw Señor Anco.

'She didn't leave a note, nothing?'

'Nothing. Just yesterday she made the last payment on the loan I gave her years ago.'

'Who's looking after Miguel?'

'Her neighbour, Señora Melchora.'

'How is he holding up?'

'He doesn't say anything. Two of his friends came.'

'OK.'

Vittorino wandered off. I turned back to Paulino.

'Why did you ring me today?'

'Because she asked me to. She told me to call you if anything happened to her.'

As I listened, I suddenly noticed a man standing in the street in a grubby shirt, hair falling into his eyes. He looked utterly filthy, his hair dishevelled, his face frozen in a rictus of stupor. Everything about him repulsed me. He stood a moment and stared at me, then went on his way.

I went to find Señora Melchora. Her eyes were red and puffy from crying. I had seen her a number of times before, but we had never actually spoken.

'Miriam never said anything to you about being ill, *señora*?'

'No, nothing. She wasn't the type who'd talk about things like that.'

'Where's Miguel?'

'He's inside, I think he's crying.'

'Can I see him?'

'Come in, *señor*.'

I went into the room. Miguel was sitting on a chair, barely moving. I crouched down next to him.

'Miguel, listen to me, I'm so sorry,' I said.

His face was buried in his hands. He didn't move.

'I'd like to come and see you again. Tomorrow, maybe. We could go for a drive.'

He looked up. His eyes were wet with tears but he looked at me with a certain coldness. I got up and went over to Señora Melchora.

'Could I come and pick up Miguel tomorrow?' I asked. 'I was thinking I might take him for a drive.'

'How did you know Miriam, *señor*?'

'I was an acquaintance. I'll pick Miguel up tomorrow, *señora*, I'll come at about four o'clock.'

The woman looked at Paulino.

'That's fine,' she said. 'Miguel needs someone who can help him.'

'Do you have his birth certificate?'

'Yes. Miriam gave it to me.'

'Could I see it?'

The woman disappeared. While we were alone, Miguel glanced at me for a moment, then bowed his head.

'Here it is,' she said.

The certificate had been issued by the Municipalidad de San Juan de Lurigancho. Father unknown.

'Thank you, *señora*. See you tomorrow.'

She nodded.

I went over to Miguel again, not quite knowing how to say goodbye. I shook his hand, patted him on the back. He barely reacted.

As I stepped out into the street again, Paulino came over to me.

'Could you give me something?' he said.

'What?'

'Could you give me a little money, whatever you've got, just a tip?'

I handed him a note and he slipped it quickly into his pocket.

'Thank you, *señor*.'

'You're welcome.'

'Could I ask you something?'

'Of course.'

'Could you get me a job in one of your businesses? Any job, it doesn't matter.'

275

'I don't know, Paulino, I don't own any businesses.'

'But you've got friends who have big businesses, haven't you?'

'Yes, I suppose I do, we'll have to see.'

He lowered his head. Everyone else was looking at us. A man came over and demanded that Paulino return the money I had just given him. They started arguing.

I got to the office at about 5 p.m. Tato Harrison had sent over the signed contracts in a manila envelope. I found myself sitting at my desk. All the objects on it appeared blurred. I blinked several times but still I seemed to see them behind a pane of dark glass. I felt rooted to my chair. When I finally managed to get up, I paced up and down the office. I went into the Gents. Then the phone rang. It was Claudia.

'Where have you been?'

'At a funeral,' I said.

'Whose funeral?'

'Miriam's.'

'Who?'

'The funeral of the girl who knew Papá,' I said.

There was a long silence.

That night I had to take a couple of pills to try to sleep. Thankfully, Claudia hadn't asked too many questions. I needed to sleep because I had a working breakfast with a new client the next morning at La Tiendecita Blanca.

I managed to get there by 8.30 a.m. The decor – the place was decked out like a miniature Alpine chalet, the Peruvian waitresses dressed up as traditional peasant girls – was so wretched I suddenly felt a wave of sadness.

I settled myself in a booth by one of the faux-wood walls. I flicked through the newspapers, glancing up towards the door now and then but there was no sign of J. J. Arteaga, my client. I ordered a coffee, and scalded myself as I took the first sip.

A group of men in suits walked past my booth. I buried myself in the newspaper. The whole place was pounding to the beat of the traffic on Avenida Larco, an incessant percussion that sounded like a lunatic drummer. I rubbed my eyes and glanced around me. I considered ordering a stiff drink. When my client finally showed up, we shook hands and before long I found myself chatting casually about his start-up company.

That afternoon, I went to see Miguel at Señora Melchora's house next to the salon.

He looked so much like his mother. The pale grey eyes, the grave forehead, the thick eyebrows, the strong line of the mouth.

'I'm Adrián, you remember?'

He didn't answer.

'Would you like to go for a drive with me? We could get an ice cream, what do you say?'

'He's always been like this,' Señora Melchora said. 'Ever since I've known him.'

I gave her a 100-*soles* note, making sure as I handed it to her that she could see how much it was. It was a selfish gesture, like giving it to myself.

'To cover your expenses. I'll give you more later.'

'Thank you, *señor*.'

That night I woke up.

2 a.m. The bedside lamp, the chair, the curtains.

I got up and stared out the window. The appalling silence of the street. I went downstairs and sat in the living room, got up again to get a glass of water.

Miriam. Miriam.

Just seeing her these past weeks. Hearing her voice, touching her lips, discovering the living body behind the stories of Chacho and Guayo. The images formed in the air in a spiral, like postcards in the darkness. I thought I could see myself in each one: the first day I saw her at the salon; the afternoon we went to talk at Misky's; the trees in the Bosque del Olivar where we first held each other; the hotel room where she told me her memories of her family; the first time I heard her voice asking if she could see me. Suddenly, the images seemed to form a sequence.

Why had she called me that first afternoon, having sent me away when I came to the salon? Maybe because she'd just found out she had heart trouble? Maybe she wanted to see me to be sure there would be someone to look after her son. Maybe that was why she'd let me be with her, why she'd asked me, *What do you think of Miguel?*, knowing that she might die at any moment.

But there was another possibility. Perhaps this had had nothing to do with why she had called.

Her body appeared before me now like a vision. For those

weeks, Miriam had breathed next to me, her hand had brushed mine, I had wanted her, held her, made love to her. I had thought about her with a mixture of inexplicable sadness and desire. Her voice gnawed away at my heart. I could feel her warm skin, the gentle pressure of her hair, her fingernails on my back. In the darkness, her body reappeared in all its fragile perfection. Her eyes seemed to stare from within me. She had come into my life like a bride. Her dowry, the truth she brought to our relationship, had awoken fragments of memory. It was as though only now was I truly prepared for the words that my father, from his lonely bed, had said as he lay dying . . . *'There is a woman in Huanta. You have to find her.'* His fierce whisper still burned in me like fire.

'Your father was like this when he was with me. He was a gentle man, like you.' Miriam's words had brought my father back to life, and now he too stood before me in the living room, with his military stripes, his green-and-black uniform. She had recreated this phantom and given it to me. I was grateful to her for that.

Miriam's appearance had thrown open the doors of the house of apathy where I had been so comfortable for so long. The walls I had built around me out of fear, out of prudence, had begun to crumble the first moment I heard her name. Vilma Agurto's letter had been a ticket for an unknown journey into the enchanted region of evil, the kingdom in which Miriam and my father had lived, a barracks policed by torturers – his officers. My carefully cultivated egotism, my brutish elegance, had protected me from them until then. I was accustomed to shrugging off the little problems of the outside world with a sneer, drawing the curtains of cynicism and settling myself in the lavish cushioned room I shared with the likes of Leticia Larrea and Haroldo Gala, with my partner Eduardo. I had seen death, poverty and cruelty, and considered them accidents of nature; fleeting moments in the lives of other people to be quickly set aside. Now they seemed to me like gifts I had not noticed before.

This pain and suffering which my family had created, had buried like a treasure and then asked me to find, was now my only possession. I should have been grateful to my father for leaving me the plunder of his past. Miriam was the angel who had guided me out of my own hell. She had shown me the abyss from which men and women just like me had returned, the very men and women I had seen in Huanta and in San Juan de Lurigancho. Every day, these people had woken up determined to carry on, not to die, not to give up the dubious blessing of being alive, first through the war and later through poverty. Again and again they had woken up in the early hours and come face to face with the pictures of their bedroom walls, the insistent voices of their parents, their brothers, their children, the ethereal bodies hovering in the air, We are here, We do not want to leave, We are here with you. For them, life had always been irreparable. The frozen silence of the night was always the silence of fear; their front door was always a door about to be broken down. The war was over now and yet still faces crowded round them, little brothers asking if they would ever escape, the fathers putting them to bed, the mothers giving them a bowl of milk. Gentle ghosts in the stone air.

This is what it had been like for Miriam. She had never

escaped from that long run through the night back through Huanta all the way to Ayacucho, had never been able to tear herself away from the thin red line her eyes had conjured to help her carry on. That line had been broken. She had had to run before morning came, before the danger that was dawn, the blue hour of first light. For as long as she kept running she was fine. But now she had stopped. Now she was in that forest of anonymous ghosts, the pit between the hills on the road to Huanta, other corpses piled on top of hers. Hugo Matta who refused to let the *senderistas* torch his car and was shot through the head; Leonidas Cisneros the lieutenant governor who refused to let Sendero Luminoso take over his village; Señor Sillipú's son whom the *senderistas* had doused in petrol and lashed to a rock in the midday sun so he would slowly burn to death; Luis Zárate, whose throat had been cut and his body hanged from the lone tree on the Plaza de San Miguel de Rayme and the six sons of Señora Paula Socca. All these people had lived, had breathed under the same sky that sheltered me, they had been so close and yet now almost no one knew about them. They did not exist. Their memory was an immense silence on a mountain road. They would be remembered for a time by a handful of people on their side. The other side.

Those survivors, those who had looked death in the face, were the only true inhabitants of this life. Empowered by their solitude they stood erect on this barren wasteland of the everyday. They alone. Not me, waking up next to Claudia every morning, going to the office, talking to Eduardo and to my clients.

My policy of cowardice constituted a more powerful law than all those I had studied at university. And yet I felt no worse and no better than people like Luis Zárate or Señor Sillipú. I was seeing them from such a distance, they seemed so clear. The fact that I had only just discovered them made me idealise their suffering. I attributed virtues to them they did not possess. They were people just like anyone else (Paulino Valle had asked me for money the day Miriam was buried). Those of us on this side once liked to imagine that the poor were good people simply because they were poor. But now we know that the poor are not necessarily good, nor are those who have suffered good, nor are all the people of Ayacucho good. It seems obvious. They are people capable of anything, just like us. They can be as stupid, as foolish and selfish as we are, perhaps more so. But though I know it is not a privilege, that it does not make them better people, I am surprised by their silence in the face of the brutal division of death into which they were born. They did not ask to be born into such a divided world, did not ask to be born on the other side. The line between them and us is razor thin. It is obvious I will do nothing to rectify this injustice which is ingrained in our society, there's nothing I can do, I cannot help them and I don't really want to. And yet finding out about all this death, the rape, this torture has left me sad and slightly ashamed, I don't know why. I won't forget them. Though this is something I promise only to myself, and to her.

But maybe I will. Maybe this is just a passing phase. Maybe I will forget them. I need to drift off again into the great sleep of the man I think I am, pull the clean white sheets of forgetfulness over my head, surrender to the trivial, forget all these things that will die with Miriam. The great house will be open again and I will be sitting in the living room. My study, my garden, my friends, this is where I belong.

I went back to the bedroom and lay down next to Claudia.

XXI

THE FOLLOWING MORNING I HAD A LONG TALK with her. She seemed to take it very calmly. She said we had no right to judge my mother, or even my father. But we couldn't allow ourselves or our daughters to be affected by this thing. They won't be affected, I said.

After a minute, Claudia said I looked tired and suggested I take a couple of days off work.

'I'm not sure, I think I've been neglecting my job.'

'Maybe the important thing now is to get through this.'

While we talked I pictured her as a statue: Claudia would be a white statue, ever vigilant – no leaf, no bird would dare settle on her.

She told me she was worried because Justina, the maid, had said she wanted to leave in order to set up her own company. She and her sister were planning to import fruits and vegetables to sell them on to the supermarkets.

'Fine then, if that's what she wants, she should do it.'

'Oh, yes, it's easy for you to say that. What about me? Where am I going to find someone else to look after the house? Are you going to start doing the washing-up and polishing the floors?'

'Maybe,' I said. 'I'd enjoy that.'

'Oh, for God's sake, Adrián – tell me what's going on with you.'

The next day Eduardo called me into his office. It was as if I was seeing it for the first time: the leather armchairs, the overstuffed cushions, the huge spray of flowers, the diplomas and the certificates. Eduardo's face was caked with moisturiser as part of his ongoing attempt to reduce wrinkles.

'Two clients have left the practice,' he said. 'I'm very worried. There are younger lawyers out there charging half what we charge. They're trying to fuck us over. We need to do something about it. We've got too complacent, and you've been very preoccupied recently, I don't know what's going on with you. I don't know what you were thinking pulling that shit the other day, just walking out and leaving Pozuelo without so much as a goodbye. We're lucky he wasn't angry, he just laughed it off. But you've been acting weird. And what's worse you're not going out any more, you hardly go anywhere. Attending meetings, going to parties and events, making new contacts, you know that's an important part of what we do, just as important as what goes on here at the office and you – I don't know – you constantly seem exhausted, you're getting less and less done at work. Let's face it, you just delegate everything to Jenny. Don't get me wrong, Jenny's a great girl, she's learned a lot while she's been here, but she's not a lawyer. You're the one who should be writing the reports, talking to the clients, not her.'

Eduardo was firm but calm, careful to say what he had to

say without making me – or himself – angry. It was as though it wasn't him talking but some anonymous voice. He might just as well have been announcing the weather forecast for some far-flung country.

I wasn't annoyed by what he was saying, I felt only a slight irritation at the noise of a power drill from the street. (Sedapal, the state-owned water utility, was constantly digging up the park nearby.)

I suddenly noticed a small crystal elephant Eduardo had on his desk. I stared at it; it seemed a strange thing for him to have and I wondered how long it had been there. There was something monstrous and ill-defined about it, like an animal frozen in the act of killing some invisible creature on the desk.

'You know when my brother was here he told me some story about my father,' I said, 'something about him and some woman when he was posted up in Ayacucho . . .'

I don't know why I said this, but suddenly I found myself telling Eduardo everything. About my mother's death, my brother's visit and his revelations about my father. I gave him an abridged version of the events I've set down here. As I spoke, I realised I was barely looking at him. Eduardo was just an excuse, just someone who would listen while I tried to rationalise what had happened. We were just colleagues, I felt a vague respect for him but nothing more, we certainly weren't friends and deep down I disliked him and he thought me a pretentious upstart. I was using him.

No, it wasn't that. I think the truth is I wanted to hurt him. That's what it was: I wanted to upset him, to piss him off with my story. Wipe the smug look off his face. He listened to me, at first wearily and then in astonishment. When he brought his hands up to his face, I felt vaguely comforted. Suddenly I stopped, I think in mid-sentence, as though someone had unplugged my voice. I hadn't finished telling him everything, but I walked out of his office, along the corridor, saying hello to one of the secretaries as I passed, then went back into my office. I sat at my desk and toyed with a pen, rolling it over and back again. I started writing.

I have the piece of paper in front of me now.

Once upon a time a little elephant was walking across a lawyer's desk. The little elephant was very thirsty and he asked the ashtray for some water, and then he asked a book, and then the desk lamp. But no one would give him a drink. So the little elephant threw himself off the edge and smashed himself to pieces on the floor.

I started laughing.

I looked out the window. The phone rang. Picking it up, I felt sure I would hear my mother's voice. '*How have you been, hijo? How are you feeling?*' '*I'm fine, Mamá, everything's fine.*'

I spent the following day working with Quique, our intern. He'd recovered from his heart trouble and these days went to bed early, got up early and had started regularly taking long walks.

'It's strange to think you might die,' he said one morning. 'It's kind of unreal. You know, for the first time in my life I feel fine. I'm only saying this because it's weird being here and thinking I might not have been here telling you this. Do I owe my life to anyone? Well, the surgeon who operated, the ambulance that came to pick me up, the people like you who helped me. Maybe. But you forget about that, you just deal with what you have to do every day, and no one remembers you could have died, I suppose it's better not to think about it.'

He was almost smiling as he talked.

My birthday was around that time. Claudia and the girls made a photo album for me, the story of our family from the time our daughters were born. All three of them came into the bedroom singing 'Happy Birthday' and gave me the album. On the cover was a photo of the girls with 'For Papi' in multicoloured writing. I was surprised to see myself as a young man running with the girls on the beach, on a merry-go-round, the two of them horse riding in La Cantuta, playing in the snow up in Pastouri, splashing in the waves of lake Llanganuco on our trip to Huaraz. Underneath the photos there were captions like 'Alicia and Lucía with Papá at the top of the world'. I felt so moved by the album that for a long while I couldn't say anything. I hugged the three of them.

At the office everyone wished me a happy birthday. Leticia Larrea phoned to say, 'Have a great day.' Haroldo Gala got his secretary to send his regards.

The next day I woke up before the rest of the family. I sat on my bed. My feet looked strange against the carpet, like two grotesque, helpless children. They clashed with the curtains, with the family portraits, with the perfect colour of the walls. I looked at Claudia lying next to me. She was sound asleep, a rare thing for her at this hour, her head thrown back.

For sixteen years I had slept next to her. I knew her so well. I understood her obsession with order, her generosity, her intelligence, her common sense. She was a familiar creature. And yet, although I understood her, although I shared her reservations, I was irritated by Claudia's unspoken inclination to sweep the story of my father under the carpet. Not that I wanted it to get out, given the problems it would cause me. I didn't want it to get out, but I didn't want it hushed up either.

I was trying to walk on water, find a path across the water back to where I'd come from. I wanted to go back and get the photos of my father making love to Miriam. It would have been interesting to show them to my uncle Federico, to my aunt Flora, even to my daughters and my wife. I'd like to have danced around the photo of their two bodies. Obviously the idea was ridiculous, it was sick. I would never have done anything like that. And yet it seemed unfair somehow that I was the only person to have seen them.

I got up and started pacing the room. I remembered what I had read when I was going over Lucía's homework with her. *'On Pluto the temperature can drop to minus 120 degrees C, on Neptune winds can get up to 2,000 kilometres an hour.' 'Do you really think the wind can blow that fast, Papi?'*

I went into her bedroom. Watched her sleeping. Her heavy lids, the peaceful set of her mouth, her smooth skin. My next pleasure would be taking her to school.

*   *   *

The day slipped by slowly in meetings with clients and reviewing a number of reports. I thought about visiting Miguel the following day. Instead I went to see Señor Vittorino Anco.

The sky that afternoon was ashen. Cars inched along more slowly than usual as though desperate not to reach their destination. I turned on the radio as I came to the National Stadium and amused myself watching a man going from car to car selling globe atlases.

Calle Emancipación seemed even more deserted than usual. I parked in the car park, went up the stairs and knocked three times on the dilapidated door. Señor Anco opened it himself.

'Hi,' he said. 'Good afternoon.'

He ushered me inside. I sat facing him, watched him lean back in his chair. There was something guarded about his polite manner that I had noticed the first time we met, a set of gestures that distanced him from me.

'I don't think I managed to tell you at the funeral how sorry I am about Miriam.'

'Thank you. I know she held you in high regard too.'

I said nothing. Regard. It was a strange word. She held me in high regard. Maybe something more, maybe less. Regard. Affection. Scorn. Resentment. Something.

'I'd like to help Miguel,' I said.

'He's a good boy. And, as you know, he has his problems.'

'What problems?'

'The problems anyone in his position would have, you know how it is, *señor*.'

'Yes. I know. Miriam talked a lot about him. She was very worried.'

I realised that I was panting for breath.

'She thought about him all the time. But if, as you say, you can do anything to help Miguel, it would be most welcome.'

I shifted in my chair.

'You don't know who Miguel's father is, Don Vittorino?'

'That's something you could have asked Miriam, *señor*. I don't see why you would ask me.'

'Yes, you're right. Did she ever talk about me?'

'Yes. She was very grateful for the way you helped her.'

'And that's all she said?'

'She said some other things, but they're between her and me, I can't betray her trust. You understand.'

I understand, I thought, she's family, you have to keep her on your side, I'm not allowed to know any more than I already know, she'll always be yours. Don Vittorino looked at me, an irritated frown forming on his broad face.

'Of course I understand,' I said. 'But I would like to visit Miguel now and then – with your permission. You being his closest relative. Would that be all right with you?'

'Anything that might help him is fine by me.'

'Thank you.'

The phone rang. He hesitated but finally picked up the receiver and said he couldn't talk just now. I shifted in my seat. I thought it was time for me to go. I watched him hang up the phone.

'Thank you for everything, Don Vittorino.'

'There's nothing to thank me for.'

'There's one last thing I wanted to ask you.'

'Of course. Ask away.'

'Miriam, she didn't die of a heart attack, did she?'

'That's what I was told. Her heart.'

I said nothing. I was convinced now that he knew what I only suspected, the plan Miriam had been working on these past weeks, waiting until she had finished paying for the salon. He was the only one she would have told the truth to.

'She committed suicide, Don Vittorino, didn't she?'

I looked him in the eye. His face didn't change.

'I don't know why you say that.'

'She killed herself, didn't she? She finished paying for the salon but she couldn't deal with the memories any more. She missed her parents and her brothers. She slashed her wrists, then she just waited, didn't she. You were the one who found her.'

He didn't waver for an instant, he simply stared at me curiously.

'I don't know what makes you think that, *señor*,' he said finally. 'Miriam had a heart attack, it was completely unexpected.'

'Did you know she talked about the best time to die? She said God would be with her whatever she did.'

Vittorino looked at me blankly.

I imagined their encounter. Had Miriam told him I'd offered to help Miguel? Had they hugged each other and said goodbye? Had she dropped hints to her neighbours about heart trouble? Hadn't Miguel spent the night at Señora Melchora's house? That distant afternoon, that first time she had called and asked to see me, she had already decided she couldn't go on living. And from that moment, all she had wanted was to leave me to Miguel just as my father had left her to me when he died.

Head held high, Vittorino stared at me in silence. The whiteness of his eyes seemed to emphasise the formal dignity of his wide-lapelled jacket. It was as though a line ran from his raised chin to the long row of buttons. This was his place. Some secret strength sustained him. The strength of someone who had managed to live long enough, to see enough of life, before death began to flourish all around him. Miriam had not been so lucky. She had been surrounded by death when she was little more than a girl, before she had had time to love or even respect life. Whatever secrets Vittorino knew, he would never confess them to me. I could only guess at what horrors he had witnessed. But I can still see Don Vittorino's face as, in his velvet tones, he said:

'Miriam's death is her own affair, *señor*, you have no business prying into it.'

Now, as I remember that sentence, I don't know why, but I feel somehow comforted.

I got up and shook his hand.

He walked me to the door and shook my hand again, murmured his thanks, then smiled briefly and said, 'Goodbye, Señor Ormache.'

I went out into the hallway. He had already closed the door.

XXII

I'M TRANSCRIBING DIRECTLY FROM MY DIARY.

Yesterday I went to Señora Melchora's house. Miguel was there. His hair straight, his big eyes anxious. He was wearing a green striped sweater and black trousers that were too big for him. 'Do you want to go for a spin?' I said. He didn't move. Señora Melchora insisted: 'Go on, Miguelito, go with the nice man, don't be like that.' Eventually he got up and walked back to the car with me. He looked at me with his big eyes and almost smiled when I suggested we go for something to eat.

As we drove down the Avenida Weisse, I put on some music and asked him what he liked. He didn't answer. Later he told me he liked Eminem. We found a burger bar.

The next day I phoned a psychologist friend of mine, María Gracia Martínez. Dr Martínez blends her medical knowledge with devastating common sense, invariably delivered in her earthy accent.

A couple of days later, I brought Miguel and Señora Melchora to see her so she could do a series of tests.

'The thing with Miguel is that he's folded in on himself, like an animal reluctant to come out of its cave. He understands everything perfectly so I think he's treatable. It will take time, but I'm sure we'll be able to help him. Obviously his mother's death has made matters worse.'

On the way back, I stopped and bought him some clothes and some things for school. He told me he liked to paint so I also picked up some watercolours, pastels, brushes and a sketchpad.

Whenever I could, I watched him surreptitiously. He had a deep voice for his age. When I asked if he wanted to go somewhere, he'd answer in a monosyllable. He barely responded while I chattered away to him, but eventually, just when I was about to give up hope of him ever talking to me, he'd say something about his teachers or his friend Martín, or about going with his uncle to visit Miriam's grave.

I met Martín, his only friend, a bright-eyed boy with curly hair. Unlike Miguel, Martín asked me all sorts of questions about my car, my clothes. Sometimes I took the two of them for *pollo con papas* in some restaurant on the Avenida Weisse. Whenever Martín was around, Miguel seemed to talk a bit more.

Every week, I gave Señora Melchora 200 *soles* to cover her expenses (the salon had gone back to being a local grocery shop selling fruit and vegetables, tinned food and drinks). I also bought Miguel clothes, CDs and books. I went to see him every Tuesday. If I had to go to an urgent meeting, I would send Nelson with the money. Nelson realised that these transactions were somewhat clandestine which made him all the more proud. He'd come back with a big smile on his face and say, 'OK, *señor*, mission accomplished.' He was clearly convinced that Miguel was my son.

Once, instead of going to see Miguel at noon, I went in the early evening. I arrived at the house and persuaded him to come out for something to eat. He seemed particularly shy that evening. As we sat down at the black formica table, he picked up the ashtray and started spinning it around.

'Why do you help me?' he asked suddenly, the words shooting out like an arrow.

'What?'

'Why do you come and visit me and give money to Señora Melchora?'

'Because I knew your mother and, well, because I think it's a good thing to do.'

I said something about how in Peru there was a lot of social and economic inequality and that those of us who were fortunate had a duty to those less fortunate. It felt as though someone was dictating my words.

'And that's the only reason?'

'Yes.'

'How did you know my mother?'

I hesitated.

'I knew her because my *papá* used to know your *mamá*. He met her when he was living up in Ayacucho. My father was Comandante Ormache. He met your mother during the war. The war against Sendero Luminoso. That was in the eighties. There are still *senderistas* around there, but not many these days. Since Abimael Guzmán was arrested, there's been very little terrorism.'

'Yeah, I know.'

'Well, anyway, that's how.'

'So how did my *mamá* know your *papá*?'

'Because your *mamá*, well, she was a prisoner and that's how they met each other up there, but luckily she escaped, she ran away and came to live in Lima.'

The waiter brought our drinks. Miguel toyed with his glass.

'She escaped?'

'Yes. And afterwards your uncle helped her a lot, you know that, don't you? Your mother was worried, she was very worried about you, she talked to me a lot about you. So that's why I'm happy that you're doing so well with Dr María Gracia. You like her, don't you?'

Miguel looked down.

'Do you think Comandante Ormache was my father?' he asked.

I had had an answer to this prepared since the day of Miriam's funeral.

'I asked your mother that same question.'

'And what did she say?'

'She said no.'

'OK.'

He gave a sigh. I poured some Coke into his glass. He didn't even look at it, but I drank some of mine. We ate in silence. Then suddenly he looked up.

'My mother was a great woman, wasn't she?'

'Yes,' I said, 'she was a great woman.'

He bowed his head again and pushed his plate aside.

'Are you going to keep helping me or is it just for now?'

'I don't know,' I said. 'Right now, I want to help you. I don't know what will happen later. I'd like to go on helping you, but I'm not sure I'll be able.'

We chatted briefly about school. The only thing he was really interested in were his drawings and his watercolours.

'I'd like to go home now,' he said later.

I paid the bill and drove him back. On the way, he told me he had a Spanish exam the following day. When I left, I promised I'd come round and pick him up next Tuesday. He nodded.

Before heading home, I drove around the *barrio*. All I could see was Miriam's face, and then Miguel's face superimposed on hers. Suddenly I thought I saw the bed Miriam no longer slept in. Several times I touched the seat Miguel had just vacated. Ran my fingers over the black leather. The same seat where she had so often sat. Seeing it I could almost discern Miriam's body in her son's, that scent of sadness bodies leave in places they have been. On either side, the street lights and the trees slipped past, the windscreen devouring the road ahead. The face I had just seen saying to me, '*My mother was a great woman, wasn't she? Yes, she was a great woman.*'

When I got home I sat in the car for a long time.

It was June. Around that time I wrote something about winter in Lima. I found it again recently:

In winter, Lima takes the concept of misery to its highest level. Misery is a coating that eats away at the surface but makes its home in the heart. It takes the form of rain and drizzle which spread an air of unreality across the facades of the houses, the edges of the cars, between the cracks. Objects have no form. The sea is the sky. The ground is the air. The colour of winter is not grey or white or leaden. It is impossible to grasp, it is the absence of colour. Lima in winter might be said to be the grandeur of desolation. For all things that exist, Lima exalts towards nothingness.

One morning, I went to Miguel's school. He introduced me as his sponsor. I spoke to Señor Guillén, his teacher, who gave me his opinion. 'Very quiet, that boy.'

We were in a room that overlooked the playground. Next I spoke to Señor Saravia, who taught Spanish and history and had a permanent frown. I told him that Miguel had problems but that he was seeing someone about them. Saravia barely listened. I didn't have much more luck with the headmaster, but Señorita Zegarra, his maths teacher, at least listened.

'One way or another, he'll have to talk to us some day,' she said. 'But don't be too worried, he sometimes speaks up in class and he gets good marks.' I met a few other teachers. Two of them asked if I could give them a job.

XXIII

ROUND THAT TIME, I MADE A PROMISE TO CLAUDIA. It's a night I remember well. It was a Friday, we were on our own, and we'd eaten at the Café Bohemia before going to see a film at the Cine Alcázar. I'd just been speaking on the phone to Miguel.

Claudia was still upset even at the mention of his name. That night, she told me I had to keep his existence absolutely secret.

'It's a problem,' she explained. 'I know you feel sorry for him, I feel sorry for the poor boy too, but we have our own children to think about, darling. If people find out about your relationship with him, it won't sound good.'

'Don't worry,' I said. I remember I was drinking a beer and looking at her. 'Nobody's going to find out about this.'

And nobody did find out. There are rumours, but I've never told the whole story to anyone other than Jenny, and Platón obviously. No one else.

Things got worse between Claudia and me. All I can think now is that Miriam came between us. One night, we were invited to dinner by Dina Arteaga, one of Claudia's aunts. Señora Arteaga liked to wear flowery dresses; she seemed determined to wear fabrics that represented all the gardens, forests and jungles of the world. She had dresses with creepers, lianas, bunches of flowers, grasses, but also tigers, butterflies and horses. I sometimes felt as though you could put on a hat, fill a water bottle, pay the entrance fee and step inside her dress for a safari.

There were only a few guests that evening sitting around the living room of her apartment in San Isidro opposite the golf club. Señora Arteaga, her husband Humberto and her sisters were all present. Being with them meant constantly fumbling for some new word, some way of keeping the evening going . . . The whole Arteaga family lined up on the sofa in this apartment, I can see them now, these people mired in their cruel tedious existences, chained to their homes, their sofas, as though their whole lives they had been hoarding silence. Everyone looking at us while Claudia and I tried to find words to praise the new curtains.

I think that what happened that night was the result of my feeling – I don't quite know what to call it – a weariness at having spent so much time with them. I'm not trying to justify myself.

It all happened so fast. As we were having coffee, I moved my hand too quickly and knocked the cup all over Señora Arteaga's dress. She threw up her hands and gave a shriek. The flower-print dress was streaked with coffee like dirt tracks through the forest. Señora Arteaga went on shrieking. I felt shocked but also elated. 'It's perfect,' I said, pointing to her dress. 'A perfect little path to go for a walk in the countryside, don't you think?' Then I bent down with a napkin to wipe her dress, but couldn't stop myself from saying aloud, 'If you didn't wear dresses that make you look like a deranged parrot, I wouldn't have been distracted.' As I said it, I saw the words hang in the air, like a trail of red letters over the astonished company, and they seemed so alien to me I didn't say anything more.

I only came out of my trance when Claudia stared at me and demanded icily that I apologise to her aunt immediately. I did what she asked. The argument with Claudia lasted two whole days including the various stages of reconciliation, but it was not the only one.

At the time, it was as though another man inhabited my body; this combination of rage and passion suddenly felt natural to me. I could think only about Miriam, I could see her eyes watching me, hear her voice. *What do you think of Miguel?* I could feel her lips lingering on mine.

'Papá is kind of crazy,' I overhead Lucía tell one of her friends.

On another occasion I went to my father-in-law's house for dinner. He spent the evening going on yet again about his trip to Miami. About this exquisite little seafood restaurant that had just opened in Little Havana. 'The seafood risotto is to die for, maybe we should all go up to Miami for a week just for the food.'

I listened to him and, before my mother-in-law could further embellish the account of gastronomic delights, I turned to my father-in-law and said:

'You really shouldn't be eating seafood risotto, it's bad for your cholesterol. You'd be better off dieting and doing some exercise.'

The whispers and laughter at the table died away as, with a smile, I added in a low voice:

'Screwing expensive hookers isn't the only way to burn calories. Though I know you've screwed a lot – and I'm sure the ones in that brothel you go to over in Surco are very pretty.'

It might have gone down well were it not for the fact that my mother-in-law, who knew nothing about her husband's visits to the brothels in Surco, was of course present. Claudia finally broke the silence, telling her mother that she thought it was best if we leave.

We got in the car and drove home, where she locked herself in the bedroom. She didn't talk to me for days. I slept on the sofa that night. Eventually we worked everything out in a screaming match.

I phoned my in-laws and apologised.

'I don't know what came over me, *señor*, I'm going to go and see a psychiatrist to find out if I've got a screw loose, but I'm begging you, please, forgive me.'

A pause, a sigh.

'Fine, let's forget about it. We were starting to think you were wrong in the head.'

Each fight with Claudia after these incidents was worse and aggravated the distance between us, a process I watched as though from a distance, making no attempt to stop it.

'Why are you and Mamá fighting? Are you sleeping with

another woman?' Lucía asked me. 'Can I meet her?' Then she asked me a series of questions I could barely answer. 'They told us about sex in school. Someone said to me, If oral sex is good, what's written like?'

The last stage in this phase between Claudia and me took place late one night as we were coming back from dinner with her cousin Dolly. She started it.

'You haven't said a word all night. Everyone was talking and you just sat there saying nothing. What's wrong with you?'

'Nothing.'

I remember it was spitting drops of rain that blossomed into mushrooms on the windshield.

'Then why didn't you say anything? You just sat there.'

'I didn't have anything to say.'

'No, it's not that, it's because you think Dolly and Pepe are too stupid for you to talk to. You think they're not up to your standard, don't you?'

She shouted these last words, I could feel her breath on my cheek. I don't know why, I was staring in front of me watching the raindrops form sad streaks down either side of the windscreen and the wipers push them aside.

'Calm down, Claudia,' I said.

I think these words were my last mistake.

'Calm down? You want *me* to calm down? You get yourself involved with some *chola* and you want me to calm down. You insult my aunt and my father, but I'm the one who has to calm down. You ignore me, behave like I don't exist, like I'm nothing, but you want me to calm down. OK, fine, just watch how calm I can be.' She held her hand up so I could see. 'See? Not even trembling. And I'm glad I'm feeling so calm because now I can tell you I want you to move out – not tomorrow, not next week, as soon as we get to the house you pack your things and you leave, you get the hell out, do you understand? Get a hotel room and tomorrow you can start looking for your own place. The truth is, I've been wanting to say this for a long time. And it's for the best because you're a terrible example to the girls, they don't want anything more to do with you, they've told me as much themselves.'

We said nothing on the rest of the drive home. I heard her sobbing. I tried to comfort her but she pushed me away. A long thread of water formed on the windshield. I was not going to leave. I was going to stay here. This was my house. At least for tonight.

The following day I found an apartment in San Isidro. It was handy because it was halfway between the office and the house.

In the weeks and months I lived alone, it was as though Miriam was with me, it was like being married to her. I felt her in bed next to me, heard her voice saying she was making coffee, felt her body lying next to mine. When I went out, I'd leave a CD playing that I thought she'd like.

I think her ghost helped me at the time, helps me still. It was a constant, reassuring presence. I felt she was the only person I could count on. When I went to visit Miguel, I was shocked when I found myself almost saying I'd just left his mother at my place and that she was fine.

I managed to have a working relationship with Claudia. I

called her regularly. I picked Lucía up every morning and dropped her at school. I spent time with Alicia. And I went on seeing Miguel. On my visits I'd managed to persuade him to let me have some of Miriam's things. The white blouse, the blue jeans with the embroidered flower, her combs and brushes, her black shoes. Over that period I visited her grave several times, always with him.

Once, during the weekly office meeting, I thought I saw her.

We are in the hills above Ayacucho. It's dark, but I can see her; light plays on her body, she asks me to follow her. She's naked and moves in great loping strides as though she's flying. She appears several times and each time her voice is different. She looks at me, but there is no love in her eyes, nor hate; she looks at me with a kind of indifference that excites me.

This beloved, exasperating ghost of Miriam with her morbid recklessness, her gloomy elegance, her brusque voice will always be with me. I hear her voice. I can't understand the words, but I know it's her. Sometimes it becomes confused with my mother's voice, which I can understand. '*I didn't want things to turn out this way. Why did you behave like that with Claudia, why don't you try to get back together, how do you think your daughters will grow up with the two of you fighting all the time?*'

Claudia was my wife, after all, the person I had lived with all these years. I wrote something about that one night:

After all the luxuries, all the flights of imagination and desire, we always come back to what is around us. The reality is the resignation. We are forced to confront the fact that our essential loneliness is the reality. We have to make the long slow climb down from our flights of fancy, face the fact that we have a family, that we have a partner, a result of the casual fact that once, before a crowd of people, in a church, we said, 'I do.' And our tragedy is not realising that we have stopped loving, stopped wanting this person, but realising that behind the bitterness we still want them without knowing why, out of the resigned passion of habit. Because we know that all of the illusions that surround us are distorted mirrors. We are the partner to whom we swore we'd be faithful. It is not even because that partner is good company. It is because growing old means realising that no one will ever be a better partner than she is. In this, loneliness is crucial, it is the cage in which we prowl like a fierce and gentle animal, constantly bumping into our own reflection.'

XXIV

ALL THIS WAS SEVERAL YEARS AGO. ALICIA IS studying law now, she's doing her internship at José Ugaz's chambers, which makes me happy. I've just given her a car. Lucía is studying fine art at the Universidad Católica. Justina doesn't work for us any more, but she sometimes comes to visit. Her job was taken by her niece Elizabeth; Claudia calls her Lisa. I've told Alicia and Lucía about Miguel. They've both said they'd like to meet him.

I wrote to Rubén to tell him the whole story. His reply was brief:

I can't believe it. I'd like to meet him.

Last night, sitting alone on my bed, it occurred to me that my mother is the real author of this story. The day she put the letter from Vilma Agurto into her trunk, locked it and went back to her room, she was leaving me her will: Find out who this girl is, find out who your father really was, who you are, who I am.

I had never had any reason to doubt my mother's integrity, but only now do I realise she was the most important person in my life: her whispers and her lullabies when she put me to bed, the confidence in her voice as she sent me off to school, the blue and white dresses, her greying hair, her indisputable flair for friendship and conversation, the little parties she threw at her house of tea and biscuits and music, the grace with which she dealt with my adolescent whining, the way she tried to reassure me when I had doubts: *'Look, son, you're the only one who can decide if you want to study law or literature, make a list of all the pros and cons. You want to marry Claudia? She's a wonderful girl, just make sure she's right for you, think about it and then decide, there's no rush. You shouldn't just forget your brother Rubén, I write to him as often as I can, why don't you just write something here at the bottom, even if it's just see you soon or something. Dear Rubén . . .'*

Platón and I still see each other. Once, when we were at Delicass, we got chatting to the waiter serving us – a thin, shy, mixed-raced guy. He told us he was studying to be a car mechanic in his spare time.

'You see,' Platón said when we were alone again, 'you can give yourself all the airs you want, but everyone in this world knows something we don't know, whether it's knowing how to mend a car or how to get somewhere.'

'So what?' I said.

It's been three years since Miriam died. Nowadays, like any other lawyer, I'm happy settled in the comfortable day-to-day routine of success. I still have a pretty good relationship with Claudia. She is someone I can't imagine being without. I don't feel close to her, but I can't imagine sitting working at my computer without hearing her voice in the next room. So, I moved back home a couple of months ago, I asked her to forgive me. The first time I brought Miguel round to the house, Claudia was very sweet to him and now sometimes she'll ask me about him, though when she does she never looks at me.

Obviously there have been a lot of rumours about my private life which I don't deny or confirm. People say I had an affair with the maid who worked for me, that Miguel is my son. They've seen him with me sometimes. Some of them laugh at me behind my back about my 'affair with some *chola*', as they put it: 'He's lucky Claudia forgave him. Though she only did it because Adrián's got money.'

Over the past three years, Miguel has made great progress with Dr María Gracia. He has more friends, he talks to me more and he's getting better marks at school. This is his last year at school and next year he might go to the National School of Engineering. His features are more defined now and I think he's very well-adjusted for a boy of seventeen. Sometimes he goes for trips with his uncle Vittorino to Ayacucho.

Jenny still works for me at the practice. I often talk to her about how Miguel is doing, I still think a lot of her. Every time I go to the office, just seeing her is a genuine pleasure. I'm afraid that some day she'll leave the practice; leave me. That's what I'm afraid of, but I haven't said it to her, and I never will.

Now I am sitting writing. It's night-time. Everyone in the house is asleep. Today is 5 July. I want to finish this story.

Earlier today, about 1 p.m., I finished up a meeting with a client and came home and sat in my office. I had a pile of contracts I needed to go over. I sat at my desk. Lucía was at the art gallery. Alicia was off having lunch with friends. Claudia had gone round to her sister's.

I went out and did what I sometimes do – drive around. I headed along Javier Prado and almost without thinking found myself at Miguel's house – what used to be Miriam's salon. I suddenly remember the first day I saw her. I could almost see myself sitting in the chair facing the mirror as she cut my hair.

I saw Miguel walking along the street with his schoolbag slung over his shoulder. His face lit up.

'I want to show you something,' he said.

He went into the house and came out with a folder and opened it. He showed me a watercolour landscape: blue sky, green mountains, yellow flowers. A road winding between two hills. The green and yellow and blue of the landscape contrasted with the black mountain peaks.

'It's Huanta,' he said. 'That's where I'm from. What do you think?'

I suggested we go out for a spin, maybe get something to eat.

I headed for Miraflores. We chatted while I drove. We came to the park by the Church of Fatima. From there, we could see the hotel, the piers, the long spit of land jutting out into the sea. We walked down to the seafront.

The waves formed a ribbon that dissolved as it reached the shore. La Rosa Náutica, the restaurant where Miriam and I had had lunch, looked like a misty fortress hovering on the water. The glass and steel conservatory, the turrets, the jets of spray, the long sinuous curve of the beach melting into the sky, the waves breaking in a surge of euphoria, dying on the shore and coming back again from far out. Everything seemed to be happening at a great distance, in a great pall of horror.

'The other day I visited a school near your place,' I said to Miguel. 'They run foundation classes for the University of Engineering. They teach maths, prepare you for the entrance exams. Why don't we drop in on our way back and see when you can start?'

I don't think he answered. But when I turned, Miguel was looking at me. Looking me in the eye for the first time ever. And in that moment I saw the reflection of those brown eyes, the eyes I had seen in that hospital bed. But unlike that day in the Military Hospital when I had turned and left him to die, I sat next to him for a long time in silence.

'I've wanted to say something to you,' he said, '. . . for a while now.'

'What?'

He looked out at the horizon. Winter crept over the sea and disappeared behind the long peninsula of La Punta.

'I wanted to thank you,' he said. 'That's all. I wanted to thank you.'